HEATHERN

HEATHERN
JACK WOMACK

UNWIN
HYMAN

LONDON SYDNEY WELLINGTON

First published in Great Britain by Unwin Hyman, an imprint of
Unwin Hyman Limited, 1990

UNWIN HYMAN LIMITED
15-17 Broadwick Street, London W1V 1FP

Allen & Unwin Australia Pty Ltd,
8 Napier Street, North Sydney, NSW 2060, Australia

Allen Unwin New Zealand Pty Ltd with the Port Nicholson Press,
Compusales Building, 75 Ghuznee Street, Wellington, New Zealand

British Library Cataloguing in Publication Data

Womack, Jack
Heathern.
I. Title
183.54
ISBN 0-04-440691-6

Printed in Great Britain by Billing and Sons, Worcester

For Nancy

With Nancy knows what,
and Nancy knows why.

From a report of the 2nd Battalion, 405th Infantry, U.S. Army, April, 1945:

We discovered near Gardelegen an atrocity so awful that it might well have been committed in another era, or indeed, on another planet.

1

A baby almost killed me as I walked to work one morning. By passing beneath a bus shelter's roof at the ordained moment I lived to tell my tale. With strangers surrounding me I looked at what remained. Laughter from heaven made us lift our eyes skyward. The baby's mother lowered her arms and leaned out her window. Without applause her audience drifted off, seeking crumbs in the gutters of this city of God. Xerox shingles covered the shelter's remaining glass pane, and the largest read:

Would like to be crucified. Have own nails.
Leave message on machine.

The fringe of numbers along the ad's hem had been stripped away. My heels wobbled, crunching

1

glass underfoot; my skirt clung to my legs as I continued down the street. November dawn's seventy-degree bath made my hair lose its set. Mother above appeared ready to take her own bow; I too, as ever, flew on alone.

'Joanna,' Thatcher said, prying loose my memory's coils that I might freely return to my present. 'You want your face to freeze like that?'

Thatcher Dryden, who with his wife Susie owned the Dryden Corporation – that is to say, Dryco – was my boss; my owner, in a conceptual sense. As Vice-President in charge of New Projects I rarely listened during the morning rundowns, as I had yet to work on a new project in the nine months since he promoted me.

'There's something I want you to look at tomorrow. See if anything's there.'

'Anything where?' I asked. Thatcher's eyes glazed as if he imagined me clad in one of those specialised designs he favoured, the sort I refused to wear.

'Got some reports in about some fellow on the Lower East Side— '

'Loisaida,' said Bernard. 'For appearance's sake we should keep the names straight.' As Vice-President overseeing Operations, Bernard made sure that when his owners left teeth beneath their pillows at night they would find shiny prizes in their place. He handled those New Projects. I'd worked under Bernard before coming to Dryco, through his mentorship learning the skills I no longer used.

'Whatever they're calling it this week,' said Thatcher. 'This fellow might come in handy. Give her the lowdown as we've got it, Bernard.'

Bernard was forty-five, three years older than

me; he held his printout that he might see over
the frames of his bifocals, and read aloud,
translating the jargon in which all paperwork, for
obfuscatorial reasons, was written. 'One Lester
Hill Macaffrey, age twenty-nine, from Kentucky.
Present address unknown— '

'Squattin' somewhere, no doubt. We'll dig him
up like a clam if we have to. A southerner,
you'll notice,' said Thatcher, keen to note his
countryfolk.

'Turn over any rock and find one,' murmured
Susie Dryden, seated as ever at the far end of
the table reading the *Daily News*, her eyes flitting
over the pages looking for referents, seeking in
the reports the usable connections that underlie
unrelated events, remaining me of a hawk searching meadows for mice. Her paper's headline read:
PROBLEM? THEY ASKED/CANNIBAL, HE SAID.
Kept Hand in Pocket.

'He teaches philosophy and theology at a
parent-run facility on Ninth Street. Most of his
students are Long Island transferees, including
test group children— ' Susie grimaced.

'Macaffrey teaches grade schoolers philosophy?' I asked.

'Nothing more inconsistent than Nietzsche, I'm
led to understand,' Bernard said. 'Our friends in
the appropriate agencies have examined possibilities I've mentioned concerning potential political
disruption and feel we're being quote, paranoid,
unquote.'

'Told you that's what they'd say,' Thatcher
said, placing a finger to his lips that he might
hush his own classroom. 'Listen now. That's all
I ask.'

'His neighbourhood is rife with tales of

Macaffrey,' Bernard said, 'most arising during the past year, most claiming that he possesses, or is possessed by, some supernatural force. It's sworn by many that through unknown agencies he provides his charges and their families with drugs— '

'Drugs?' Why would Dryco care? 'What drugs?'

Bernard winked at me. 'Food, clothing, shelter. Old-time silencers. As so many these days are mad for apocalypse no matter how arbitrary, more outré stories have begun to circulate, silly even by Nasty Nineties standards and far beyond recent fin-de-sièclivities— '

'English, Bernard,' said Thatcher.

'Sources claim he foresees and tells of the future.' Bernard smiled. 'Must be a fount of joy for his neighbours. Supposedly he restores sight to the blind. As predictable within such subcultures a consistent belief is that he changes the weather to suit or punish as he pleases. I don't think these tales can supply his public with the fix they need much longer. Any day now we'll probably hear stories that he's cured millions of cancer, turned water into Coca-Cola and parted the East River to ease the shipment of weapons into Brooklyn.'

'Damn good research,' said Thatcher. 'Good talking. Thanks, Bernard.'

I remembered how so often to me Bernard referred to Thatcher only as Stonewall's revenge. 'It sounds so charismatic,' I said. 'So cultish.'

'The snakecharmer's air clings to him,' said Bernard. 'These types rise up in ebullient times such as ours as scum rises on stew. Good to have an accomplished hand lifting the lid now and then to see what's boiling up.'

'I got a hunch about this one,' said Thatcher,

making a series of tiny x's on his notepad with his pen.

'Like the hunch you had about that fool last May?' asked Susie.

Thatcher paid her no mind.

'Messages from beyond could be useful even if true, depending on the beyond,' said Bernard. 'At least Swami Lester doesn't claim to have once lived in Atlantis. So many do you'd think the weight of the populace was what sunk the place.'

'Makes him more believable, doesn't it?' Thatcher asked. 'You got to follow these things up.'

Spring's oracle had professed the ability to lift the shrouds from Elvis. When he conjured up no incubus of higher rank than one claiming to have been Grover Cleveland's postmaster general Thatcher felt more assured that Elvis was still alive, or at least for now sat waiting in the lounge of heaven's airstrip until he heard the boarding call for the return flight to earth.

'This boy didn't come calling on us, it's cost-free so far. If there's something usable he's got it'll be a damn smart investment, getting in on the ground floor.'

'Send a magician if you're sending a safari out,' said Susie. 'A *stage* magician. Someone who recognises tricks and lies and knows what to do about them.'

Bernard, stonefaced, lifted his hand. Thatcher smiled, ogling me for the tenth time that morning, his attitude implying that he's told all of his classmates a secret I'd asked him not to tell.

'Go down there tomorrow, hon. See if his shoes match his suit. Report to me once you get back.'

'May we proceed?' Susie asked. 'More pressing matters require notice.' She turned to Gus, who'd thus far remained silent. Gus oversaw Security, and so spoke only of matters about which we didn't want to hear. He was in his sixties, and worked for many in many ways before signing on with Dryco. 'Fact me on this Jensen thing, Gus.'

'Mr Jensen, who worked with Latin American accounts— '

'Dog bites man,' muttered Thatcher. 'Who doesn't?'

' —left Chicago two nights ago, arriving at the Newark terminal on our jet number 12AR6. Jake and I were to bring him into town and we met him there.' Jake was Gus's protégé and trainee. 'It startled me, how pale he looked, but Jensen said he was fine. I sat with him in the back, Jake sat with the driver. Halfway through the Holland tunnel he clutched his chest and slumped. A coronary, I thought, and pulled him closer to me. When I tried to place the oxygen mask over his mouth he pushed it away. His face was grey and blue. He felt very cold. He spoke.'

'What did he say?'

'"Can you keep a secret?" he asked. I said yes, my friend. But he could keep a secret as well and said nothing else. He entered a paralytic state, almost a coma. In his eyes you could tell he was thinking.' Gus sighed.

'What's the moral to the tale?' Susie asked.

'None, so far,' said Gus. 'Our doctors examined him after he was admitted to our ward at Beekman. Within an hour he died. Poison, the doctors said.'

'What poison introduced how?'

'Fugu,' said Gus, 'derived from a Caribbean species of blowfish— '

Thatcher nodded his head, as if thinking. 'How much was Jensen allowed to know? He must have been aboveboard if he was using one of our planes.'

'High enough,' said Bernard. 'Sometimes I saw him at various dos, always resembling a librarian on speed. Just the same he was vouchsafed and seemed no less competent than the rest. Probably he only took the wrong path in life, at some stage— '

'No ifs about it,' said Thatcher. 'Sushi boys are in the bush.'

Bernard frowned, and when he spoke his offering was no less serious than I would have expected. 'If those little yellow people weren't so little they'd be easier to spot.'

'They hid on Guam for thirty years after the war,' said Thatcher.

'We believe the poison was on a projectile fired into the back of the leg, behind the knee, by means of a nondiscernable microbioinoculator,' Gus said. 'Dartgun,' he added, seeing that none of us save Bernard knew what he meant. 'Easily concealed within an umbrella, for example. In a car exhaust, in a child's party whistle. Innocence doesn't deny death.'

'Sounds like Russian tomfoolery to me,' said Bernard, examining his nails. Whenever he dieted he fed upon his fingertips to supply the calories forbidden. 'Those crazy Krasnayas, they eat up those Bond movies. I've told you so often it's our Moscow trolls we should be keeping an eye on— '

'They need the business too bad,' said Thatcher. 'We're partners, boy. Russia's at war with the country, not us.'

'The recovered pellet fits instruments of Cuban make,' said Gus, his own Cuban accent shading his soft voice.

Thatcher shook his head. 'They're in the damned Caribbean,' he said. 'Finally getting into the market.'

'Quit fixating,' said Susie.

'You've no reason to suspect,' I said. 'All somebody has to do is say Tokyo and you act as if samurai were running down Fifth Avenue.'

'Stick to your assigned projects, hon,' Thatcher told me. 'You know something about conspiracy we don't?'

'Returning to this other supposed conspiracy of which we have no evidence,' Bernard said, 'if Jensen was into freebooty he may well have been flying solo.'

'Loose cannons sink ships,' said Susie.

'Somebody else must have been involved, since somebody killed him,' said Thatcher. 'Wish to hell I could remember the bastard. These low-level boys, it's like looking at ants— '

'He was higher on the hill than that,' said Susie. 'Investigation's essentialled.'

'Of course it is,' said Thatcher. 'You can bet Japs'll be holding the dartgun when we catch 'em. Talk about watching too many Bond movies. Fugu poison, my ass— '

'You're such an idiot, Thatcher,' said Susie; her snow-pale skin darkened as if she'd been rinsed in cheap wine. Whenever her control over anything slackened Susie rushed to teeter wildly at hysteria's edge so that one among those who watched might rescue her as she desired. In all situations, and especially since aligning with her husband, Susie lived by her balance.

8

'Aren't there plots enough without your making up ones that don't exist?' Standing, she walked to the window to sightsee while she bided her time, but it was Bernard and not Thatcher who spoke anew.

'Let's forget Pearl Harbor long enough to approach this logically, why not— '

'Give it a try,' said Thatcher.

'The negotiations at Kyoto have been ongoing for a year and a half— '

'Year and eight months,' said Susie, without looking at us.

'On Tuesday you'll be meeting with the closest Japan has to your equivalent— '

'Oswego— ?'

'Otsuka,' said Bernard. 'You know his name, use it. He's the one who made the bid to us and he's worth hearing. Nothing wrong with forming with Japan the same sort of benevolently hostile relationship we have with Russia and with Japan there'll be no need for military interaction. So long as we postnet options— '

'English,' said Thatcher.

'What will Japan matter in ten, twenty years? We'll be in full Chinese production by then and all we'll have to do for the Japanese after that is draw up their retirement programme.'

'Like they don't have enough to retire on. Property, farms, factories, stores, banks— '

'And all assets frozen since the troubles,' said Bernard. 'Once this deal is done the freeze goes off. They make profits again, of which we receive a thirty percent cut.'

'Thirty percent,' Thatcher repeated. 'You're serious?'

'They know there's no other way around it.

9

They're willing. Once we sign, though, we have to abide by the agreement. No funny stuff later on. That's our sole requirement— '

'Sounds good. Too good. We'll settle, all right—'

Susie stood before Gus, sounding much more tranquil as she spoke. 'Security's on double alert?'

'Absolutely. All guards are undergoing allegiance checks. Master Dryden is safe at your house in Westchester.'

'It's Wednesday,' Thatcher said. 'Settle this Jensen thing by Monday, if possible. Get the police to make pertinent arrests whenever necessary.'

'We've surrounded the usual,' said Gus. 'The actual assassin may prove untraceable.'

'Wouldn't be the first time,' said Thatcher, staring at him until Gus looked away.

'There's so much else that needs attention,' Susie said, rubbing her forehead as if shifting her brain into bizthink; as she slid into her traditional role even her speech began to change. 'What's tagged for intersits? List me.' Intersits were, in our economical shorthand, international situations.

'Three point seven million imperial gallons at our Vancouver plant primed for disposal,' said Bernard, reading from a different printout. 'Dispersal, excuse me.'

'As what?' Thatcher asked. 'Cancer in a jug?'

'Barter unfeasibled in *this* instance,' said Bernard, resting his chin in his palm. 'Call it charity.'

'Third-world writeoff,' said Susie. 'India it. Next.'

'Dryco's Caracas unit to return online January first— '

'December fifteenth,' she said.

'They ever figure out what happened?' Thatcher asked.

'Major malfunction,' said Bernard.

A guess; no one was left alive to ask. I gazed into Thatcher's face as if to divine the future, found myself again unsuccessful as a seeress. His actions were ever unpredictable, but this day's whim puzzled me, that he should make advances to a teacher in a ghetto. Beyond his claims I could yet discern no higher purpose.

'What's this I heard about some delay with the wall?' said Thatcher. 'What's up?'

'The river.'

Workfare recipients built the wall that would shield downtown from rising waters in the event Greenhouse predictions proved accurate. Without working they received no government assistance; for twelve daily hours they received thirty cents. There was a two-month wait for those wishing to sign up, but new spaces opened daily. 'Higher tides this fall than expected. At Cortlandt Street they ran out of bedrock. Schist one of those things.' Bernard paused, as if hoping for a reaction other than the one he drew with his pun, before reading on. 'Struck quicksand at forty feet. Geologists say additional tests are essentialled— '

Thatcher's finger rapped my knee as if he was testing to see if I'd gone bad. He slipped a note to me beneath the table.

'Check it out, Bernard, whatever they say.'

I want to see you tonight.

On the message's note I scribbed my reply

11

and passed it back, watching his reaction from the corner of my eye. Thatcher glanced over it, his dark eyes fixed. His features could have been called Lincolnesque, had Lincoln been forty pounds heavier, beardless and worn his hair tied in the back with a short pony.

'Precautions. Can't trust nobody on faith.'

Not tonight, he'd read.

I agreed to drink with them after work; so long as Susie accompanied he usually kept his passions reined. During this season, I settled for going with such company as would keep me. Through the years, spending the Thankgiving-Hanukah-Christmas circuit carving turkey rolls instead of turkeys, decorating bushes rather than trees, I should have convinced myself without reminder that each new year's holidays might prove more memorable than those preceding, but no; the mind rejects too many lies as the body rejects too many sleeping pills.

'Look at that sunset,' Thatcher remarked as we rode the few blocks from Wall Street to Fraunces Tavern, seeing slivers of sky between buildings through which glory might be found. Old downtown's narrow streets held a medieval feel, hemmed in as they were by stone battlements and wide walls. Evening's lingering heat slapped our faces as we stepped from the car; we saw two visigoths who'd long leapt the wall into the city, bond traders giggling as over a bug in a bottle while they poked umbrellas into a trashbag. The bag groaned; the man within hid his face with his hands.

'Amateurs,' Thatcher murmured, commenting upon their style, evincing so much concern as

I or anyone I knew ever evinced toward those who'd lost that we might win. The queen of the snows, Bernard laughingly called me; ice princess, glacier girl, hoar with a heart of frost. Was I better for having noticed, and not remarking? That was another lie I couldn't keep down: I saw but didn't see, cared yet didn't care; couldn't stop long enough to think about what I might do if I tried. There was nothing, I thought, that I could try to do, and so did nothing.

Susie took Thatcher's arm as we entered, holding him tight; he didn't pull away. He'd had involvements before ours, yet Susie never left him, nor did he want her to go. They never spoke of their unavoidable symbiosis, as if embarrassed to admit that neither could have dealt with their world by themselves. There would be no breaking of their ring from without; I'd tired of battering myself, trying. Soon enough, I lied to myself, I would fly away from it all, not knowing how, not knowing when; wanting only to let what time we had left together pass silently and uneventfully away, that he wouldn't notice my leaving until after I'd gone.

Our drinks were on our booth's table. Gus sipped from each before we drank. He and Jake took the outer seats, walling us off from the crowd. Jake crushed debris from my corner of the booth and I sat across from the Drydens. She looked at her husband as if recounting the ways she'd loved him.

'I hate this place,' she said. 'These animals.'

'Can't isolate yourself all the time, darlin',' he said. 'Look at poor old Elvis. It's the courtiers kill the king.'

'Fuck Elvis,' she said. 'Look at you. Mr man of the people, indeed. Some man.'

'Some people.' Something brushed my foot; I jerked it away, having seen rats in better places. Beneath oak beams, amid tankards and pewter and steel engravings were hundreds at drudgeful play. A post-teen broker barked, crawling on his fours, his tie sweeping the floor; two women armwrestled, their flowcharts forgotten, keeping their sneakered feet firm against their chairs as each struggled to toss the other; I-bankers shook breadsticks at one another as if casting untried spells. An ageing mentor at barside held forth before his adminassists and executaries, forking his hand into a cheese-ball, licking his fingers clean as he spoke. Any abomination was excusable so long as you lived in New York.

Gus illustrated a proper table setting with the unused dinnerware for Jake; to his mind social graces were so essential as social control.

'Salad fork always to the left of the regular fork.'

'AO,' said Jake, examining the tines of each.

Something returned to caress my leg. Slipping off his shoe so as not to ruin my hose, Thatcher ran his foot along my calves, appearing to his audience so expertly vacant that he might have been running for office.

'Anyone here might try and do the do,' said Susie, rescuing her olives, drying her hand by rubbing her short hair, perhaps hoping to bleach the grey into more platinum tones. 'Pop out of the crowd and bingo. You know that.'

Gus frowned; in this season he wore his memories so poorly.

'What are you trying to prove?'

14

'Not trying to prove nothing, darlin', just enjoying myself while I can,' he said, his foot writhing over my knees. I froze, showing nothing to anyone. I dreamed of assassinating him while he prodded my thighs with his toes. 'It's the edge that makes life worthwhile. Dancing through the minefields of life. Like flying over the border at night with all the lights off. Like dropping in on the competition when they're not expecting company. Just cause somebody lives straight doesn't mean they don't need a rush now and then.'

'You're such a fool— '

'Too damn paranoid, darlin', that's your problem,' he said, laughing. 'My boys'll keep me covered.'

Clamping his lips onto her cheek as if to feed, he simultaneously thrust his foot between my legs until he could push it no further; he wriggled his toes as if squeezing mud between them. Choking, I dropped my glass; Jake caught it, not spilling a drop.

'What's the matter, hon?' he asked, his eyes postcoital as he drew back his foot.

'Went down the wrong way,' I said, pressing my legs together, then relaxing them, having expelled my offspring anew. 'I'm all right.'

Susie stared at me, anxious to convict, keen to execute, no less sympathetic than any judge. My innocence was no less real than any defendant's. 'Paranoid,' she repeated, forgetting me for the moment. 'You're the one with the lock on every lid. Always claiming you'll be spooning it out next Christmas— '

'I've helped you grasp the intangibles of the situation,' he said.

'Imagine what I could do with whatever's in your files.'

He nodded, saying nothing.

'You're so good keeping secrets when you want to. This thing you're sending her off on tomorrow. What is it you want her to look for? What's she going to find? You act like you think you're really onto something.'

'Maybe.' A feigned guilelessness came easily to him. 'Let's not talk business after work, darlin'—'

'No better time to talk it,' she said. 'What's this creep got that you want?'

He looked toward the ceiling as he spoke, seeming to visualise something he didn't yet own. 'Somebody drops by your house on their way someplace else,' he said, 'and they go to the bathroom while they're there, and stop up the pipes shittin' gold, you're not going to call a plumber.'

She had no response to his homily. Susie had known him from before the beginning, when he and his friends owned nothing but a plane and a field in the Colombian highlands. He admitted to me only once that her business acumen brought them to where they were, and then only because he had, as he put it, such blind fool timing. I can't imagine she'd ever gotten used to him.

'If there's something you're not telling me, I wish you would,' I said, doubting that I would be heard, much less answered. 'What've you got me walking into?'

His smile resembled a new incision, a caesarean scar. 'If I knew for sure I'd tell you, but I don't. Just take a look and let me know,' He raised his glass. 'A toast.'

16

'To what?' Susie asked, lifting hers; a waiter refilled it.

'Everything,' he said, a whisper to his mother.

Jake held my jacket for me when we rose to leave; I smiled at him, and he grinned in return, his face full of blessings. Gus led us, Jake tailed us; the crowd parted for our movement as if for a clump of bellringing lepers. Everyone in the place must have worked for Dryco, directly or indirectly; reason enough for circumspection. We waited in enveloping night for our cars. From the west a blur breezed by Thatcher and Gus; a bicycle messenger racing a delivery to one who couldn't wait, each knowing nothing more valuable than a little more time.

'Watch it!' the messenger shouted, flashing past. As he shot beneath an unbroken streetlight Jake fired. The bicycle passed some distance beyond the light's cone before falling over. Gus held Jake's arm.

'You rushed,' he said. 'That's why I didn't act. I could see he was unarmed.'

'I'm sorry,' said Jake, covering his mouth with his hand.

'And remember your breath. Breathe in as you fire and hold it. Then let it go a few times after.' Gus demonstrated, lightly hyperventilating. 'Like a train. Gets air back into the head.'

'Just wing 'em next time, Jake,' said Thatcher, dry of emotion. I knew that within he rocked as if in an earthquake. 'Low-key. That's the way.'

I rode home in a Dryco car to my apartment on King Street, which Dryco also provided; Thatcher gave me many nails that I might use. I lived in the bottom two floors of an 1825 townhouse refitted

17

to postmod standards by the previous occupants. They'd lost it during the Readjustment; maybe they never deserved it, I'd tell myself. Maybe I passed them each morning as they raked at my clothes, calling for pennies, crying for change. On the street and on my stoop were syringes and shards of bottle-glass left by passersby to remind the street's residents how long we had lingered at our own edges, relying only on our own balance.

My neighbour on the third floor wasn't screaming. Wrapping my comforter around me when I got into bed as if expecting recovery a thousand years hence, I let my memory squeeze me unconscious. A friend who lived in the neighbourhood I'd be visiting told me a story that never made the news. Sixty problem people were shot in Corlears Hook Park by the Army. Sanitation men came in white trucks and buried them in red bags. A woman went to the landfill, after. With bare hands she tore away the earth until she found her husband. Retucking the others beneath their blanket, she carried him off that he might sleep alone. One who watched as she patted the earth down upon his new bed asked where she'd go now. To the grocery, she said, I got mouths to feed.

2

While waiting at the stoplight we watched tanks roll down First Avenue. In the Readjustment's early months so many control vehicles collapsed through the pavement into the subway that those remaining assigned to Manhattan now only travelled those streets with thicker crusts. A semblance of calm prevailed for the moment in the city's more disgruntled neighbourhoods; many within the government, especially Army personnel – some even within Dryco – wished to remove the soldiers from New York as they'd been removed from other cities and send them into Long Island where they were needed. The Drydens said no; the Army couldn't control trouble if it wasn't around to start it.

'It's sad that so many hope for better,' said Avi, staring into the one-way glass as if watching

19

his favourite show. 'Hope's the truest opium. Better that people work with what they have. But no, they dream of better. The man on the white donkey riding up, putting everything in its place. As a dream, it's cancer.'

'Hasn't cancer a purpose?' I asked, still dreaming that one day I might win an argument with Avi that he admitted to my having won.

'It has,' he said. 'It makes people appreciate the world for what it is.'

One tank lagged after the rest, the litter's runt. Had the driver not recognised our car as one of Dryco's own and, for laughs, turned its turret toward us, I don't know what Avi would or could have done. All in Security were able in all fields; Avi, after Gus, was ablest, but I never hoped that he might always save us.

'I've always told you you'd be happier if you took your life for what it is. As would they. It's only karma.'

Our car inched eastward on Ninth Street. During the night a cold front swept the clouds from the sky; morning sun glinted off the tears of millions.

'Karma?' I repeated. '*Schmeggege*. You're some Hindu.'

He smiled, hearing a word from a language he chose to lose. Avi's family were Lubavitcher Hasidim; he left his old world while still in his teens. During his twenties he feasted from faith's buffet, swallowing and passing Unitarianism, Catholicism, Reform Judaism, Buddhism and more, at last assembling a plate of scraps from which he might thereafter nibble. His unshaken tenet was a belief in an afterlife so redemptive of the life lived before that he saw no greater purpose to his own existence than to relieve others of theirs.

'Take it as a brandname,' he said. 'Like Kleenex or Lasereo or God. A word you understand without knowing the meaning.' He cleaned his glasses with a silk handkerchief his fiancée had given him. 'Even media agree,' he said, handing me his copy of *Newsweek*. FOR THE SIX BILLION, the cover's blurb read, referring to those who'd left our station on the twentieth-century train. I'd scanned the article earlier, finding simple words that presumed to summon understanding from the years during which the perfect Victorian world became our neopost one. Perhaps the editors hoped that unexpected patterns might emerge from what they threw across the pages, but the only pattern these days was the one from which everyone's clothes were cut. There was image upon image, familiar scenes from the family album: Elvis beside Hitler, Joyce next to the Beatles; the sailor kissing the girl in Times Square on V-J Day side-by-side with the burning girl running down the Vietnamese road; Gorbachev's face was shoved between frame 313 of the Zapruder film and the first soldiers marching over the Fifty-Ninth Street bridge.

'It seems to me that what we live through are only birth pangs, that the deepest pain awaits after delivery,' Avi said. 'Who knows? Because ours is a sick world doesn't mean we shouldn't love it.'

At the street's far corner was an abandoned Benetton. On its Ninth Street side was a mural limnedd by locals, showing a line of ill-drawn skeletons wearing grey pinstripes resembling my own, raising metatarsals higher than their skulls in synchronised kick. 'Hell's Rockettes,' he said. 'Terrible perspective.'

'They've painted over the numbers along here,' our driver said, slowing so we wouldn't miss the place; secondarily that we wouldn't run anyone down.

'It's a few doors west of Avenue A,' I said. 'That's it.'

Except for the entrance the building resembled its six-storey neighbours, one of a row of corpses. The old tenement designers often had names chiselled above their building's outer doorways, allowing new-arrived immigrants an introductory dream, that their hovels were not so much less than the Dakota or the Belnord. The steel door of Macaffrey's school was painted crome yellow; the name above – *Hartman* – gleamed with smudged gilt. The worn faces of stone seraphim poked from twin circles that bookended the word; each circle was formed from three pairs of wings. The angels' eyes poured down their cheeks, as if without suspicion they'd glimpsed this world's Trinity.

'Don't bother them, Avi,' I said, referring to those yet unblinded, the ones on the curbs and steps and stoops.

Figures claimed that Loisaida's population density approached that of what it had been at the turn of the previous century, but that didn't seem possible; too many of the old buildings were gone, and the streets could not have lodged so many.

'If it's necessary I act, Joanna. You know that.'

The grace of Avi's that doomed and saved was that he understood his own purpose so well. After we emerged the driver locked the car from

22

within; electrified its body for our visit's dura-
tion. Dozens at once encircled and separated us,
waving empty cups in outstretched hands, their
cloud buzzing as might a beehive's.

'Money,' they cried. 'Please. Money for food.
Money.'

As always I allowed my eyes to blur out of
focus, that it would seem they were not truly
there. Shaking lesioned fingers from my shoulders, I tried to push through. Someone shoved
a fist into my pants pocket, restraining me. 'You
got money, bitch,' my assailant said, yanking as
if to rip away my clothes; he was too weak. His
eyes were so dead as an angel's. 'Give it to me.' I
tried to escape but he wouldn't, or couldn't, free
his hand.

'Avi,' I shouted; he swam toward me through
the crowd. 'Get him away— '

'Gimme money— '

Avi's hand encircled his neck. I pulled him from
my pocket as Avi lowered him to the sidewalk.
The crowd dispersed, seeming much calmer. Avi
let go, took my arm and led me off.

'You killed him?' I asked, my leg still warm
with the man's touch.

He nodded, and we dashed up the school's
worn stairs. Avi used unarmed methods that shed
no blood and therefore left him sinless. Forget? I
tried. Though I'd housebroken compassion, I still
wet my bed at night.

Once buzzed in we entered a hall that was
enlarged to serve as foyer. Posters taped asym-
metrically around the walls bandaged the plaster's
wounds. Some ennumerated medical litanies and
the ninety-eight warning signs of cancer. Another
gave numbers to call in event of rape, robbery,

accident or suicide, with no assurance of any answer to any question. A third, drawn in garish colours, diagrammed the proper use of contraceptives. One poster was but a photo of kittens sitting among flowers. They looked stuffed. A fiftyish woman sat behind a paint-speckled desk. She had fresh mums in a jar and fresh gauze around her arm.

'We're from Dryco,' I said. 'We have an appointment to see Lester Macaffrey.'

The doctors must have taken her larynx in removing her cancer; when she spoke she lifted a microphone to her throat, her generated voice sounding more mechanical than a Toyota's. 'Third floor, second door on the right.'

As she returned to her work we began ours, ascending the narrow stairs at the rear of the hall. Former residents, the apartment-dwellers past, left nothing behind but their vegetable tang, the faint odours of cooked lentils, boiled cabbage and, as if we passed a marketstall, a whiff of cilantro. It seemed too quiet to be a school. The drawings of students hung on the walls we passed.

'Good colour sense,' said Avi. 'You expect a thematic repetition, considering their age.'

Some of the pictures might have been drawn by any child living in Beirut or Belfast or Johannesburg. Others were identifiable as designs of our neighbourhoods. In those, crowds raced from distant buildings that spewed inky clouds, soldiers shot young men in their yards, children ran after wagons carrying off their dogs. An artist of a traditional school sketched a suburban design, unexceptional but for detail: a mother and father stood before their house, holding the hands of half a child. The gallery continued beyond the third floor; we went no further. Hearing at last the sound of children's laughter, I wondered at whom they laughed. On the glass of Macaffrey's door a stencilled message read *Knowledge is Danger*.

'Visitors,' called a man's voice when I knocked. 'Come on in.'

Avi slipped ahead of me, opening the door; I saw him, inside. Macaffrey's look was that of a million's; once out of my sight, I couldn't have more accurately described his look than I could a cloud's.

'Sit with the rest or stand in the corner.'

Choosing to stand, we noted absentees: there were no desks, no chairs, no books or blackboard, no TV or tape-player. Only half the windows had glass; on this cool day all wore their wraps. The unobservant might have found the pupils no more memorable than their teacher. They must have had homes, for all appeared washed, and if Macaffrey supplied their clothes he must have provided detergent as well. Perhaps he had trouble with shoes; most wore sandals fashioned from strips of tyre and rope. A girl sitting in the front row, her hands clasped before her in her lap, spoke to us. The rest of the class was preternaturally still.

'We were— ' She halted, and scratched her head, searching for the word she wanted; each of her hands bore an extra thumb. 'Discussing, that's it. We were discussing the fall of man.' She laughed. 'Man's first disobedience. The fruit of that tree.'

'You're studying Milton?' I asked. 'As an aspect of theology?'

He looked at me; I stared between his eyes as he spoke, as if I were being interviewed. 'Biblical interpretation of every sort has its purpose, you know.'

Avi and I frowned in unison, as might twins, each of us surely thinking that we had found nothing more than the usual fundamentalist continuing to eat through the woodwork. Scholars suspected that American students would find the legend of creationism no more comprehensible than the theory of evolution, therefore remaining untainted by either, but I had my doubts, and suspected Macaffrey of being one of those keen to demonstrate to the young that the only proper logic is none at all; so I imagined, until he began.

'Let's recap for the benefit of our guests,' he said. 'The key to understanding the first chapters of Genesis is remembering that nothing in it is written as it happened. What do we call such writing?'

A girl with hair the colour of crow's wings lifted her arm, her hand reaching no higher than her head. Another child of that test group; her legs were little more than stubs propping her squat body aright. 'Allegorical,' she said, her voice raw, sounding as if she'd smoked and drunk heavily, awaiting exit from the womb. 'Truth bedecked in Hallowe'en drag.'

Neither game nor video could have seduced Macaffrey's audience into taking their eyes off the screen he presented. 'Good, Marge. So face facts. Seven days represent billions of years. Keep in mind that this was written for people who didn't know years from hours. With that ground planted, let's get to the growing. What was that snake, and what made it special?'

'They meant Neanderthal people,' said a boy. 'Godness like Neanderthal people. They couldn't talk but they communicated.'

'They had flowers at their funerals,' added another boy, perfect enough but for the ragged scar transversing each cheek.

'They saw Adam and Eve,' said Macaffrey. 'Who were they?'

'Cro-Magnon,' shouted a girl. I looked and looked again, but saw nothing wrong with her. 'God liked them. They acted without a script.'

'They yearned to burn,' said a boy standing on his hands; without legs, he waved like wheat in the wind. 'No patience.'

'There're two kinds of people in the world,' said Macaffrey. 'The Garden was the world as it once was, as it was intended to be. Everything was very peaceful for a very long time. Both groups kept to themselves. They did as they'd always done. There were no problems. No disruptions. They were very afraid, and didn't know why. What was the matter?'

'They knew they weren't complete,' said the girl with four thumbs.

'Their creation, though perfect, wasn't whole. It was divided, as They were. Godness knew that our intermingling would cause no end of trouble but knew as well that the choice would have to lie with us. She put the flea in the serpent's ear – symbolically, of course.' The students laughed, as if knowing well the answer to a riddle just heard. 'We've known responsibility for our actions ever since.'

'So what happened?' Avi asked, as if hearing it for the first time.

'Opposites magnetise,' said the crow-haired girl. 'Wanting to mindblow, they aimed bedways.'

'Cain and Abel were the first children,' said a boy, scratching his ear with his toe as he spoke. 'They suffered for being first.'

'For being human. Their children's children were as us,' said Macaffrey. 'They knew They put too much of Themselves into us and it drives Them crazier than They already are. As we forever throw ourselves off cliffs to see if we can fly, so They forever strive to sort things out, certain that one day an imperfect being will fit into a once-perfect world. They're still learning, too,' he concluded. 'Class dismissed.'

Once undammed the children flooded from the room. Macaffrey remained where he stood as his listeners left, looking to have reached the chopping block and wondering what delayed his executioner. His natural speaking voice was different from his teaching tones, looser but yet clipped, and possessed of a heavier twang than Thatcher's.

'I been expecting you,' he said, his eyes turning toward ours; I looked away, wishing not to be so quickly lured.

'What on earth are you teaching them?' I asked.

He grinned. 'Kind of adapted to circumstance over the years. Only way to get some things across is to lose them in the packaging, you could say. Like putting vitamins in sugar. What're you here for? Come by for private lessons?'

'The head of our company wants– ' What did Thatcher want? 'Wants to see you tomorrow, in our office.'

'There's a reason for this honour?' he asked,

his voice sharp with the same edge that Bernard's sometimes bore.

'He seems to believe you might have something to tell him.'

Had Bernard not told me Macaffrey's age I could only have guessed it to be somewhere between seventeen and forty, his appearance varied so in the room's shifting light. 'Does Macy's tell Sears?' he asked. Did southerners speak only in riddles? With such responses he and Thatcher might prove made for each other.

'How do you conceptualise?' Avi asked, an unexpected miracle for him to stir from his solipsism long enough to hear a stranger's words. Still, for Avi to grant attention did not assure trust.

'They come to me,' he said.

'You've got the sound of a state Christian,' said Avi. 'Just doing the police in different voices.'

One night Avi told me about his fiancée. On a morning during the troubles she's been on a bankline. A gang burst in, members of a sect who frowned upon the sins of moneylenders and their clients. Avi hoped she'd been thinking of him as she died, but I doubted it; they watched as she watched her blood wash the marble pink beneath her. The truth later emerged about poor old Jesus, so conveniently released that it might have been by design, settling the restless, eliminating old troubles that the new ones could crowd in. The particular guilty were never punished; during his retreat Avi conceived a readjusted creed, and upon re-entering the world came to Dryco as Bernard and I did, our memories of the lost world wilfully erased. Amnesia came so easily as hunger, after a while.

Macaffrey seemed ashamed to be so accused.

'My father was a minister who passed out grape juice, lying it was wine.' I wondered who I might see staring back at me if I looked into his eyes. 'My family knew their purpose. Doesn't matter. You like our school?'

'You have a refreshing approach,' I said. 'Your students are remarkably articulate for their age— '

'When they want to be, they are,' he said. 'They saw you staring. It doesn't surprise them or please them, you understand— '

'I'm sorry,' I said. 'I've read about them but never seen— '

'Social worker words,' he said, smiling. 'Sideshow eyes. They're in their own world, after all.' He lowered his voice, as if to detail his own conspiracy. 'Some of them talked minutes after they were born, you know. Doctor I once knew explained that their vocal cords had already lowered, or risen, or however it works. Generally that's why babies don't talk, but they did. That's not the most wonderful thing— '

'What is?'

'If they knew how to talk when they were born, think how long they must have been listening.' His cheeks crushed his eyelids together as he smiled, burying his gaze beneath wrinkles. 'Why's your boss want to see me?' he asked, his eyes suddenly open, and I staring into them. When I first tried to speak, I couldn't; finally I stammered a reply.

'If I knew I wouldn't be allowed to say.'

'Fair enough,' he said. 'I'll be there at noon tomorrow, once my classes are done.'

'We'll send a car— '

'I'll get there,' he said, opening the door. 'Let

me walk you downstairs, make sure you get out all right.'

As he led us out I knew an uneasy comfort, the feeling a beaten child might know if her parent suddenly tossed aside the whip to gather her young one into her arms. Other teachers passed us on our way down, patting Macaffrey's arms and shoulders; students slowed, rushing by. He nodded to all, an incumbent cruising his electorate.

The man's body still lay on the sidewalk. Macaffrey sighed as he saw him. 'Your handiwork?' he asked Avi, who murmured admittance, his hand caught in the cookie jar.

Kneeling, Macaffrey placed his hand on the man's chest and shook him. He turned his head to look at us, fixing his unblinking eyes upon mine. My knees gave way, for I hadn't fought off his look; I started to slump, and felt Avi's arm encircling my waist, holding me up. The one hitherto lost to the world blinked his eyes.

'*Behave*!' Lester said, helping the man to his feet. 'How old are you, friend?'

He looked sixty. 'Eighteen.'

'Then you ought to know what can happen when you bother people you don't know. Go on, get out of here. Don't do it again. Go on.'

The man stumbled toward Avenue A, patting his head as if trying to remember where he'd had it. Avi and I looked around. Word of Macaffrey's appearances passed quickly; peering from windows, gazing out of doors, poking faces above the roofs of cars, the block's hundreds showed themselves, none speaking, none moving, all watching Macaffrey. He looked back at them with emotions I hadn't allowed myself to feel publicly for years, shivered and spoke.

'Noon tomorrow, then,' he said, almost whispering, rushing back to the yellow door, seeming so haunted by the neighbour's eyes as I was by his.

'You don't know where it is,' I said.

'I do.'

'Send kids to the circus and all they tell you about are the clowns,' said Bernard. We had no more trouble recounting what we'd seen than we would have had explaining it. I felt I should have worn cap and bells during our presentation, so foolish it sounded away from his presence.

'A con,' said Susie, certain that we'd failed, certain that she'd predicted as much; by her inerrant prophecy reaffirming her worth. She spread her eyelids with her fingers as if threatening to pop her eyes out at us. 'It's all in the peepers. Nothing but psychohypnosis.'

'Sounds like he's got the look to me,' said Thatcher.

'The Hitler look,' said Susie.

'That could be usable, depending on the circumstances— ' said Bernard.

'He obviously believes what he says, it sounds like,' said Thatcher.

'Then he's even crazier than we imagine,' said Susie.

'His messages would seem to be comprehensible to most nine-year olds, so you could reach a large enough audience in time,' said Bernard. 'It's more helpful if he does believe what he says, you get that unmistakable burp of honesty muffling the more obscure parts of the text— '

'Could he work on a mass scale?' Thatcher asked.

Bernard shrugged. 'We'd have to run the usual tests. See if he washes. It could be done, perhaps. Religion's simply an aspect of popular culture mutated. Only— '

'We saw what was there,' said Avi. 'I certified death.'

'How can you tell any more?' Susie asked. 'They must all look the same by now.'

Avi shook his head.

'He look dead to you?' Thatcher asked me.

'I'm no expert,' I said. 'I thought so.'

'Macaffrey could have told you the sun was the moon and you'd've thought so,' said Susie.

'There, see— ' Thatcher began.

'It is odd he had you so enthralled and ignored the chance to go all the way,' Bernard said. 'While he had you two fisheyed he didn't pass along any idle commentary on the brotherhood of life? No sidebars concerning meaning? A better race?' Bernard wrinkled his nose. 'Natural diets?'

'All he talked about was what I've told you,' I said.

'Pretty small-bore ammo here,' said Bernard. 'You're working with a nondescript who tells Bible stories of his own devising to special children and who, in his spare time, brings muggers back to life.' He chewed his thumb as he spoke. 'Wouldn't be the easiest sell to any market.'

'Let's subtext this for the moment,' said Susie. 'We have to examine the Jensen situation.'

'It's being seen to,' said Bernard.

'This boy sounds like he can talk some trash,' said Thatcher. 'That's good. I need somebody convincing.'

'He can't even keep his anthropology straight,' said Susie. 'Neanderthals. *Goddess*— '

33

'Godness,' Avi corrected.

'Fucking hell— '

'This time tomorrow,' Thatcher said, 'we'll get ourselves a good look at God. Next best thing, anyhow.' Throwing his head back he laughed with a delight of a boy racing through a thunderstorm, unmindful of lightning. He glanced at me, hoping to glimpse my response to this day's invitation. I nodded my head; he could have me, that night. 'What a wonderful world,' he said, his smile uncharacteristically beatific.

Wishing forgiveness for previous trespasses, Thatcher hadn't entered me for almost a year. He took pleasure rubbing himself raw against me, laying out the scenario desired that I might serve as metteuse-en-scène. 'I'll remember you in my will, hon,' he always said, after. Though he provided it I never invited him to my place. We met that night at his apartment in the north Trade Tower, a reconverted ninetieth-floor suite. At such altitude drapes were superfluous; moonlight shining through the narrow windows threw bars of shadow across our bed. Tossing aside the sheets I broke from my prison, walked over and looked out, the moon seeming so close that it could have been part of the décor. Thatcher beat his belly as if it were a drum when he rose, sending his victory cry to all his fellow beasts. His city pieds-a-terre served as warehouses as well, where purchases were stored until the executors might sort them out. From a stack of packages he removed a box, pulling from it what appeared in the dark as some archaeological relic.

'Jim Beam did a lot of figurines,' he said, proferring what I realised to be a two-litre bottle in the form of a bejewelled, bloated Elvis. 'Wanted one since I saw it in a liquor store, when I was a punk. Two thousand dollars.' Two hundred thousand old dollars; with that sum he could have fed a fraction of the starving, once. 'He'd have drunk it, if he'd drunk. He did touch the bottle. Got a paper with it authenticated.'

I discerned a date stamped on the bottom; I'd only been graduated from Middlebury that year, and believed as I exposed myself to the real world's virus that the country could never be worse off. 'He was dead when they made it,' I said.

Even when he loved, and he did, in his fashion, Thatcher condescended. 'One of these days E'll come again,' he said, shaking his head. With worshipping touch he rewrapped his icon within its mylar winding-sheet. 'Jerusalem Slim struck out like all the rest, but E'll turn up at the bottom of the ninth. Wait and see.'

'Maybe you can buy him when he shows up,' I said.

'Let's make do with what we have, for the moment,' he said. 'How'd this Macaffrey bird really strike you, hon?'

'He's got something,' I said. 'I'm not sure what. He'll cause trouble doing whatever he does, I'm sure. He seems rather independent— ' Thatcher's shoulders shook; he failed to hide his laughter, and I slapped him across the back of his head. He stopped laughing, overcome with emotion. 'If you're going to ask for my opinion, would you at least pretend to listen?'

'I'm not laughin' at you, hon,' he said, slipping his arm around me. 'It's the concept's got me going. I'm listening. Go on.'

'He seems to mean well in what he does. Probably makes him feel less guilty— '

'Guilty?' Thatcher repeated, as if learning the phonics of an unfamiliar word. 'Guilty about what?'

'I don't know, most people are— '

'Whose feelings we talking about here?'

'It's how it struck me— '

'You got a crush on him already, don't you?' I ignored him. 'That's sweet. He sure had you all convinced of something over there. Never heard such carrying on as when you all got back.' Slipping again into the shadow, he seemed no more than embodied dark. 'Avi doesn't get fired up too easy. And as for you, you worked with Bernard so long that an awful lot of him's wore off on you. Always bitin' the hand that feeds you. Not enough respect to pour into a thimble. Vipers, that's all you are.'

'I'm not like Bernard.'

'Bernard's got a different wound than you have— ' he started to say.

'Not by much.'

'You both got what I need.'

As he leaned forward his head re-emerged into light, his face reflecting city and moonshine as he kissed me. 'What the fuck are you planning, Thatcher?' I said.

'Walls always have ears, hon. Let's keep things general.'

'Couldn't get less specific.'

'Say somebody came along that seemed to be the messiah,' he said. 'Seemed that way often enough to enough people, at least.'

'What sort of messiah?'

'How many kinds are there?' he asked. 'I don't

mean palm readers, no gypsies reading tea leaves. No California babes talking about Egypt or Atlantis or Mars. I mean the real McCoy. What if you caught him in the wings while he was waiting to go onstage?' His eyes held the light, shining like beacons, cleaving the dark. 'How would you affect a co-opt? Could you interface him into the corporate frame? How much weight could he throw in the marketplace?'

'What if he's not— '

He lifted his arms, seeming to catch one tumbling to earth. 'Making a tree grow fruit in the wilderness. That's business, plain and simple.'

Hearing screams I remained mute, not having to convince myself that my actions could not prevent a crime. 'You're crazy, Thatcher.'

'Say he isn't anything but a good talker with the look, like Susie thinks,' said Thatcher. 'So? Doesn't mean he can't get things done with our help. She's good with the details but she can be blind as a bat with the big picture. If the idea's too – what's the word I want— '

'Crazy.'

'Transcendent,' he said. 'With a little coaching fellow like Macaffrey could do us a world of good. Show him which side of bread to put the butter on. How to slice up the loaf.'

'Why do you want a messiah?' I asked. 'Why?'

'It's not like it hasn't been done before,' he said, ignoring me so well as if I were but another lost in the surrounding crowd, one whose words went unheard, whose existence was so inessential as fog. 'Tell people somebody's something often enough and everybody comes around to believe it in time.'

I could never be such a devil's advocate as Bernard, but I had my moments. 'What if he is the messiah?' I asked. 'What then?'

Thatcher walked across the room to look over his land, staring into Long Island's crimson air. Retrieving my clothes I began to dress, wondering if in his reverie he could even see me. He kept the air conditioning so low in his rooms that even my soul felt chilled; I shivered, feeling as might a traveller lost in a blizzard, collapsing into a drift, ignoring all coming down around me, overcome by entombing cold, allowing my eyes to shut slowly beneath the weight of the snow.

'Different runway,' he said. 'Same approach.' He turned to look at me as I zipped up my skirt. 'Heathen might just get what they want for a change, or what they think they want.'

Heathern, the word emerged, mangled by his accent. All were heathern in his eyes; why had they so become in mine as well? A heathern world deserved a heathern messiah, yes, but what of our world, our sick world, our wonderful world? Which did it less deserve, its creators or its keepers?

3

In morning's more transcendent glow we awaited
Macaffrey, thinking or speaking of anything else.
'We examined Jensen's office files,' said Gus,
lifting a sheet of notepad. 'With police I searched
his apartment in the Bronx and his sister's in
Chelsea. That's where they found it, down there.'

'Did she know?' Thatcher asked. He reclined in
his chair, gazing out the wall-wide window onto
40 Wall Tower's pyramid crown and the ocean
beyond. Sparrows and gulls flew by, not looking
in. Susie sat sheltered beneath her paper's tent.

'Our silence was so effective that she was un-
aware of her brother's death until we told her. In-
terrogations proceed. No results. She's not much
in a mood to talk.'

'Let's see what you got,' said Thatcher. Looking over his shoulder, I read what was written,

seeing carefully inscribed black letters: MAHAICA *Conrad Taylor* MYSTIC *Mitch Moseley 3 days 25 percent.* Susie declined to examine it. 'What the hell's it mean?'

'As it has no evident meaning it must be pertinent,' said Gus. 'Mahaica is the name of a small port southeast of Georgetown, in Guyana. No other references to this name exist in the files. What remains appears shorthand rather than code. In either event, the names, the figures, the word mystic, the meaning of those is still unclear.'

'Guyana,' Thatcher repeated. 'Jim Jones territory?' Bernard nodded. 'Nobody wants him, he's dead. What else's Guyana got?'

'The usual raw materials,' said Bernard. 'It's an inessential state, except perhaps to Guyanans. No information received suggests Japanese interests presently operating in Guyana.'

'No evident interests,' said Thatcher.

One night while I was with him he drank to excess and began rambling about hiring Godzilla to destabilise Japan. I had to have Avi put him to bed before I went home.

'They've been taking all this time figuring out how to get into it right. Cut their losses before they even begin— '

'Who wrote this note?' asked Susie, tossing aside her paper as she might a kitten she'd tired of petting. 'Jensen?'

Gus shook his head. 'No ID thus far. The lettering is done with felt-tip pen such as any criminal might use.'

'What's the provenance of the paper?' Bernard asked.

'Standard notepad with a difference,' said Gus,

40

holding it against the light that we might see the watermark's modification, the fang protruding from the empty face's smirk on our company's happy-face logo. Bernard designed both versions of the trademark, the open and the closed. 'The paper came from this floor.'

'Jensen ever come up here?' Thatcher asked.

'Never,' said Gus. 'The guard wouldn't have accessed him.'

'So either he came in with somebody, or somebody was already here doing his business for him. Who's allowed on this floor?'

'Many,' said Gus. 'Politicians, Army representatives, publishers, your friends, company executives, government officials— '

'Charwomen, maintenants, anyone in the upper three levels of Security,' said Susie.

'Messiahs,' said Bernard.

'We can clear most of those,' said Thatcher, 'but there's still a rat in the cheese factory. Whoever's behind this is using our people. Who among us is most corruptible?'

'Blessings are equal, all around,' said Bernard. 'I'd suspect the Army. They're certainly enough of them running around here. You'd think it was a VFW hall some days.'

'It's not the Army— ' said Thatcher.

'If he had Latin American dealings he would have had to liaison with Army personnel at times,' said Susie. 'Any reports of renegade elements within the ranks? Conceivably he was contacted— '

'Reports in from all fields are analysed by sociopathologists for disturbing motifs recurring in the subtext,' Bernard said. 'That way those branches may be swiftly pruned. They're exam-

41

ined for signs of the boys enjoying themselves too much, or for patterns of fatalism, signs of disagreement with stated policies, the usual things. The prizewinners this year were a group of pilots who were flying copters into central Jersey at night to land in fields and mutilate farm animals.' He laughed. 'Those guys. Wannabe devil worshippers off on a toot.'

'What happened to them?'

'Transferred to the Turkish theatre,' said Bernard. 'Busy there mutilating Turks, I suppose.'

'If Jensen couldn't get in up here no one in the Army ranks could have helped him access, whether they were in or out,' I said. 'Army involvement would assume knowledge on the part of some in Command, wouldn't it? Who analyses their reports?'

Bernard shrugged. '*Quis custodiet ipso custodies*?'

Thatcher spoke again, ignoring Bernard's sudden lapse into tongues.

'The Army's not in this, I tell you,' said Thatcher. 'They're all right. They just see things differently than we do, that's all. They may not be too grateful but they don't forget who kept 'em going when times was hard.'

'Why would Frankenstein mind being given a gun?' asked Bernard.

'Let's be realistic,' said Thatcher. 'You and I know who we're looking for— '

'While it's possible the Japanese are involved I'm sure it would be only coincidentally. They've had so little involvement in the area in the past— '

'Think there's a possibility, though?'

'Anything's *possible*, Thatcher,' Bernard said.

'We still have to get this agreement signed, whether they're involved or not. After that our problems are over, wherever they arise.'

'Over?' Susie asked. 'Done?'

Thatcher nodded. 'You say this guy's into a lot of things— '

'So many that conceivably a renegade within his organisation might possibly be in on this. As, possibly, ones in ours have been involved. But he probably wouldn't be the one behind it, not at this point. The Japanese aren't crazy— '

'They play golf on top of skyscrapers,' Thatcher said, speaking slowly, as if to children. 'Keep robot fish in their aquariums. Put fresh air in spray cans. Watch movies of little girls killing each other with swords— '

'So they're crazy as Americans,' said Bernard. 'Neurosis is no reason for running before the gun's fired.'

'They got fifth columnists in half my businesses and I can't fire the bastards, they're too good. They're trying to get me in bad with the government.'

'Aren't you constantly telling me not to worry about the government?'

'It's not as cut and dried as I'd like it to be,' said Thatcher. 'You all act like we're already the government but you can't hurry love. That's why things still have to look halfway right. We'll always have to have elections, for example, there's no getting around it— '

'Subtleties,' said Susie, 'or so you always say.'

'You're safe as milk, Thatcher,' said Bernard. 'The populace has been so sober since it broke that terrible addiction to truth. No one cares what you do, they know it doesn't matter.'

43

'Never know what might get leaked,' said Thatcher. 'To the media.'

'Even the media you don't own want nothing to do with unlocking your closet,' said Bernard. 'More pressing problems need attention. The scams of beggars. Serial killers in the ranks of environmentalists. Subliminal messages on cereal boxes. All we ever have to do is put the cap over the lens, Thatcher, you've got to remember that.'

'Mr Dryden,' Lily called over the intercom. It was noon. 'Lester Macaffrey to see you.'

Susie tapped her jaw with her fingers. 'Glory.'

'Send him on in,' said Thatcher. 'Never enough time to do everything. All right, Gus, keep on Jensen. Go out there and give Macaffrey a rubdown, why don't you?'

As the door slid open Gus patted Macaffrey down as if flouring him. 'Three times for luck?' Macaffrey asked, his arms outstretched. 'Or ritual?'

'Precautions,' said Thatcher. 'Have a seat. Good of you to come see us on such short notice. Never heard such good things about a teacher before, Lester.'

'Mr Macaffrey will do for now,' he said, sitting down. 'You understand.'

Gus relaxed enough to cross his ankles. Avi had been invited to the meeting; when I asked if he was coming he shook his head, and walked away. I always knew when he was scared, even if he didn't.

'Nice offices you got here. I'm surprised it's not the penthouse.'

'Precautions,' Thatcher reiterated.

A question of blast direction, Avi told me;

the roof blew up if anything heavier than a pigeon landed upon it, destroying as well the floor immediately below, the observation deck.

'Mr Macaffrey, then. What I've heard about you makes me think your talents might be going to seed. I'd like to offer you a bigger field to sow.'

Macaffrey's stare seemed not so withering as it had the day before; I wondered if his mesmerism's effect could be likened to that of a drug to which one became addicted without ever feeling the high.

Susie slipped on sunglasses, looking as a gorgon lifting her own mirrors against those who came to harm her.

'Maybe you've heard of Dryco,' said Thatcher. 'We keep a low profile, but we're into more things than you could shake a stick at. What we lack is consistency. Got lots of material and no grand design. No theory.'

'You need a moral outline,' said Macaffrey. 'How could a teacher teach that?'

'For a teacher your educational record is refreshingly free of degree,' said Bernard, reading his printout. 'We have no evidence that you were even graduated from high school. How did you come across your present position?'

'Fell into it,' he said. 'Neighbourhood folks saw me as a natural, I suppose. I don't think the Board of Regents especially minds my taking my students off their hands.'

'Yesterday you told them your father was a minister,' said Susie. As she sat there, her eyes unreadable behind those shades, she seemed only to lack a cup filled with pencils. 'That's an interesting field. Of what breed was he? Something respectable? Fundamentalist? Racialist? He have any interest in politics? How much experience has your family already had in this area?

'Were the standard old ladies fleeced is what she's asking,' said Bernard. 'Did he molest innocent minds? Could he convince the flock that hell was worse than what they had? Or had he gone to graduate school and dreamed of something more encompassing?'

Macaffrey answered, his face totemic, showing nothing, holding all. 'My father was an Episcopal priest. He found good in unlikely places. I think he was happy with his life. In the fall he blessed the foxhounds before the hunts began.'

Bernard winked. 'Who blessed the fox?'

'Is this a genealogical society?' Macaffrey asked. 'I don't understand what my family has to do with this— '

'Following up on background checks. Precautions,' said Thatcher. 'That's all. Looking for the man behind the mask. It's easy to lose the human element in all this if you're not careful.'

'Heaven forbid,' said Bernard. 'Much of a churchgoer yourself, Lester? Not really much point these days, don't you think?'

'I'm no joiner.'

'In our service economy,' said Bernard, 'who do you serve? God?'

'No less than anyone.'

Bernard loved a challenge – to a point – and responded at full tilt. 'I wish my teachers had been so creative. Such curious invention you have. It's way above the norm, I assure you. Tell me now. It's tricky to describe a creative act without tossing the Lord in somewhere, I suppose, but I

46

find such vagueness unholy. I'm told these concepts of yours came to you, How? In dreams? A bottle? Do you file through some heavenly fax? Do you consider your truth to be true?'

'I've said it long enough that I should.'

Bernard's net was ready but the butterfly wouldn't settle. More familiar with Thatcher's sort of logic, Bernard reconsidered, and readied the killing jar.

'Good man in procurement, we hear,' he said. 'What's involved in that? You look up in the sky until you see it falling? Does some geyser of bounty shoot up between your feet? Where do you come by your gifts?'

'Everybody has connections,' said Macaffrey. 'No mystery in that.'

'Tricks are fine for television but we have no cameras here.' Thatcher once told me that there were twelve in the room. 'Some here in our audience gave boffo reviews for your act's finale. Can you raise the dead?'

'To be what?' Bernard pursed his lips, and looked down at his printout.

'Maybe you're not taking this in the right way,' said Thatcher, leaving it purposefully unclear as to whom he spoke. 'Mr Macaffrey. If Gus was to throw you through that window, would you fall?'

'Under the circumstances you'd risk it?'

'I wouldn't be putting in an investment to lose, if you fell. You get used to taking risks in business like you get used to breathing, you know. It only seems to me that there's mighty big stuff being hinted at here and I'd like to see something more impressive. I want to know if you're all you say you are.'

'I'm nothing,' said Macaffrey. 'I'm here at your request. If you're so sure of what you see, why should I give you glasses?'

'Gus,' said Thatcher, 'go out in the hall, bring Jake in here a minute.'

'Why?'

'I won't hurt him.'

Gus went to retrieve, and the dialogue continued.

'Is there something you're planning?' asked Macaffrey.

'You're probably aware that most everybody in your line claims some degree of medical skill,' said Thatcher. 'None of 'em ever come claiming to be a psychic accountant, say. Guess God never has to balance His own books— '

'I'm no doctor.'

'Bringin' somebody back to life's damn good doctoring, I'd say, long as they were dead,' said Thatcher. 'Course if you could do that we'd have a new problem deciding who to keep— '

Gus returned with his protégé. Jake stood silently, awaiting his orders, clasping his hands over his groin.

'You been working over a year for us now, right?'

Jake nodded. I don't believe he'd ever been in the boardroom before.

'You've done a good job for us. Good potential. You don't fuck around, Jake.'

'I sting the bees.' With quick fingers Jake smoothed his clothes, an unconstructed white jacket and ironed jeans.

'That's the way God planned it. I hear you never let on when it hurts.'

'Not overmuch, nada nohow.'

'What hurts you?'

'Tooth Nazis,' he said.

'No root canal this trip,' said Thatcher. 'You don't mind blood tests, do you? How often you get those?'

'Bimonthed as required.'

'Think of this as a blood test,' said Thatcher. 'Jake, Gus is going to break one of your fingers and then we'll see if this boy can fix you up. You pick the finger.'

After a moment's hesitation Jake lifted his left arm, extending a pinky no larger than my own.

'There's a purpose to this, Mr Dryden?' Gus asked.

'Told you I wasn't going to hurt him,' said Thatcher. 'Get to it, Gus, don't have all day.'

Gus broke bones with the greatest finesse, I was told, but I still closed my eyes and covered my ears. Looking again I saw Jake still motionless, his arm pressed against his side, his finger jutting away from his hand; he seemed a statue of smooth cold marble.

'What do you suggest?' Thatcher asked Macaffrey. The look Macaffrey returned held no threat of trance.

'Take him to the hospital,' he said. 'He'll go into shock.'

'You don't think you can fix it?' asked Thatcher.

'I always fail tests.'

'You passed, son. If you'd tried faking it you'd've already hit the street. Jake, that hurt you much?'

Jake's mouth barely moved, as if he intended to throw his voice through a dummy. 'No.'

'AOK, Gus. Take him to the clinic.' Jake

49

shook Gus's hand away from his shoulder as
they walked away. Bernard tapped his pencil
against the tabletop. Susie's eyes were unreadable
behind her sunglasses. I tried convincing myself
that I wasn't fully there.

'You're everything I've heard, Mr Dryden,'
said Macaffrey, standing. 'I'll be on my way.'

'I understand gut reactions,' said Thatcher. 'Sit
back down. I want you to see how valuable you
could be to my organisation. Sit down.'

'What good could I do?' Macaffrey asked.

'You got to have more self-assurance than that,'
Thatcher said. 'It's essential. Haven't you ever
once stopped to think what you could paint with
a bigger brush?'

'What do you want from me?'

'People always want more than what those who
have can give,' said Thatcher. 'It's gotten to the
point where we can't let expectations get any
lower— '

'How could they?' Susie asked.

'Time's come to raise a few hopes. We need an
inspiration, not just for us but for them. Help 'em
get out of bed in the morning. Help keep a lid
on things when need be. Main thing is we can't
forget that we couldn't do what we do without
people.'

'You want me to pass out the Kool-Aid,' said
Macaffrey.

'Are you making unwarranted references?'
Thatcher asked, a century's sorrow at command
soaking his voice. 'Unfair lies, that's what you
might have heard. Makes me sick to think that's
what's still believed.' He calmed down shortly,
taking comfort in truth. 'Not ten percent of our
money comes from drugs any more, and we're in

the process of phasing that out. We've diversified into a number of fields.'

'In a number of places.'

'It's so simple to go global these days,' said Thatcher. 'Only limit is how far you can see. Think of it, son. Hundreds of millions of people everywhere and every one listening to you. You can give peace to troubled minds. Help groups settle their differences. Solve the problems of tomorrow today. Get that camera in front of you and a few satellites and it's all yours— '

'Thatcher,' Bernard said, interrupting. 'Don't overstate— '

'Think of what things might be like today if TV'd been invented twenty years earlier.'

'Television has great power to confound and distract,' said Macaffrey. 'It saps the soul. I have no desire for unnatural congress.'

'Most people'd kill and eat their grandmothers to get on TV,' said Thatcher. 'Worse. We'll start you at six thou per year and see how it goes. No more having to preach to gimpy kids from Farmingdale, that's for sure.'

Bernard and Susie looked no less stricken than I must have appeared; I made two per year, and Bernard not that much more.

'Appropriate raises with suitable results. Fair and equitable. We scratch your back, you scratch ours. Everybody comes out ahead.'

'You want me to make people render unto Caesar what Caesar already has,' said Macaffrey. 'Not much point in that, I don't think. I'm sure you'll get along without me.' Turning, Macaffrey went to the door, and left.

'What's this?' Thatcher said, watching him leave.

'I think he's saying no,' said Bernard.

Susie laughed, flushing so with colour that I thought her happiness might kill her.

'Found a smart one for a change,' she said, her words seeming to choke her as she laughed them out.

'Thinks he is,' said Thatcher. Having seen his seduction foiled, he appeared now to be toying with fantasies of rape.

'He obviously doesn't want to be bothered,' I said. 'Leave him alone. Hire an actor for your plots. Hasn't that worked before, I think you said?'

'Thatcher must feel he needs this kernel of winsome sincerity,' said Bernard, 'to grow his new crop of threats.'

'Can't get an actor for this kind of deal,' said Thatcher. 'Be like a white boy singing the blues. We'll play it by ear. I got a hunch he'll come around with the right prompting.' As he turned to me he paused, as if to make me more aware of how soon I would learn of my next role in the drama.

Susie spoke to her husband as she walked out. 'I'm going to the infirmary to check on Jake. Did you have— '

'That's what we pay 'em for.'

That afternoon I stopped at Bernard's office, suspecting I'd never see Macaffrey again, finding it impossible to remove him from my mind. Bernard sat surrounded by the remnants of his personality that covered his desk: a photo of his wife, a Clio award he used as a paperweight, a pencil sketch of their late son; he was in a coma for a year before he died. Bernard, maker

of millions – old millions – was bankrupt when
he signed on at Dryco; I had my jewellery. In
the centre of his desk, near the edge, was a
brass-coloured pen and pencil holder in the shape
of Dealey Plaza.

'You're here to see our newest commercial,' he
said as I entered.

'Must I?'

'Sweetness, overseeing new projects means
feigning interest even in the inanimate ones. Here
we go.'

His set was a flat screen on the far wall; pressing the remote he rolled the spot, which not so
much played as richocheted. Sequential images
flashed on during the first twenty seconds, coming too quick to grasp individually but showing myriad aspects of the worst of our world;
the music backgrounding was the orchestral run
swelling along the scale as it led to the bridge in
'A Day in The Life.' Before the mind overloaded
the sound and picture changed, the music segued
into a full chorus singing the *Song of Joy* from
Beethoven's Ninth; the blurs vanished into clean
clouds seen at angel's altitude, the light aglow in
bright blue air, sunrays lending that Nuremberg
touch. As the company's motto superimposed itself onto the clouds it seems to rise from the
depths of heaven.

D R Y C O
Worry not. Wonder not.

'Does the signifier need the sign? It's meaning-
packed at the core level. We've entered it for
several awards— '

'It's unreal even for television, Bernard.'

He pulled clippings from a folder on his desk.
'Unreal,' he said. 'Listen to what we have here.
Elvis appears on Mexican woman's taco, hundreds come to be healed. Pregnant by alien, woman sues NASA. Teacher at Dartmouth divides
polisci class into Gestapo and Jews to illustrate
the limits of power – three dead. All of this is
just from last week's *Times*. What's the second
leading cause of death among white American
teenagers?'

'Boredom?'

'Casually,' he said. 'Autoerotic asphyxiation.'
Men tapped into inexhaustible strength so long
as they possessed a battery of irrelevant facts;
Bernard owned more than I could count. Men
had a way of using their facts to propel them toward imagination, and not to truth. 'You couldn't
make it up.'

'I need to talk to you,' I said.

'Work-related?' he asked, shutting off the set.

'Coincidentally.'

'Pity,' he sighed. 'Does it involve Thatcher's
new avatar? At least it helps keep him dis-
tracted— '

'I've never seen anyone get under your skin
so.'

'Halfbaked Jesus freak,' said Bernard. 'Too
stupid to lie.'

'You hate him because you couldn't out-talk
him,' I said. 'It's so obvious.'

Bernard's mood was changeable as tropical
weather, and as he glared I feared I'd roused
a typhoon. He didn't blow; the moment passed.

'Bernard, what if you'd gotten so sick of working here you couldn't look at yourself in the
morning?'

'Where are the mirrors?' he asked, with mimic gestures delineating the room.

'I've got to get away from this,' I said. 'I spend all my time doing nothing. I see no one but him. It's driving me crazy.'

'A benefit of the position,' he said. Bernard never responded as I might have preferred, but unlike all others he always listened. 'You arrived at any preliminary decisions yet? Been examining options? Besides complaining, what have you done?'

'Avi thinks I should live with my reality.'

'That gets tricky after a while, doesn't it? Jobs, people, fish, they all rot after three days. Say you quit. What happens?'

My tracks seemed to lead to a single terminal, whether I took the express or the local. 'No income. I lose my apartment. I'm out on the street.'

He nodded. 'If you get yourself fired?'

'The same.'

'If you find another job and then quit?' Bernard asked. 'Shouldn't leave one job until you have another one lined up, you know.'

'I'd still be working for him.'

'What if you request a horizontal promotion?' he asked. 'Not in the sense with which you're most recently familiar— '

'Transferred where?' I asked. 'Data? I'd be blind in a month.'

'You could always go on Workfare,' said Bernard. 'Enter a shelter. One way or the other, you wouldn't be there long.'

'People get by with less than I have— '

'People eat their dead in Brooklyn,' he said. 'Thatcher's not the worst man I've ever known.

It's bound to happen eventually, so you should enjoy yourself while you can— '

'Some mornings I wake up and just want to run away,' I said. 'Anywhere. Get in a car and drive and keep on driving.'

'Through our great and good land?' His face brightened as if he'd already received his awards. 'You've flown over it, sweetness, but I've been there. You think New York's bad? And the people, well. They'd give you the willies for weeks. Whole time the axe is coming down, they've got the smiles turned up full. You'd be a fish out of water, for sure. Dead in three days, I'd bet.'

'Something's happening to me, Bernard,' I said. 'I don't know what. It's as if somebody else is running away with me before I can get away myself— '

'You're getting older,' he said; Bernard always listened, not always intelligently. 'Listen to what Avi tells you. He's a sensible sort, every once in a while. Ignore the worst and do your job well. Forget the day as it passes. Go enjoy your life as it is. That's all— '

'That makes me no better than they are,' I said. 'Worse, because I don't feel as they do, I don't believe— '

'Or you already feel as they do and don't want to face it,' he said. 'These things sneak up on you, you know. Get that look off your face, sweetness, you wanted inspiration? I'm no messiah. I can't tell a crystal from a crack vial.' He read his appointment book, his glasses low on his nose. 'Pity me, my angel, I have to roll in the gutter with the mayor tonight. He's demanding specific dates as to when the Army might be expected to pacify Queens and I have to leave the

56

date as being sometime during the twenty-first century. He's been causing a lot of annoyance lately— '

'You see no other options for me?'

'See any mirrors?'

'Travelready?' Jake asked, appearing at my office door as I prepared to leave. It was after eight.

'All set,' I said. Whenever I left late, alone, Jake assured my safety. It struck me that somehow I intimidated him; though never loquacious, he seemed especially numbtongued around me. Jake's was a prodigal's soul; his divine talents so influenced his every action and word as to overwhelm any would-be friend. I noticed a volume of Shakespeare, rather than the expected truncheon, stuffed into his jacket pocket.

'Gus teaches you literature?' I asked as we rode down.

'AO,' he said. 'Litcrit twicecovered this month.'

'So many wonderful characters,' I said. Jake's presence aroused in me a deeply buried instinct that was still conceivably maternal. 'You have any favourites?'

'Ariel.'

A car waited at the curb to carry me home. Before we reached it I heard my name called; there was no forgetting Macaffrey's voice. He walked toward us, across our building's plaza; Jake, recognising him, allowed him to get to us.

'You haven't been out here all day?' I asked.

'I came back.' In the streetlight his face held a hundred years' lines. 'Would you walk with me?'

Run was what I wanted to do. 'Yes,' I said, hearing a stranger speak for me. 'Jake, I'll be going a different way tonight. I'll see you Monday.'

Jake remained where he stood, cautious as a cat. For the first time I noticed the bone-white cast gloving his finger and, suggesting no medical purpose, the scalpel attached to the tip.

'Tell the driver to go on, Jake,' I said. 'I'll be all right.'

'You're chancing,' he said, his sea-changing voice sometimes soprano, sometimes tenor, this night unexpectedly clear and deep. 'You know who lights the lights.' Jake had only turned fourteen.

'Worry not,' I said, attempting to sound official. 'Have a good weekend.'

After we walked away he cried out in higher pitch, perhaps only making sure that I still heard him. 'Joanna— '

'Jake?' That must have pleased him; without responding, he went inside to go home. With Macaffrey I wandered down Broad Street's gully. Small buildings plugged the rifts in the range, seeming no more than pebbles eroded from the sides of their mother boulders. Billboards of two year's vintage or older stood atop their low roofs. One sold the winner of the most recent Presidential election, and whenever I passed his face faded further away. Vice-President once, he was shot on the last day of March. His Vice-President died five weeks after being sworn in, when Air Force One collided with a sightseeing helicopter over old Shea Stadium. His successor tried to escape, the day of the crash; after the jets forced his plane down the crowd, seeing at last a reason to vote, decided that he should be soundly beaten in their election. His successor and Thatcher worked something out that suited Thatcher for three months; Gus settled matters in Seattle.

The present President, the fifth to take office that year, appreciated whose butter smeared his bread.

'You'd never guess what your company does from the name,' said Macaffrey. 'What do you do for them?'

'Less and less,' I said. 'Nominally I oversee new projects.'

'Like me?' he asked. 'You must stay busy. Did they get that little fellow fixed up all right? I don't think he took too kindly to your going off with me.'

'Jake takes his job seriously,' I said. 'Gus took him in off the street as an apprentice a year ago. He's grateful. Why were you out there waiting?'

'Nowhere else to go,' he said.

'I'd think your schedule'd be booked— '

'On the way back this afternoon I stopped for lunch. When I returned to the school it'd been closed by order of the Army as a disorderly house. It's a subtle approach, I'll admit, but still— '

We stood there for a moment as I estimated what I'd done. So many wings, so many flies. 'I'm so sorry,' I said. 'Thatcher thinks he can bully anyone into doing what he wants.'

'He can,' said Macaffrey. 'I suppose he thinks he wants me.'

'So you've reconsidered,' I said. 'Well, what choice you got. They've left for the weekend, but I can get access. Tell them you came back to see them— '

'To see you,' he said. I hoped I wasn't blushing, but my skin reddens even when someone calls me by my first name. Craning my head I looked at anything but Macaffrey. When I was young and visited the city with my parents I remembered how I could look down any of the cross streets and see a river; I glanced into an alley-wide street whose vista was not of water, but the wall of a riverside tower resembling twenty thousand elevator buttons stacked one atop the other.

'Why?'

'We have a mutual interest.'

Thus far he differed from other men I'd known only in that he apparently believed what he said at all times, and not solely when it was convenient. 'I am sorry you lost your job. Those poor children— '

'They'll be all right,' he said. 'My job's just starting.' A trace of disappointment in his voice made me aware of his sorrow, his sadness over not having yet been able to hook me. The street we travelled ended at the island's toe. Battery Park's old trees were cut down by the Army so that mortars might be strategically aimed in the event Long Islanders attacked by sea. The floodwall started rising soon after, and now the guns pointed directly at downtown's only defence against the water. Siren's sound echoed across the ocean air; damp salt breezes wafted over the wall, bearing dry leaves from trees far afield, their currents rich with smells of rain and oil and dead fish.

'You mean your job at Dryco?' I asked.

'Let me help you see what I mean,' he said, lifting my arm before me as if to restrain me from flying away too soon. 'Take my hand.'

There it was: the first shake of the buck's antlers, the sly valentine hand-drawn in crayon, the molester's unwrapping of the lollipop, the first phone call promised. Southerners wasted no time, I thought, recalling Thatcher's unctuous chivalry during our first month together, before events removed my presence from his mind's upper slot. Men behaved so perfectly until their attention spans failed them.

'Why?'

'To see something pretty.' Pressing my hand into his, I marvelled at how wilfully I fell into any new trap. Then, as if in brownout, all city light dimmed, outshone by the sky as it unexpectedly took fire. Over Upper New York harbour no spires or towers disrupt the view of heaven's bowl; I stared freely into its millions from below, gazing up into the crowd as if into a tornado, a mandala, a spiral of DNA. In the midst of the angel's hurricane was an eye of blinding white light. I heard the angels' sight, saw their music as a sound like the roar of the sea in a shell. In knowing their movements I looked into the painful light for so long that I thought my own eyes might melt, but I couldn't turn away.

'They figure it's what we'd expect,' he said. 'I'm sure it's different in reality. Sometimes you'll hear music, too. They like Wagner.'

I let go his hand; the vision faded as it came. The street's chiaroscuro reappeared beneath New York's sky, free again of angels as it was free of oxygen or stars. Others passing along their nightly circuits seemed to have seen no more than the sidewalk lying ahead of their shoes; New Yorkers looked up only to see what might be falling toward them. As I looked at Macaffrey I thought I'd never felt so secure in my fear. 'Call me Lester, Joanna,' he said. 'I don't hold much with labels.'

4

'You'll see me home,' I asked, knowing he'd agree. A million words raced around our silence as we sailed uptown between Broadway's palisades. In our day the thumbrule was that bony lies became truth rich and strange if the need for belief was great enough. A child might rub her stuffed animals bald, trying to wish them into life; what if she started with a living pet? Reality was never so flexible in fact as in theory. Angels, I told myself: there could have been nothing to see; all was but a blend of sky and delusion. Closing my eyes, I still saw angels. Why was I chosen to receive revelation? It made as little sense as those stories of flying saucers landing on lonely Nebraska prairies, desiring that farm girls alone would know the secrets between the stars. That I liked being with Lester held nothing of heaven.

'That fellow you came to the school with,' he said. 'You were lovers once?'

From distant Brooklyn came the sound of bundled papers being thrown onto a news-stand's curb, the nightly cannonade. No doubt I'd opened my mind wide enough that Lester might now easily slip anything in.

'You couldn't know that— '

'It's in the way you stood next to him,' he said. 'The tilt of your pelvis. It's all in the details. Let's go this way.'

We headed west down Rector Street; Trinity Church's encircling boneyard was on our right, bright beneath floodlamp glare; arcs hung from the trees, appearing as fruit passed over at harvest time. The yard's retaining wall rose higher as the street sloped toward the unseeable Hudson river. Turning north again we passed beneath a slender wrought-iron bridge arching above the street, running from the cemetery to an office building, as if the sextons, foreseeing Doomsday, provided for the dead a short walk between grave and Workfare office.

'You broke up with him a while back?' Lester asked.

'It was a work relationship. We got over-involved. Not long after we started working there. Our jobs got in the way. His job.'

'What happened?'

'We had this awful conversation one night,' I said. 'I called him a golem. Worse. We kept talking and stayed friends, but the moment passed.'

Midtown's distant lights enflamed Manhattan's sky until it appeared no less bloody than Long Island's. The breath of the underworld rose through cracks in the pavement. The Trade Towers stood on our left behind a low wall of outbuildings. Soldiers guarding the plaza searched and taunted a man delivering pizzas; a lateworker's dinner always arrived cold. 'Why am I telling you this?'

'I asked,' he said. 'Seems so quiet down here at night. Like the old days, I guess. Army's really necessary still?'

'Seen as necessary,' I said. 'Thatcher gets nervous unless he's surrounded.'

'Except when he's with you?' Lester asked, no trace of malice in his question.

By moving further away from him, I thought, I could keep him from driving deeper into my mind, deliberately forgetting that I walked with one who showed me God's lack of face.

'Please stop,' I said.

'I read people well. I wish I was illiterate.'

'It's as if you've had me investigated,' I said. 'Watching me come and go and I never knew it. It's an awful feeling— '

'Do you hate me as much as you hate him, then?'

A third pair of feet paused a second after ours; stopped, the sound adding a grace note to our chord. I saw no one near. A soldier, I thought; some worker, a clerk leaving a store. A nominal curfew was on, though as a Dryco exec I could probably have stepped to the curb and hailed a tank, had I wanted.

Lester kept alongside me as we moved uptown through ever-darker streets. Helicopters overhead thrashed the city with sticks of light, searching for those with whom they refused to share hegemony. Wind glued newspapers to our ankles as we walked, the day's words lost in the wind.

'I'm sorry,' he said. 'It's too easy to see what people think.'

'That means you have to tell them?' I said. 'Like people don't have enough to worry about without having strangers come raping their minds?'

'People never worry about what they should,' he said, 'and so often rape happens with someone you thought you loved. You wouldn't trust me if I weren't a stranger.'

'Don't they hate you for this in your neighbourhood?' I asked. 'Reminding people of what they want to forget?'

'It's a sin to see wrong and do nothing about it.'

'So God's the greatest sinner?' I asked, the Bernard in my soul leaping forth.

'Yes and no,' he said.

We passed an old post office recycled years ago into a Health Service clinic. A long line of silent people awaited entry into the waiting room. Brass railings green with verdigris guarded its graffitied walls. A sign affixed to the granite tallied late additions to the six billion:

NATIONAL REPORTED
  CASES NOV 17 1,623,958
DEATHS 783,521
NEEDLES AVAILIBLE DAILY
9 AM 1PM
Hope Will Find A Way

'Even They have to make the best of what They've made,' he said. 'Does it make sense that in a better world this would be a better world?'

I wondered what might be expected of God-Godness if Their apparent messenger could sound so transcendent. 'You see what you showed me all the time or only if you want to?'

'How else?' he asked, laughing. A wild wind, an angel's breath, swept his hair across his forehead, for a moment taking twenty years from his look. 'I've learned to live with what comes to me.'

'Can you see the future?'

'Can't you?' he asked, sweeping his arm out before us.

The familiar whoop of an oncoming siren sounded as an infant's wail. Facing the street we lifted our arms above our heads. The mayor's limo rolled uptown, surrounded by motorcycle cops, preceded and followed by flatbed trucks carrying soldiers thrusting their rifles forth in every direction, pins in pincushions.

'He never visits my neighbourhood,' he said. 'When they pass I'm always tempted to keep walking as the hearing-impaired do— '

'You'd be shot as they're always shot,' I said.

'Considering how he treats the innocent, how does your Mr Dryden deal with the guilty?'

'Depends on who's guilty of what,' I said. 'He never gets his own hands dirty.' My earlier question at last returned to mind. 'You never said if you could see the future. Can you?'

'Some people's futures,' he said.

'Whose?'

'Mine,' he said. 'Yours,'

Reaching the corner of Duane Street South we stopped for the light; someone else stopped. There was nothing Thatcher had taught me so well as the acceptance of fear. Seeing no one,

I knew they were there.

'We're being followed,' I said.

'No, we're not— '

'Listen.'

Food wholesalers still plied their trade along Duane Street from their old brick buildings; trucks idled beneath overhanging metal awnings as teamsters loaded them with milk and cheese. The din was conveniently loud.

'I don't hear anything,' he said.

'Let's get out of here.'

A dark triangle of park lay between Duane Street's legs. Within the small plot were dozens of sleepers wrapped in the blankets upon which, the next morning, they'd peddle magazines retrieved from dentist's offices. Bernard always said it was easier, now, to live in Calcutta; it was never cold in Calcutta. We started across. Growing used to the pounding of the truck's heartbeats I heard again what I didn't want to hear, footsteps racing with quicker rhythm than ours. Wishing I'd worn lower heels I trotted leftward, Lester close behind. I heard the pop of a firecracker; having heard the sound knew I hadn't yet been shot.

'God,' I said. 'Run!'

We did, up a side street on the north border of the square, our feet slipping over the Belgian block. The street was so narrow that its low buildings seemed three times as high as they were, and only a solitary lamppost broke the two-block gloom. An enclosed bridge of almost Venetian appearance ran between buildings nearest the light, several stories above the street. We could have as easily run into the last century and not known, so unalterably ancient were our surroundings. Where the dark was deepest we pressed ourselves into a wall.

'Why are we running?' Lester asked as we waited.

'They're shooting.'

'Who?' I shook my head, knowing a deli's wealth of selections. The assailants of Jensen, working their way through the repertoire; Jake, having acted upon second thoughts; soldiers taking target practice, a sniper warming up before performance, an accountant upset with her husband. Some shot only for love of the sound.

'Anybody after you besides us?' I asked.

'Not any more,' he said. 'Do you think he's behind it?'

'We'd never know. Gus would be handling it if that's the case— '

'The old guy?'

'He's had experience— '

'Breaking children's fingers?'

'He shot three Presidents.'

All remained quiet, but it didn't matter. Patience was all; we couldn't move if we were perhaps to be missed. Had I been left to simmer in my own juices I might never have moved again. A door slammed, down where the trucks waited to pull out, and I glanced down to look at their lights. When I turned around again I saw that Lester had walked into the middle of the dead street and waited there, as if to see who might notice. As he stood beneath the streetlamp's half-light Lester seemed to glow from within, his aura assuredly no less radioactive than it was numinous.

'Nothing's happened to us yet, Joanna,' he said. Returning to where I stood yet fastened onto the brick, he took my arm and led me out.

Down on Duane Street the trucks revved, pulling away to make their deliveries. My stomach burned as if my ulcers were newly aflame; I sank to my knees, my strings cut. Wanting to throw up, I threw out only tears, crying without sound so that no others might hear, gaining an awareness I didn't want them to have.

'No,' he said. 'It's all right. It is.'

As he stroked my back I began to recover, drawing long, dry breaths; my head reattached itself to my body.

'A truck backfiring. Must have been. If somebody was after us we've given them plenty of opportunity.'

'They have that anyway,' I said; it did seem safe enough, for the moment. Lester helped me to my feet; when we walked off I noticed the street's name. I'd never heard of Staple Street but others must have, for they lived there. A nearby window showed kitchenlight; boxes of catfood on the sill, a dead plant, a plastic hanukiah. We turned right, toward Hudson Street.

'This happen to you often?' Lester asked.

My mouth ached as I answered, so harshly had I bridled myself against my tears.

'It didn't use to,' I said. 'This is too much. I hate being afraid all the time. I hate what I am. How I live— '

'Don't say that.'

'I hate what I've done. What they've done to me. I hate so much and I can't let it out.'

So often so-called new men purport to admire the inherent gentleness of women, only demonstrating they know women no better than old

69

men; too often a woman recirculates her rage through herself, settling upon the likeliest victim in the most practical way. Men play at anger, as at a game; so many times, then, I could have as uncaringly taken a machete and hacked through any subway-car's passengers.

'You hate what you've let them do to you?' he asked.

'That too.'

Hudson Street looked so much more of our time than did Staple Street that you could almost imagine people still using it. Cars two to twenty years old lined the curbs; traffic restrictions ended a block below Canal Street and as we drew closer the streets began filling with traffic. On the city entrance of the Holland tunnel, at the end of Canal, the Army ran a haphazard checkpoint, stopping and searching vehicles for improprieties that they might seize and resell for themselves. The line of cars awaiting entrance into the city ran, at all hours, five miles deep into Jersey; Dryco and Army cars had their own lane, and so could pass through much more easily. The rumour was that the soldiers, to cut costs, reused their testing needles on their successive suspects.

'We cross north?' Lester asked.

No taxis grazed our flanks as we raced across Canal; no tanks flattened us, rolling down their centre lane. One of several double-length semis almost blew us over with its wind, careening past. On the trailer was the Kraft logo; superimposed upon that, the Dryco smile.

'You were right, what you said. I'd trust a stranger before I'll trust a friend.'

'For the right reasons?' Lester asked.

'People you know, friends, they always expect you to act a certain way. When you don't, they get disappointed, or they get to hating you. I think people have friends only to guarantee they can always be let down.'

'So you behave differently around strangers,' he said.

'I'm looser,' I said. 'Thatcher likes everyone high-strung. And the people I've known the longest and have been the closest to are also the biggest liars I know, so— '

'How much do you think has rubbed off on you?'

On the far corner an enormous office building had been torn down years before for luxury apartments never built. Hundreds of smaller residences were scattered across the lot in its stead: boxes and crates, ill-pitched tents, tin-walled huts, clusters of cardboard. At the neighbourhood's centre stood a small frame shack, surely the home of that community's Thatcher.

'Enough, I'm afraid,' I said. 'I used to have so many more friends.'

'What happened to them?'

'Bankrupt between breakfast and lunch,' I said. 'Lost their jobs. Their apartments. If I saw them I wouldn't know them now.'

'You would,' said Lester.

'I was just luck it didn't happen to me,' I said. 'Bernard moved to Dryco just before. I moved as well. The right place, the right time. I couldn't help it.'

'It's all right— '

'It'd never happen again,' I said. 'Everything hinges on his behaviour. My life depends on how crazy he gets. I don't like it.'

Along these blocks the remnant of a more traditional neighbourhood remained: a diner, a deli, a row of shops partially rented. In the deli window was a sign written in Korean and English, reading JAPS KEEP OUT, looking so old as to refer to Axis-allied Japan. The doors of stores were open to catch cool evening breezes. Two young girls thrashed about on the sidewalk, arguing and cursing, pinning one another with pipestem legs; they looked Jake's age, or younger. A gang of boys hooted; several older men watched, keeping their hands in their pockets. The girls screamed, oblivious to sideshow eyes.

'You said that older man killed three Presidents,' Lester said. Three teenagers, their shaved heads making them resemble mad insects, shoved by us as they made for the brawl. 'Who was the third?'

'Gus was on the grassy knoll,' I said.

The crowd's scream faded to a whisper, the further we drew from it. Lester took so long to respond that I wondered if he'd heard me.

'You're serious?'

'That's what Thatcher told me. As I understand it Gus didn't know Oswald was there until they started shooting. I suppose they were as shocked as anyone.'

'Who fired the shot?'

'Gus isn't sure.'

One last small shop sold mineral specimens, petals of stone, roses plucked from the rock. I doubted the owners had a lease. After that the street passed through dead blocks, every building's windows and storefronts boarded up as against the flood. Flowered decals brightened some windows' blinders. Sprigs of colourless

72

grass sprouted through the broken sidewalk. So abandoned in haste did all appear that I imagined entering any of the buildings, finding coffee still warm in cups, toothpaste still wet upon brushes, but not even a scrap to show where everyone went.

'That your company's mark?' Lester asked, pointing toward an upper floor.

Plastered below the cornices were block-long posters advertising the new development on that lot shortly rising. They'd missed the target completion date by three years. It seemed too late to idly seek logos, but at last I saw what he saw, a small design in no way resembling Dryco's empyrean leer.

'Bank of Nippon,' I said. 'Their mark. These are some more frozen assets. I'm sure he'll wind up with them eventually, he always seems to. I've lost track of half of what they have.'

'Do they own everything?' Lester asked, seeming overly aware of what everything contained.

'Every business has a little bit of Dryco in it.'

'How'd they do it?' he asked. 'Just luck? Did they plan it?'

'Their government reps found out about the revaluation before it went into effect,' I said, explaining as I'd heard it from Bernard. 'Some of them suggested it, apparently. Before it went through they'd already traded their old money in for the new bills. It's understandable, I think, they wanted to see their competition in the drug field out of business as badly as the government did. When the market crashed Susie was the only one able to buy. She bought fifty percent of seventy companies. That was all they needed.'

'What was he doing at the time?'

'Conferring in Washington,' I said. 'By sunset the deals were done. I can't imagine what all they must have gone into. I don't think either of them knew before it happened how far they'd be able to take it.'

It was such an odd feeling to speak to another without interruption, certain that I was being heard. 'She seems the more pragmatic of the two,' he said. 'She knows about you and— '

I nodded. 'Everybody knows, I think. Sometimes I talk to Avi about it. Bernard never wants to hear.' Somewhere to the north something blew up, and I wondered if we would find my house where I'd left it. 'Thatcher was sort of a rebound, after Avi.'

On the side of a building was another ageing billboard, this one older than most. *God Sees Those Who Come Unto Him* was the message printed below the photo. Swastikas were scrawled across the picture's faces, the survivors on their day of liberation. Avi's father had been in Maidanek during most of the war. With his family he left Crown Heights when the Army entered Brooklyn. Avi sent half of his salary every month to their upstate *shtetl*. Does he know how you earn your money? I asked him, on our last night.

He knows a purpose beyond understanding, Avi replied.

A guard's supposed to defend. Thatcher says kill and you go after anyone he wants.

It's my job.

Nazi, I called him.

There's no comparison. The Drydens are like a mother animal rolling over and suffocating her young as she sleeps.

They're not so unconscious.

Nor are you, he said, kissing my hands.

I allowed myself to re-enter my unavoidable world. 'Joanna?' Lester asked. 'You there?'

'I'd never thought about Thatcher before,' I said. 'Not in that way. Not until later. So much could have been avoided. I might still be myself.'

'Or might not,' said Lester. 'They provide maps without roads. We have to clear our own path.'

'They,' I repeated. 'Are there really two of Them?'

'Way I describe it isn't strictly accurate,' he said. 'Problem of popularising. Everybody understands it, at least, the way I tell it. The split between Their aspects is a decided one. I'm never immediately sure which One I'm addressing until I listen for a spell. I can always talk to Them, see, but They don't always talk to me.'

'But you talk to Them—'

'Not incessantly,' he said, 'and They don't tell me everything.'

'If They're separate,' I asked, 'what tore Them apart?'

Signs noting the curfew were so peppered by gunblasts that they could have been used as graters. As two halftracks rumbled downtown no fresh shots rang out, no footsteps echoed but our own, and none in command chose to stop us for interrogation. I dreamed of safety, so close to home.

'Creation,' he said.

'How?'

'A difficult birth,' he said. 'Whether They're truly split, I'd hate to say. I don't know that They even know. It's a spiritual division more

75

than a physical, I believe.'

'If They are split could They ever reunite?'

'There's a problem in that.'

'What else is new— '

'If They do reunite, the world will be made anew. But that means the world as we know it must end.'

'It must?' I asked. 'You know that?'

'They pull up the corner of a blanket sometimes and show me what's underneath. When They feel like it They show me something else. It's up to me to draw the inferences. The blind men and the elephant, nothing more.'

King Street was a block away; something hung from my corner's lamppost but it didn't look as if it had ever been alive. Tank-treads rutted the new-tarred pavement, looking as fossils on the land.

'Thanks for walking with me,' I said. 'I live around the corner. Would you like to come in?'

'Sure.'

'I'm sorry I ask so many questions,' I said.

'You know the story of Job?' Hearing no response, he continued, 'Job questioned God. God questioned Job in return. They made an arrangement and Job returned to his life. Years later a stranger called on Job, demanding to know the answer to a question. "He tells you to speak to Him as an equal and you let Him treat you like that?" the stranger asked, and Job answered, "Listening to Him as He spoke I realised that the Creator may need neither sense nor sanity to do as He does, and that our failings in such may be more godlike than we know. It seemed most reasonable to agree with everything He said."'

I brushed the day's debris from my steps with

my foot into a neat pile at the bottom. My
neighbour screamed, welcoming us home; Lester
seemed afraid until he saw I could no longer
respond to her voice. Bernard once told me how
the screams of children in his building kept him
awake at night.

'That wasn't all that happened,' Lester concluded, reassured of my fearlessness. '"You have
no more questions?" God asked Job, he told the
stranger, and Job had one more question, but
worried that he'd tested God too much, and so
for an endless time only mouthed the word with
his lips. "You don't learn if you don't ask," God
said.

'"Why?" Job finally asked, but God was gone.'

5

Switching off the alarms I flipped on the over-heads, spreading light throughout my house.

'This is all your place?' Lester asked, hovering behind me as if fearful to step further into the entry.

Once he came in I reset the alarm, locked the five locks, slid the police bar back up. If anyone lay in wait I had a gun in my purse, but I had never had to use it.

'Plus the floor upstairs. They call it a duplex but it's enough for thirty. It's Thatcher's place, really. A gift until he wants it back.'

The previous owners favoured the sort of décor that resulted in its having appeared in several expensive journals years before. Most of the rooms were the width of the house, divided by walls painted in Navaho white and floored with blond wood. Had I roller-skated I would never have passed through the apartment unless I was on wheels. Lester wandered into the living room, narrowing his eyes against the glare of the furniture. He studied an abstract I had hanging above the fireplace. Looking anew into its painted swirls I wondered how my friend had known what angels swarmed through heaven.

'It's called "Driven to Pieces in Pursuit of Love,"' I said. 'A girl friend of mine painted it. She did a number of works that no one ever bought. Except this one.'

'It's awful dark,' he said. 'She did this recently?'

It was dark; the angels smothered in vast clouds of dust, tumbling wing over wing as they spiralled down into the deep. 'She bought a factory loft in Tribeca,' I said. 'Her fiance came down to see the place. She stepped into the elevator to take him up to the roof to show him, but the elevator wasn't there.'

'That's terrible,' Lester said. 'I'm sorry.'

'Probably for the best,' I said. 'She'd be even unhappier now than she was then. It was years ago. Would you like a drink?'

'Bourbon'd be good,' he said. 'Just a little one.'

'I wouldn't want to corrupt.'

'You won't,' he said. 'Don't worry.' We walked into my apartment's Food Preparation/Interpersonal Interaction Core; here the designers had so unyieldingly followed a pattern of black and white in both fixture and wall that to enter the room made one feel to have fallen into a crossword puzzle. There were burners and microwaves and convection ovens; cabinets and blenders and gadgets enough to supply several large restaurants. In one of the cabinets I kept one knife, one fork, one spoon and three plates.

'I've never seen a refrigerator this large,' he said, staring up at its bulk; Bulganin refrigerators were the best made, I'd always heard, but then I suppose Russians understood ice. The thing was large enough to hold half a steer. 'Do much entertaining?'

I poured our drinks into the two glasses I kept ready for such socialising. 'Bernard tells me I more often depress.'

When I handed Lester his bourbon he took small sips, as if drinking too rapidly might sear shut his mouth. 'Strong enough?'

'I don't drink much,' he said, sitting on a black stool, leaning one arm on a white countertop. 'I don't understand what got him so interested in me. It's not as if I just started doing this.'

'I have no idea what set him off,' I said. 'He thinks he can use you to intimidate, I believe.'

'Intimidate who?'

'A limitless number of candidates.'

'Seems to me he sees too many squirrels in the trees,' said Lester. 'What does he think I am, anyway?'

'It should be obvious to you at this point— ' I began to say. As I looked at Lester it struck me that it was obvious, that he simply wanted to hear me say it. 'He thinks that if you're not the messiah, he can use you as such.'

'To intimidate,' Lester said, smiling, but not appearing happy. He ran a fingertip round the top of his glass as if wishing to make it sing.

'Among other things, I suppose, but he's been playing it very cagey. He's impossible to figure out after a point, he doesn't even tell his wife what he's up to— '

'Would it be more to my advantage to be the messiah or to pretend to be the messiah?'

'Same difference to him, I think. I don't know. He'll keep working on you, I can tell you that. Whatever advantage you have will come with no help from him— '

'She seems preoccupied with something besides me,' he said. 'Is there something else going on that might tie in to his plans?'

'Definitely a couple of other things going on. Whether you'll get involved, I can't say. Two situations are ongoing at present, besides yours. A member of our organisation was murdered without our consent. He's already decided who's guilty and you never know what the punishment he comes up with is going to be— '

'Murdered?' Lester said.

'It's business, what do you expect?' I said.

'That's why you were so afraid,' he said. 'When you thought somebody was shooting at us. You thought it was whoever killed this other person?'

'There's a limitless number of suspects,' I said, again. 'The other situation is that he's meeting a Japanese representative on Tuesday. Bernard's cooked up some sort of deal, some treaty of alignment. I don't gather that Thatcher is too keen to go along with it. When he's left to his own devices he tends to see connections where none exist, and I think he's seeing a connection between the murder and the alignment. They love to plot, they're dysfunctional unless they're lurching from crisis to crisis— '

'At some point, then,' said Lester, 'I might wind up as part of a connection as well?'

For several moments I stared into my drink's melting ice, gazing into its smooth translucence as if to read the future; saw nothing that either comforted or disturbed. 'You might. I might. You never can tell.'

'That must make for a certain uncertainty— '

I nodded. 'If he gets his paws on you he'll adhoc it for a while, until something gets rolling. Figure he's set his sights low, in the beginning—'

'It's good to have low expectations,' said Lester. 'Messianic hopes are the worst kind. He's bound to be disappointed.'

'He doesn't like to be disappointed,' I said. 'Show him the angels. That'd shut him up.'

'He couldn't see them,' said Lester. 'Not even if he wanted to. Are you sorry you saw them?'

'I'm not sorry,' I said. 'I'm not glad. I can't really grasp it— '

'They were glad to see you.'

'Must be pretty boring up there, then,' I said, standing and rinsing my glass in the sink; pondering for an instant if I should fix myself another one before picking up the bottle, and pouring again. 'I'm sure Bernard'll be stuck with the details, if you were to go along. He always has to tie up the loose ends.'

'What do people expect of a messiah?' Lester asked. 'People in general, I mean. What do you think?'

'How should I know? It's nothing I've ever thought about,' I said. 'Somebody to clean up the mess, I suppose. Bring about a better world. Cure disease, rebuild cities, sweep the streets.' My soul's Bernard eased out once more before I even knew it had reached the surface, and I

barely contained my laugh as I continued my enu-
meration. 'Wash the dishes, fix the sink, make
the bed— '

'People can do those things,' said Lester. 'The
big things and the small.'

'But they won't. They don't even try any more.
Too afraid they'll fail, I suppose, and so they stop
caring, or pretending to care— '

'As I understand it,' said Lester, 'They love us
most when we try and fail.'

'Lessens the competition,' I said. 'Of course
They would. It'll never happen in any event, so
there's no point discussing it.' I marvelled at how
manipulative I could be, sometimes; watched his
face after I realised what I had said to see what
reaction might appear there. It wasn't that I was
drunk, I told myself, for I wasn't; perhaps I only
wanted to test him as he seemed to be forever
testing me.

'The messiah will come,' he said. 'But the
messiah won't be the one anybody wants or expects. It's only natural.'

A memory rose up in my mind; I saw again
the books in my parent's den, their books and
the dusty volumes passed down from my mother's
grandfather, shoved into the highest shelves,
unread for years. One afternoon when I was
thirteen I remembered climbing up and poking
around, seeing what I might find there. He was
a rabbi; most of his old books were in Hebrew
and so I could never read those,, but some were
in English, and I recalled now finding one on
messianic traditions, coming across a paragraph
concerning Waldo Frank as I idly flipped open
the pages, the dust rising from the book in clouds,
steam rising from a lone rider's white donkey.

Frank believed that if the messiah were to come, the messiah would come as a woman, and now it occurred to me again what an unfathomable, yet charming concept that seemed. The rest of the book seemed drier than the dust that covered it, and I replaced it on the shelf, and ran outside to soak up the sunlight, and let the wind blow the dust from my skin.

'How do They feel about the messiah?' I asked. 'Have They told you?'

'They know that when the messiah comes They'll blend together again. They don't know what'll happen after that. They know They'll change, They know that everything will change. But They don't know how, and so They've never been in any rush to have the messiah come.'

'So They'll keep putting it off until— '

'It's nearly time, though,' he said. 'They've nearly had all of Their doubts confirmed, at this point. They've run out of options, I believe. It must give Them pause. You could say the messiah's Their doomsday device.'

Picking up the CD's remote I switched on the radio, tuned as always to WNEW-AM; 'Highway 61' rang out through the apartment's speakers, and I quickly switched it off again.

'Want another drink?' I asked; he shook his head. 'Want to see the rest of the place?'

As we walked through I showed him the backyard garden, the dining room, the two bathrooms on the first floor. Pictures of my parents hung on the stairway's wall, and he stopped to examine them.

'You favour your mother,' he said; the shot he saw was taken on their twentieth anniversary, when she was a year younger than I was then.

'She coloured her hair,' I said, fluffing mine without thinking. 'She went grey early on.'

'Do they live in town?' he asked.

I preserved what remained of them: odd pieces of small furniture, a few of the books, the dishes I used; a family album, images embedded in black and white amber. My father stood in Pen Station's old iron greenhouse with his fellow soldiers in those old photos; my mother skipped rope on Pitkin Avenue, in Brooklyn, out in long-erased Brownsville. Sometimes I found photos of myself that I couldn't recall being taken, shots where my colour was greyed by distance and time, looking no more than a child hired for some special event. For so long I remembered my dreams so much more clearly than I remembered my past.

'They're dead,' I told him. 'I grew up in Short Hills, in Jersey. They sold the house a few years after dad retired.'

He's bought it for ten thousand, sold it for seven hundred thousand; were I to have repurchased it myself, that day, I would have paid the same number of dollars as he paid but the cost would have been even greater. It was a comfortable house, near the arboretum and the train station; in those woods I knew my first boys. In the backyard was a gas grill, layered with the ash and soot of a thousand barbecues; I remembered staring into its blue flames as a child, thinking how cool those icy blue feathers looked.

'I guess they were old— '

'They were young,' I said. 'They moved to a retirement community. In Florida. After the revaluation they lost their savings. They couldn't afford the maintenance on their co-op and they got an eviction notice. I didn't know until later. They must not have wanted me to worry, and I never thought— '

'Joanna, it's all right— '

'Let's go upstairs,' I said.

He preceded me on the ascent. The second floor's vacuums were broken, and dust settled over us as might sea-mist at the shore.

'They didn't tell me. It was such a— '

'Joanna?'

'Such a— ' I began again, but was unable to think of a suitable conclusion.

'Are you all right?'

'Fine,' I said. 'I'm fine. They were fine. Their lives went so smoothly. Too smoothly. I'd never learned to worry about them. How they were.'

'Joanna, it wasn't your fault, whatever happened—'

'I should have been there,' I said, stopping, leaning against the wall; I'd not let myself think about it since it happened, even immediately after it happened. They'd decided upon their course of action with the usual logic they brought to all situations; decided to kill themselves and obtained poison from a reliable source. 'Why didn't they say anything— '

'Say anything about what?' he asked. 'Joanna, it's all right.'

Lester held me, keeping me from shaking.

Every Saturday night they would fix a candle-light dinner for themselves, once I was old enough that I could make my own arrangements; I remembered leaving the house, seeing them sitting there, staring into each other's eyes as if they'd been married the day before. Perhaps they'd hoped to draw such romance as they could from their final tableau; more likely the electricity had been cut off, and they'd needed candlelight in order to see the doses they measured out for themselves. An untended candle caught the bedroom drapes on fire, the fire department said; maybe they'd passed out before blowing out the lights.

'I didn't know,' I said. Mom might have slept through it; dad got halfway across the living room. 'The fire department sent me a bill for their services the next day on the fax. That's how I found out— '

'It's all right,' Lester repeated, not letting me go. 'It's all right. Go ahead and cry— '

'I can't,' I said. 'I haven't been able to in years. Not really.'

They wanted their ashes sprinkled over Coney Island, where they'd met. Early one morning, the next week, Avi drove me out to the beach and stood guard to make sure no one else came near. I walked out to the surf; almost jabbed my foot on a needle. The wind was blowing; I tried to wait until it settled, but a gust came along as I let go of the ashes and they blew back onto the beach, mixing with the grey sand until I couldn't tell where they'd gone.

'You're crying now,' he said; I felt the tears running down my cheeks.

'Not really,' I repeated. 'Come on,' I said, pulling away from him, wiping my face dry. 'I'm sorry. Let's go on. Up here.'

At the top of the stairs we turned, and walked down a short hall. 'This is my bedroom,' I said as we walked in, seeing my bed, my dresser and the television as I'd left them. When I turned on the lights I turned on the set as well, hoping that something immediately distracting might be

87

playing. A commercial was on; to sell watches
the narrator quoted the second law of thermo-
dynamics as an old Otis Redding song drifted
over the images of women nearly nude and dyed
blue. I couldn't deal with such neo so late, and
turned it off.

'Better?' he asked. I nodded. 'You have a
beautiful home.'

'Thatcher has a beautiful home,' I said. 'I didn't
mean to get so upset. It's just— '

'I shouldn't have brought it up,' he said, touching my face. 'Don't worry. Everything's all right.'

'I haven't been able to cry for so long,' I
said, sitting down on the bed; Lester remained
standing. 'They've had me all dried up. It hurt
too much to feel so much. I couldn't.'

'There's nothing wrong in that, Joanna, take it
easy— '

'I haven't cried since that last night with Avi,'
I said. 'When we talked. Not since then. Thatcher'll never see me cry, you can rest assured.'

Lester sat next to me on the bed, keeping
distance enough that while I might take comfort
from his nearness I wouldn't be pressed into some
unwarranted embrace. As I tried to calm myself
I took long, deep breaths, drawing so much air
into my lungs as I could; feeling, as Jake surely
had, that I had killed without reason. 'You and
he must have been very close,' he said.

'It's funny,' I said, 'we broke it off just as we
were getting closest. That night. That's how it
always seems to work when you get to know
someone too well, I think. Peel off one too many
layers of skin and then you can't bear the touch
any longer.'

I stood, straightening my skirt, and walked

88

across the room to my closet where, ducking
behind the door, I could peer into the mirror
there to see what a shambles I had made of
my face. With tissue and cream I removed my
makeup, kicking off my shoes as I stood there,
out of Lester's sight. 'So where do you live?'

'Around,' he said. 'It's good to keep moving
after a point.'

'You're originally from Tennessee?'

'Kentucky,' he corrected. 'Everybody up here
always confuses them. I grew up near Lexington.
My mother's folks came from over the mountain.'

'What's it like down there?' Some of Thatcher's friends owned horse farms in the state, and
at every business function were prone to weave
shimmering tales of plantation life. I'd always
suspected they'd poured us watered bourbon. 'It
always looks so pretty in the pictures.'

'I haven't been there in years,' he said. 'I
don't know what's left. I guess it's probably like
everywhere else by now.'

'When I moved out,' I said, unbuttoning my
blouse, 'I didn't go back home again for months.
I understand how it is.'

When he said nothing in reply I wondered if I
could possibly understand. 'Why do they call it
the Bluegrass?'

'Don't know. It's the same grass as in Central
Park, I think. Just as brown.'

I shut the closet door, coming into his sight
once more wearing only my slip and undergar-
ments. Could a messiah desire, I wondered; I
didn't see why not. He didn't look away as he saw
me, but neither did he seem pleased; his cheeks
flushed red for an instant, as if he'd received a

89

sudden transfusion.

'Are your parents still down there?'

'Yes,' he said. 'They built a Toyota plant across the road from where our house was, I heard. It must be closed if it hasn't gone out of business, I suppose. Probably Dryco will reopen it one day— '

'Probably,' I said, walking toward him. 'Do you want me to leave the room while you change clothes?'

'No.'

So many times during my life I knew a suspicion, that for periods of time not all of my actions were my own; that my dybbuk rose up from the void to settle for a while in my body to know the life inside my head. Reaching down, I began unbuttoning his shirt, staring at my hands, seeing someone else's. He remained so still that I might have been undressing a mannequin.

'You're very pretty, Joanna,' he said.

'You don't think I'm fat?' Thatcher once told me he could set a teatray on my ass and I'd never notice until I sat down, and he intended it as a compliment. 'I don't take very good care of myself.'

'It wouldn't matter— ' he said.

He evinced a certain reluctance as I pulled his shirt from his body, but made no overt move to stop me. In clothes he seemed slim; now I saw how wiry he was, how tightly his muscles were drawn across his bones. Seeing his right side I backed quickly away, feeling suddenly as he must have felt, in the hall, when he asked about my parents. From his waist to his armpit his skin appeared so strip-mined as any Kentucky mountainside, pitted where it should

have been smooth, smooth where it should have
been rippled. The original design was forever
lost.

'Who shot you?' I asked; Avi had similar scars.
For the first time since we'd met he averted his
own eyes.

'It was deer season,' he said, laughing once
more. 'Hunter mistook me for a cow.'

So many men lie as if to their mothers,
stammering out denials with such bravado and
so blatantly that one could only imagine that they
dreamed of being caught.

'Lester— '

'It was a while back,' he said. 'Didn't hit anything important. The newspapers called me the
miracle child.'

'What happened?'

He shook his head; for the moment I decided
to let the subject drop. 'You're lucky you lived,'
I said, but he seemed uncertain how he might
respond to that, and so said nothing. He wore
the semblance of a smile on his lips, as if having
heard an old family joke for the umpteenth time
he had done his duty by responding as if he'd
heard it all anew. I sat down on my dresser's
chair, facing him.

'We can't, Joanna,' he said. 'I wouldn't feel
right.'

It should have been understandable, and was,
but I was sorry just the same.

He shrugged, and folded up his shirt. 'It's all
right— '

'Their means are difficult, whatever Their
ends,' he said.

How long, I wondered, had he told himself
there was a purpose before he could finally

believe it? Against his better judgment had he
wound up hoping, after all, instead of knowing?
As I looked at him I watched him shiver, as if the
room was so cold as Thatcher's; maybe somebody
walked over his grave.

'Do you ever think about Kentucky?' I asked.

'I'm not much for nostalgia.'

We sat there a few minutes more, wordless and
slumped, perhaps at last eroding beneath our rain
of events, this heaven-sent plague.

'Will you stay here tonight anyway?' I asked.
'To talk?'

'I'll stay longer,' he said. 'You have questions?'

'They must have given you some answers,' I
said.

'Not the sort of answers anyone wants to hear.
What questions do you mean?'

'Is there an afterlife?' I asked.

'What's the matter with the one you have? I'd
be surprised if there were— '

'Say there is,' I said. 'Say there was a more
perfect world beyond ours. Why would They keep
this one, in that case?'

'Why do you think?' he asked, in return.

I lay down; Lester remained seated.

'Practice,' I said, guessing at first. 'They
couldn't bear to part with the original. They kept
it as an object lesson.'

He nodded, and looked away from me, pondering questions of his own. 'I can't help but
disappoint him,' he said. 'When that happens,
what'll he do to me?'

'Depends on how disappointed he is. Don't
worry about it,' I said. 'He's such a bastard.
He'll hound me until I leave and hound you until
you start, and it won't matter what happens in

the process— '

'He'd be right in that,' said Lester. 'Perhaps it'll lessen the damage to go ahead and get things underway with him, then— '

I shook my head. 'Disappear before he has a chance to get you. It's not worth getting involved. You don't know what you'll do until he makes you do it, and by then it's too late. Don't give him the chance— '

'It's a chance that must be followed through on,' he said. 'There's a purpose for what has to be done. I can't go anywhere, Joanna, I have to do as I'm told. I doubt I'll need to be at the company very long.'

'I won't leave until you do, then— '

'I know,' he said. 'Such a strange organisation. The immediate circle he seems to rule over as if it were a family.'

'He does,' I said. 'He and Susie take turns doing the beating while the other looks on. Everything's roses so long as they get their own way but let one little thing slip out of place and there's all hell to pay.'

'But families have misunderstandings,' he said. 'That's part of the situation. After a while they stop seeing one another. Each becomes no different from anyone else passed on the street.'

He stood; I stared at the ceiling so intently as I could, attempting to conjure up angels of my own. After a few moments I gave up.

'Everyone goes blind after so long,' I said. 'That night Avi and I talked, he said anyone could become a Nazi once they stopped seeing their Jews. He's so— '

'Was it his child you had?' Lester asked, unexpectedly; I couldn't see his face from where

I lay. I could tell he stood now near my dresser, looking at a pair of booties I had hanging on the knob of the mirror's frame. 'These weren't yours, were they? You'd have had them bronzed— '

'I knitted them,' I said.

'You had a baby?'

'Once.'

'Recently?' he asked, walking back over, sitting next to me, gazing down as if he might look directly into my mind from his vantage point above.

'January.' I said. 'Things happen.'

As I closed my eyes so that I couldn't see him he leaned closer down to me, whispering:

'Where's your baby?'

'Where're your parents?'

The effect was as desired; he said nothing else. After a second or so he walked over and switched off the room's light, returning to my bed and laying down beside me, facing away. As we bundled in silence my eyes accepted the dark, and I could see in his silhouette his side's unnatural curve. Keeping my touch so light as that of a butterfly's I landed my fingertips onto his back, feeling hard rubber sheathed in satin, a tuft of lamb's wool at the root of his spine. When I began to cry I pulled away from him. He clasped me as he rolled over; I remembered my father holding me, as a child, feeling so safe; I never wanted to feel safe, never asked for protection.

'I'm sorry, Joanna,' he said. 'It's difficult to tell what you want to talk about.'

'Feeling's mutual,' I said, feeling my face grow warmer and wetter. 'You make me remember too much. I feel like I'm on overload, my head can't hold it all— '

'It's impossible to remember too much,' he said. 'Everything should be remembered. So much is lost over time. Every moment should be honoured for having existed, even the bad ones.'

'Every moment,' I repeated, knowing I could never recall a thousandth of my own. 'Why would They send a messiah if They don't even know what'll happen? Why would They risk it?'

'They have hopes,' he said, laying his head on the pillow next to mind, looking in the dark so tired.

'You said you could predict our futures,' I said. 'What are they?'

'Unavoidable,' he said, putting his arm across my shoulder; as he touched me I felt the fine hair rise from the nape of my neck.

Why do the heathern rage? Why not? A siren outside sang through the night, the scream of an onrushing train.

'You know why everyone has this?' he asked, tapping the shallow groove between my nose and upper lip.

'I don't even know what it's called.'

'Before you were born you knew all there is,' he told me. 'You knew the beginning and the end. You knew why the dinosaurs died, why blue is blue. You knew why pain doesn't ennoble us and why we wouldn't be human without it. You knew what your life would hold.'

I touched my face, brushing his finger with my own.

'When it was time for you to be born They pressed shut your lips, using an angel's thumb to make the print. The angels cried for having done it but knew it had to be done, you had to forget all you knew upon entering this world, because the one thing you'd have never known is how it feels, remembering it again.'

Though we could never be lovers, as I kissed him I knew that feeling lovers know in their first minutes together, a false commingling of fear and relief and the peace that comes upon believing again that the world can be wonderful even in its illness. Our kiss, unlike an angel's thumb, did not press our memories away. At nine Monday morning we reported to work.

6

On Monday afternoon we discussed our newest
project. 'Don't try to deny you didn't have your
doubts,' said Thatcher. 'I'd hate to think you
were just humouring me.'

'After Friday afternoon I never suspected anything would actually come of this,' said Bernard.
'I thought he'd race back to his flock and that'd
be the last we heard of him.'

'Told you I made arrangements.' Susie looked
up at her husband; shook her head as if he'd
told her he'd accidentally mowed over one of
her flower beds.

'That shouldn't have changed things. By all
rights he should've simply sprung up like a toad-
stool somewhere else. Perhaps hearing our words
issuing from a different mouth decided the vote.'
Bernard turned to me, smiling with lips so per-

fectly curved, so remarkably still that they might have been painted on his face.

'She's learning,' said Thatcher. 'Need good role models in business.'

'So if all's roses, what's the problem?' Susie asked, unable to take shelter from her world behind sunglasses or newspaper. Not even the residue of a smile lightened her face.

'The problem is that from here out I'll be working from theory alone,' said Bernard. 'As I understand it you want to spread Macaffrey's cult of personality more thickly upon the populace.'

'Without any public connection to us, just yet,' said Thatcher. 'We can backchannel him in the meantime when we need him for company work.'

'But what's desired? The usual sort of thing? You want the audience entertained with sermons, blessings, the occasional odd miracle? You want to see what ripple effects might result once we toss him in the pond?'

'Sounds good to start,' said Thatcher. 'You're acting like this is all something new to you, Bernard. It's just the old question of figuring out the best way to sell something.'

'Apples and oranges,' said Bernard. A grey world showed through the room's great window; it rained, several hundred feet further down.

'How do you figure?'

'How do you sell a messiah, Thatcher?' Bernard asked.

'Above cost,' said Thatcher, laughing. 'In the fastest way.'

'You'd use television to do that?'

'How else?' Susie asked. 'Weren't you referring to some tests or other last week that you could run?'

'Tests, eventually. That's not the problem here. If the audience first sees Macaffrey on television, they won't see him. Not really.'

'Don't give me this analysis bullshit, Bernard, that doesn't make sense,' said Thatcher. 'What are you trying to say?'

'Explicate and deconstruct,' Susie added.

Bernard rested his chin in his hand as if the weight of his head proved too great for his neck. 'A car needs gas,' he said. 'A messiah needs belief. Nobody believes anything they see on television unless they've seen it before in real life. His followers, sure, they'd tune in every night. Anyone else'll zap right past.'

'What are you talking about? We can put any damn thing we want to on TV and people believe it—'

'Apples and oranges,' Bernard repeated. 'When we put most things on television it's not to make them immediately believe, it's to make what they're seeing part of their background. Assimilation, that's what you aim for with television. Shooting your image through the skull enough times that, eventually, enough of it sticks that it seems to have always been there. In most situations that works fine, but it won't in this.'

'Ridiculous,' said Susie. 'Eye the tube any day of the week. New faces show up every hour. Hundreds megatime it once they get their minute, why shouldn't he if that's what we want to do with him?' Looking to her husband she lowered her voice, speaking to him as if they sat beneath moonlight. 'If he's a wash, we cut our losses all the sooner.'

Bernard gnawed the end of his thumb, drawing from the cuticle a red droplet resembling a ladybug at rest. 'We're talking image equivalency here,' he said. 'People appear on television and for a while someone might tune in specifically to see them, but it works only until a fresh distraction appears on a different channel. Nobody knows what keeps people watching. A democracy of images is impossible to deliberately subvert.'

'We only need to find the right sales pitch, Bernard— '

'You're not pushing detergent. You want this fool to show up one night after the news, claiming to be God. You might as well put him on Telepsychic— '

'You're being negative,' said Susie.

'Realistic. This'll necessitate serious real-world preparation and even then every time he appears on television a certain amount of symbolic worth will be lost unless we exercise complete control over surrounding programming.'

'Oh, hell, we could do that,' said Thatcher. 'What if he got on and performed some miracle?'

Bernard shook his head, glancing to me as he explained, holding back his laughter. 'The only miracle Macaffrey seems able to perform is convincing otherwise sensible people that he's anything other than a sociopath. So what if he would work miracles? He could make the moon dance in the sky and no one would believe it unless they saw it for themselves. But no one would. You know why? They'd all be inside, watching it on television.'

'Can we do anything with him, in this case?' Susie asked. 'If not, can we— '

'Hold on, now,' said Thatcher.

'If you want this done right it'll be a longterm

project. Longterm projects take a long time. Face it.'

'So how do you propose we do this?' Thatcher asked.

'News of this sort is most effectively transmitted only by word of mouth,' said Bernard. 'The old-fashioned way. Not to say we can't push buttons as we go along. Stooges and the like can be hired and trained to pass whatever disinformation we want passed, as you know. Computer networks can then be used, after the introductory period. We can't televise before attaining saturation. Long as we do that then we can rest assured that once he's finally seen, he'll be heard as well.' Bernard stood up to stretch as if his bones needed shifting, having been freed of confining ideas. 'I hate to admit it but the timing is perfect for this tomfoolery. Our premillennial fields possess fertile ground.'

'How long'll this take?' asked Susie.

'Two years, certainly,' said Bernard. 'Unless our interest flags before then.'

For more than two years Thatcher had lived with the awareness that when he wanted, he received.

'Two years,' he repeated. 'It can't take that long— '

'It will,' said Bernard. 'Of course, we haven't fully examined the premise that Macaffrey has, in the first place, anything to say.'

'We'll burn that bridge when we come to it,' said Thatcher. 'Where is he right now?'

'Gus is babysitting him in my office. I left the television on so they'd stay calm. They seemed to hit it off, which I find inconceivable. Dealing with Macaffrey's like dealing with an idiot savant,

but then Gus has had so much practice with
Jake— '

'I say disinvest,' said Susie.

'That's what you've been saying all along,
darlin'— ' Thatcher said.

'Throw him back,' she said. 'Let the sharks
have him.'

'Got to do the R and D first,' said Thatcher.
'I'm optimistic. He'll probably come in handy in
the meantime with a few things I got in mind.
Go to it, Bernard. I trust you.'

Susie seemed considerably more troubled by
Thatcher's verbal cuddling of Bernard than she
ever did of her husband's physical assaults upon
me; her jealousy was always professional, and I
doubted that she took me seriously enough to
worry. Rarely was I jealous of Susie, and then
only because he admitted to hearing her when
she spoke.

'Let's go see our boy, Joanna. See how's he
doing.'

Bernard rose to follow; Thatcher motioned for
him to retake his seat. 'Fill Susie in on what we
were talking about while we're doing this,' he
said.

'There's something I have to do you don't want
to?' she asked. 'Afraid you'll get your hands
messy?'

'Darlin', there's such a thing as being too cyni-
cal. Come on down to your office when you're
finished, Bernard. Call first.'

Bernard's quarters were at the far end of our
floor. Creeping through a lacing of halls, attempting to keep up with Thatcher, I let my eyes
pass over the hundreds of photos attached to the
walls, each holding the image of a Dryco product,

wondering to myself if the shot of Macaffrey,
Lester, might be larger, for ideology's sake if
for no other. When we spoke our sound bled
into the building's breath, droning all around us
as we wandered through its lungs.

'You have a cat's smile,' I said, seeing his grin
swell so that I believed his face might burst.
'Where's the canary?'

'Trying to swallow the cat, seems to me,'
he said. 'We'll get into it momentarily, hon.
Macaffrey can help us out a lot sooner than they
think, that's for sure— '

'How?' I asked, almost running to keep up with
his long stride.

'Ears,' he said, shaking his head, glancing at
the walls. 'Can't tell you how pleased I am you
and Macaffrey get along so well.'

'That's big of you,' I said. 'I get along with
anyone I can talk with— '

'Talk? Looked like Siamese twins when you
two came in this morning. Messiahs have a great
need for affection, I guess— '

'Thatcher, he's— '

'You must feel like a dinosaur,' he added,
with surprising tact. 'Nothing wrong robbing the
cradle long as you're not the one has to change
the diapers.'

Unexpected chords transposed the melody of
his song. Curious to discover how he might deal
with the situation as he seemed to perceive it
I refrained from explaining the nature of my
relationship with Lester, not that he had any
right to know of it in the first place.

'I'm glad you're taking this so well,' I said. 'I
thought you might be upset.'

'Oh, hon, it's just business. We all have to play

the whore sometime.' Before I could comment on that remark he added: 'How'd Bernard convince you to do it?'

'Bernard has nothing to do with this,' I said, feeling my own colour rising in my face. 'I told you Lester came back here— '

'Oh,' he said, looked at me and smiled. 'So it was your idea after all. That's a good sign. I knew my influence'd wear off on you eventually. That's good.'

You get nowhere participating in a conversation with a ventriloquist who perceives you as a new dummy, and so I said nothing more.

Lester and Gus stood beside the desk in Bernard's office, their backs turned toward the door. Gus circled around as we entered. The commercial playing on TV was one of Dryco's; the spot commanded the viewer to enjoy life. One inspiration after another appeared onscreen as the narrator sang: pink children romped with golden dogs, Christmas lights of a dozen colours outlined the gables of a Victorian house, oreads and naiads lounged on skislope and at surfside barely hidden beneath particoloured shreds of quilt; innumerable scenes of a perfect world's perfect people flashed by, scenes that to my eye could have been filmed perhaps on Mars, but never on earth, not any longer.

'Who knows?' Thatcher asked.

'None but God.'

By this ritual Gus signalled that he'd deafened the room's ears and blinded its eyes. The window-panes rattled as they vibrated within their frames, shaken by the air conditioner's wind, assuring that none without could eavesdrop by discerning the tones with which our voices helped cause the glass to waver. Thatcher, collapsing into the leather chair, lifted his feet onto the desk, knocking the photo of Bernard's wife against the drawing of their son. I sat next to Lester, on the sofa, took his hand and squeezed it, for a second forgetting the world around me.

'What have they done to you?' I asked.

'Bored me to death,' he said. 'Till we came in here, at least. Gus and I get along pretty good— '

'How's it hanging, Macaffrey?' asked Thatcher, 'You need anything, just ask Joanna. She'll see to your every need, but I guess you figured that our already— '

'Call me Lester.'

'Nothing like a first-name basis. Lester, I got something I want you to take a look at. See if you can pick up anything from it.'

'What do you want picked?'

'Anything in bloom,' said Thatcher. 'Here you go, bud. Looks like a list, doesn't it?' Lester studied the note for a minute after Thatcher passed it over to him. 'Can you see who wrote it?'

'Of course not,' said Lester. 'Does this have anything to do with the employee who was murdered?'

I knew nothing more showed in my face than I noticed showing in Gus's; Thatcher tried to give the impression of one novocained but his eyes held the most disconcerting blend of desire and fear, the look of a molester listening for the unexpected interruption. He looked to me as if wishing to see some confession; I gave him none.

'It does,' he said. 'Somebody's in something

bad and I'd like to help 'em out before they get in over their head.'

Lester, returning the note to Thatcher, wriggled himself deeper into the sofa, that his shoulders might brush against mine. 'I'm sure you have the best intentions. What do you know about the note so far?'

'Mahaica's name of a port in Guyana,' said Thatcher. 'Michael Moseley is the pseudonym of a local exporter down there, we're pretty sure—'

'Mystic means the one in Connecticut,' Lester said.

Thatcher received this knowledge as if hearing the weather report, and I could only imagine that the earlier shock must still be insulating his system from the effects of repeated jolts.

'You're sure about that?'

Lester nodded.

'How?'

'I don't know why,' said Lester. 'It came to me.'

Thatcher looked Lester over as if measuring him for size. 'That's to be expected, I suppose. All right, then. That sounds likely as anything. Let's take it and fly. Hey, Gus? It seem to you that there might be something to interest us in Mystic?'

'It could seem that way.'

'Look into it. It's funny, you know,' he said, taking from his jacket pocket two folded documents. 'You never know what'll turn up where. Looked for one thing this weekend and found something else entirely. Something might shine a different light on Jensen's killing, seems to me.'

'What?'

'He's not dead.'

Early on in our relationship Thatcher conceived the notion that his secretary was attempting to eavesdrop upon his office conversations by means of radiowaves, projected through the fillings in his teeth. After she was retired electronic equipment was found in her desk; it was never discovered for whom she also worked. Though Thatcher's manias were many, and in my absence he could have fallen prey to any of them, there could be no discounting the possibility he might, again, be right.

'I know a dead man when *I* see one,' said Gus.

'You never saw him dead,' Thatcher said. 'Saw him close to death, but that's not close enough.'

'Where is he, then, if he's still alive?'

'Don't you think I'm trying to find out? Am I correct in thinking that had there been a body it would have gone to Campbell's in fulfilment of the usual perks?'

Gus nodded. 'Personnel would have handled arrangement, not Security— '

'Am I correct?'

'As an unmarried employee,' Gus answered, 'Jensen's body would have been taken to Campbell's for standard treatments and the cremains would have been urned as per.'

'We'd have never known he never made it to Campbell's if I hadn't called to follow up. Funeral records aren't automatically sent to our floor. Things get too damn compartmentalised in this outfit. From here on out, anybody in this company sneezes, I want their file on my desk. Got me?'

'Because the body didn't get there doesn't mean he's still alive— '

107

'Somebody wanted a souvenir?'

'What did the doctors say?' I asked.

'Depends on which ones you talk to. The ones seeming most culpable are presently being talked to.' Thatcher paused. 'Don't have any answers yet, but they're still kicking. We'll see.'

'When were they brought in?'

'Last night.' said Thatcher.'They're denying they know anything but if that's true then they're just as guilty. I suppose we might have to bring their families into this. Might help 'em remember, showing 'em that carrot on the stick— '

'Why wasn't I told?' Gus asked, sounding no less angry than Thatcher. 'As Head of Security, why wasn't I told?'

Lester said nothing through all of this, watching intently as if struck dumb by the workings of industry made flesh.

'Be realistic, Gus,' said Thatcher. 'For one thing you were up on the estate with us. You think I wanted to send you down to New York and leave us unprotected— '

'By a force of sixty-five— '

' —when Avi could take care of the situation? Second, I did have to be sure you and Jake weren't in on this in any way. I've ascertained matters to my satisfaction now.'

'You didn't trust us?' Gus asked, his face darkening. 'You didn't trust me?'

'If I didn't trust you, Gus, would I be telling you now?'

Something seemed to have shifted anew within Thatcher's personality, on the one hand allowing him to speak so much more freely about company business with comparative strangers present; on the other showing every sign of having locked that personality up behind yet another door.

'What were you looking for that you found this out?' I asked, hoping to distract them before anything could go further. 'What did you find out? Besides what you say— '

'As an afterthought, on Sunday,' Thatcher said, 'I asked Beekman to send up a copy of the attending physician's report,' he said, passing a Xerox across. 'I wanted to see the medical specifications. Tests they got now they should be able to tell what bay that fish came from that they took the poison out of. Anyway.' He leaned forward; the chair groaned beneath his weight. 'Now the average person wouldn't notice a thing wrong with that, you think?'

'Whose thumb?' Lester asked; Thatcher smiled. A seeming shadow showed at second glance to a long thumb lying a top the line where the attending physician should have signed, blocking the space in the copy made.

'Be nice to think whoever did this did it intentionally,' said Thatcher, 'but I'd be fooling myself. Just the sort of thing to give one pause, isn't it? If the rest of the gang's no smarter than this, running 'em down'll be easier than pissing on ants.'

'Whose signature is being hidden?' I asked.

'I wondered that myself,' said Thatcher. 'So I had Avi go down and bring back the original by hand. When he called ahead they told him they'd looked but just couldn't find it. When he went there he took Jake along. They found it.'

'Jake went with him?' Gus asked. 'He's said nothing to me— '

'Well, I asked him not to, Gus. You understand.' Thatcher passed me the original. 'Shame they don't teach penmanship like they used to.'

'This doctor,' Gus said, his mouth tight, 'is in custody?'

'No— ' When Thatcher wanted to laugh but desired more strongly to keep a straight face his feet would shake, his joy always finding an outlet by passing directly into the ground. His shoes tapped against Bernard's family photos once more, and they fell over on the desk. 'I remembered the front page of the *News*, morning after Jensen's little melodrama. It was the sort of thing sticks with me.' I remembered Susie's paper that day; remembered a photo beneath the headline CRUSH HOUR. A woman walking to work was pinned between a tank and parked cars, trying to cross the street. The photographer took his shot as the rank rolled away. 'Probably wouldn't have made the front page if she hadn't been a doctor.'

'Her signature?'

Thatcher demurred. 'They probably had it ready before he was even brought in. Doubt she knew about it. Sure as hell bet they had it ready before they brought *her* in. If they even realised it they probably just hoped nobody'd notice. She and Jensen must have been in ER at the same time, but I doubt they had much to say to each other. Which doctor you say you'd spoken to, Gus?'

'One of the residents,' he said. 'Doctor Lu. A young Chinese woman. Our doctors took over the case from her when they arrived.'

'When the bastards washed the ink off their hands, you mean. Took over the case and when enough time passed, they told you he died. She backs you up, all right— '

'I don't need backup— '

'We talked a while,' Thatcher said. 'I hired her. I'd started to think they might even have made up the cause of near-death but she's seen fugu poisoning before, when she was an intern. Some toxiterrorist used it in San Francisco while she was out there. When she found out Jensen hadn't pulled out of it she said she was shocked. Told me she never dreamed he wouldn't'.'

'Why?'

'Didn't have a strong enough dose, she didn't think,' Thatcher said. 'Strong enough to cause problems, sure. See, when you go into storage like that not enough blood tends to reach the brain. She said he's probably been under long enough he wouldn't even be all right again, at best. Now whoever did it, for whatever reason, you know what I think they wound up doing?'

We shook our heads. Thatcher had an innate talent for research and detection which could but be rarely discerned from his actions, or distractions.

'They zombified him. Like the Tontons Macoute used to do with their prisoners, you remember.' Gus pursed his lips, as if such practices were beneath him. 'Fugu poison, yeah. But from a Caribbean fish.'

'Haitian techniques are not often adaptable,' said Gun. 'It's a strange country.'

'It's a rather outlandish thing to do, don't you think?' I asked.

'I didn't say it was done deliberately,' said Thatcher. 'This opens up all sorts of possibilities, doesn't it? Somebody more'n likely just screwed up.'

'Then the doctors would have finished up

the job in the back and sent the body on to
Campbell's— '

'They didn't, though,' said Thatcher. 'Maybe
they didn't have permission to. Maybe they didn't
want to kill him. Just make him sick and went
a little overboard. Maybe they *did* intend to
zombify him, for whatever outlandish reason— '

'All entries where his prints or eyes could be
used to gain access have been recoded?'

'Yeah,' said Thatcher. 'He won't be much more
use to 'em than a coatrack if they were going
to try walking him up somewhere so he could
get 'em in.' Thatcher watched Gus shrug, and
turn away. 'Could be Jensen had himself taken
care of. Could be somebody mistook him for
someone else. Could be random and senseless,
nothing more.'

'Avi's been apprised of the situation?' I asked.

'Not entirely.'

'Do Bernard and Susie know?'

'Told Bernard this morning,' Thatcher said,
toying at the edges of the note with two fingers.
'You know how excitable's she's gotten herself
about this. He's been talking to her about it while
we've been down here, seemed like a good time
to fill her in.'

'Why are you letting me overhear all of this?'
Lester asked. 'It really seems like none of my
business— '

'It's company business,' said Thatcher, winking.
'You're company.'

'What do you trust me to do?' Gus asked.

'Don't take everything so personally, Gus,' said
Thatcher. 'Everybody has an off day. Listen, go
down there and you talk to the doctors. If they
don't spill by tonight, well— '

'Is the service over yet?' Bernard's voice broke in over the intercom, coming in as if on cue, seeming that he knew when to best enter for suitable dramatic effect.

'Come on down,' said Thatcher, hauling himself upright. 'Keep all this under your hat for the moment, Lester. We wind up keeping lots of little secrets around here, you'll get used to it. You have anything to add from what you've heard?'

'If the wound wasn't self-inflicted,' Lester said, 'I suspect it wasn't unwelcome.'

Thatcher nodded, scratched at his chin as if judging his beard's growth. 'If there's reason to this, we'll find it.'

When Bernard returned to his office he entered without immediate comment; took his seat behind his desk and replaced his family portraits, shifting them again into their proper angle.

'What's eating at you, Bernard?' Thatcher asked. 'Have a good talk?'

'We made progress,' he said. 'I've been thinking that we should have his speeches written for him. We can't take the chance— '

'What're you talking about now?' Thatcher said, seeming exasperated by Bernard's endless qualifications.

'I was reading the transcripts of the questions put to him earlier today,' said Bernard. 'It's even worse than I imagined. If God speaks through Macaffrey, all I can say is He's a bring-down kind of guy— '

'You can't have a speechwriter for a messiah, dammit.'

'Macaffrey,' said Bernard, turning to Lester, 'what's the purpose of the universe?'

'Purposelessness.'

Thatcher shoved his hands into his pants pockets and glanced at the TV screen. Whatever presently played appeared so obscure in meaning that I believe even Bernard might have hesitated to attempt exegesis. Gus stared at all of us, wondering perhaps who was capable of the greatest betrayal.

'It's all a matter of phrasing,' said Bernard. 'He says one thing and we can say another.'

'What would you say about Mystic, Connecticut?' Thatcher asked.

Bernard blinked his eyes as if worrying away a cinder. 'It belies its name,' he said.

'In this note,' Thatcher continued, 'mystic refers to Mystic, Connecticut.'

'Does it now?' Bernard asked, looking at him, and then at Lester. 'Should you be discussing family matters around the help? Or was this conceit from downstairs?'

'Mystic and Mahaica,' said Thatcher. 'Two ports. One importing, one exporting. There aren't many possibilities. Think New England's smuggling clams down to Rio?'

'If those two ports are involved,' Bernard said, 'and that's a definite if, then if any smuggling's going on it would only be shipments of the usual product. Someone stepping into where we've left off.'

'That's just what someone's doing,' said Thatcher. 'I can smell it. Bringing it up from Bolivia in raw, maybe, or across from Colombia over the Amazon highways. Probably using those damn minitrucks to run the shit. Could we doublecheck those on satellite photos?'

'With their resolution we could count the

change in the driver's pockets, said Bernard. 'So may some operation along this line is ongoing. Why should it matter at this stage? We don't even have to keep that aspect of the operation going any more, you've been saying that for a year now. Maybe it's some of the old Medellin boys, they never quite gave it all up— '

'They'd have tried getting in direct touch,' said Thatcher. 'It's not them. And it's not amateur. Jensen wasn't running this, that's evident.'

'It's certainly corporate,' said Bernard. 'Too many aspects of it are too senseless for it not to be. Whoever's involved here simply used Jensen as they'd be subcontracting any number of locals, here and there.'

'My locals,' said Thatcher. 'Wouldn't mind getting reimbursed for all this free labour I seem to be providing.'

'The operation isn't large or we'd have seen traces of it by now,' said Bernard. 'Besides what we've found. It strikes me as test marketing.'

'Then I reckon I know who's trying to break into the field— '

Bernard picked up the photo of his wife and pushed it an eighth of an inch to the left. 'Possibly,' he said. 'Even if they are in it, Thatcher, what difference does it make? We're getting out of the field, or so you claim— '

'Drugs make the world go round,' Thatcher said, his eyes shut tight. 'They need cash. Something to barter with other than electronics gear. If they're getting involved with the product not only will they be hauling in stupid amounts of money, but can pick the market as they choose, long as we're not in it. Guess which market they'll take over if we get out.'

'It would be best for Americans to be drugged with American drugs, no doubt,' said Gus, seeming serious.

'What if this Otsuka bird is behind it? This agreement, I've only had a chance to look at it once. Isn't there something in there about promising to support them in new Latin American ventures?'

'Purely proforma,' said Bernard. 'We agree to discuss with them any proposals of theirs involving countries in this hemisphere before giving our approval. If we don't agree, we don't give our approval, they can't go ahead.'

'This is some agreement you all cooked up,' said Thatcher. 'Why do they want to sign it? There's a reason.'

'So they can get back to business, simple as that. Free up their assets. They've had to coast for too long— '

'There's another reason,' said Thatcher. 'And if Otsuka's big as you say he can't help but be in on this.'

'Well, so we stay with the product and drive them out of the market,' Bernard said. 'If you ever want this damned computer to go online we need their assistance. Our boys can't take the development any further by themselves. We get their boys in on it as agreed and we're over the top. That's inescapable. We don't sign, we don't get the help. I doubt we could pull off a kidnapping in this circumstance.'

'Always good to keep our options open,' said Thatcher. 'You say he's pretty sharp?'

'He knows his yen from his yang,' said Bernard. 'You'd never guess. He looks like a root you'd find in a grocery in Chinatown. Don't do anything to upset him, Thatcher. No confrontations, no escapades, no backup plans. He'll want to sign and he'll want to talk. Let him.'

'Talk about what?'

'Follow his lead. Talk about whatever he wants to. He likes hockey, talk about that. He loves old automobiles, flower arranging, bondage cabaret. He writes poetry.'

Thatcher sneered.

'Talk about his grandchildren— '

'Grandchildren? How old's this guy?'

'Is it pertinent?' Bernard asked, smoothing the wisps of hair above his forehead down with a dry palm.

'Was he in the war?'

'Probably. What does it matter? We dealt with Griesing in Frankfurt constantly until he died last year and we had proof of what he had done— '

Thatcher shook his head, as if by denying it he could even more assuredly swear that it had never happened. 'Don't worry, Bernard. I'll handle it fine, you've seen me do it before. I'm taking Joanna along. It's another new project, after all.'

'It'll be a shame to split them up, if only for a while,' said Bernard, suddenly staring at us as if he was a doorman and we, messengers. 'They make such a cute couple.'

Susie's voice suddenly cried out over the intercom. 'Some matters need attending, Bernard,' she said. 'I'm coming down.'

'So tomorrow keep Lester going through the preliminaries,' said Thatcher. 'Once I get a line on this character I'll have a better idea of when we can start putting him to work.'

'What are you talking about?' Bernard said,

laughing, evidently finding little humour in what we said, all the same.

'Mystic, Bernard. Check it out.'

As Gus stood, preparing to leave, it struck me that he had, during the course of listening to the conversation running around him, discovered one of Susie's tricks, one that so often I'd wish I'd been able to perform. Never one of the more approachable men I'd known, an almost palpable shell seemed to have formed itself around him, protecting now so well as giving isolation and distance, protecting from those protected. Lester motioned toward him, and he saw Lester, and stopped, standing before Bernard's desk.

'No one stopped you?' he asked Gus, pointing at the pen and pencil set, to the plastic knoll.

Bernard stared at them both as if watching a movie never before seen take an unforgivable turn.

'No,' he said, apparently completing the conversation we'd interrupted. 'They trusted I had nothing to do with it.'

He left, brushing past Susie as she entered; she cringed at the feel of shell against shell.

'Bernard didn't know,' I told Lester that night as we lay on my bed. 'Thatcher told me he didn't. If he did know I don't think he wanted to be reminded.'

'He doesn't seem to be a very sentimental person otherwise,' said Lester.

'He is. And everybody had heroes.'

Does Bernard enjoy what he does?'

'It's grown on him,' I said. 'He's a natural at advertising. He started in product development but couldn't stand the sight of blood.'

'Thatcher trusts him?'

'More than anyone except Susie, I think.'

'What sort of relationship does Gus have with Jake?' he asked, after a minute or so more. 'Besides that of a teacher?'

'Nothing abnormal,' I said. 'Avi once told me Gus wanted to get married and have a son. I asked him how he knew and he said he could tell from Gus's handwriting.'

'Did you want to get married?' he asked me.

'Once,' I said. 'Nobody wanted to go all the way.'

Some did, truly, but that would have ruined it; I could never allow the men I'd loved the most to become my lovers. Genuine friendship between men and women was such a rare thing that to admit sex into such relations was unfailingly destructive, as if to carve your initials into a pearl.

'Lester— '

'Did you want to have a baby?'

'Not until I had him.'

'Abortion's not illegal if you make enough money,' he said, embracing me as if assuring that one of us could not abandon the other before the time was right. 'We both know that. Why didn't you— '

'Thatcher's pro-life.'

After Lester left I fell asleep and dreamed I saw his family's house. The ruin stood so desolate as an old English church, yet it couldn't have antedated America's Civil War; its stones could never have known the touch of a slave's hand. Attached to the chimney's outer wall was a bloody diadem, a rusted basketball hoop. Opening the front door I tiptoed in as if entering a nursery. No rags of memory clothed the room's nakedness; his house's amnesia was so profound as mine. I saw Lester standing in the kitchen. The pantry door was off its hinges and the room beyond appeared only recently unsealed. In the centre of the far wall's fairness an aureola of punctures ringed an abyss blown into the plaster; an inoculation scar, the mark of an angel's bite, Saturn gathering his children around him.

What happened to your family? I heard myself ask.

Misunderstandings, his image said.

7

Susie left the next morning for the Westchester estate, departing ahead of the others that she might oversee Thanksgiving preparations. Her personality's buds took full bloom, taken from Thatcher's shadow; Avi had heard that the year before two members of the kitchen staff killed themselves within a day of her arrival.

Sitting in Bernard's office the next morning, waiting for Thatcher, I thumbed through the pages of the newspaper, seeing signs that the season was upon us. In Ohio a woman found her herald of the new millennium emblazoned in mould on the wall of her garage; analysts agreed that those stores which remained open would show profits this year, for there were no other places left to shop. There were stories of devil-worshipping cults soon to be exposed in the north of England. There'd been a murder in St Patrick's Cathedral: while confessing a venial sin the confessant was overcome by the need to commit a mortal one, and so kicked his priest to death in the stall.

'Isn't Thatcher overreaching himself?' Bernard mumbled. Before I could answer, he responded, 'No. Not this time,' and I realised he was only voicing some mental catechism as he dallied over his paperwork. 'What can he do to the Japanese except turn people against them?'

I threw the paper aside, having seen inspiration enough within to last me a lifetime. Deciding to dawdle additional time away myself under the guise of work, I pulled a thick folder marked *Otsuka* from Bernard's outbox. Within were snapshots of the man taken many years before, photos that by their angles suggested he had no idea they were being taken. There were pages of statistics referring to his businesses, and his buyouts and mergers and steals. I came across one of his poems within, its lyric transcribed from Japanese into English.

They're on my nose now, inside of
Twenty miles.

Master arm on. Master arm on.
Fox one. Fox one.

God oh God.

Good hit. Good hit on one.
Roger that. Good kill.

Good kill.

'It reads like a transcript,' Lester commented,

studying the page from over my shoulder.

'No petals on wet black boughs for our connection,' said Bernard, taking his eyes from his
insolvables long enough to interrupt. 'He's fond
of using found material in his constructs. You'll
not have time to discover that even in Japan he's
quite askew from the norm.'

'He seems almost interesting,' I said.

'Thatcher would seem interesting, seen from
Mars,' said Bernard. 'Otsuka's older, that's all.
He's had more time to develop and elaborate.
His followers worship him for having stayed alive
against all odds.'

We might as well have not been there; Bernard
could have been talking to his computer, so trans-
fixed he was by his desktop screen's fluttering
green auroras.

'Try not to evidence untoward fascination,
Joanna, they've distractions enough.'

'We're no longer involved, Bernarrd.'

'Oh, you'll be involved, long as you work here.
I forgot we're playing minister and the choir girl
for the nonce. Just keep an eye on both of them.
Prepare to duck.'

'You're as paranoid as they are.'

'With reason,' he said. 'Make sure the agreement gets signed. Progress on this computer is
essentialled— '

'Which computer?' Lester asked.

'What interest could you take in technology?
I'd imagine you'd believe it superfluous,' Bernard
said. 'But apparently we keep no secrets from
you, I suppose. All right. Thatcher requires that
a new super-super oversee company operations
by the end of the decade, or preferably next
week. Without Japanese assistance it won't be

done. Our team goes into conniptions dealing with fifth generation models. Our masters from the east play with number sevens for relaxation. Thatcher's logic is such that he believes if we combine the groups we'll have a number twelve soon enough, or what in theory they call the Algorithmic Logistical Interactive whatchamacallit hoozis. How the language suffers at the tongues of these buffoons.'

'It'll be a talking computer?' Bernard nodded. 'How'll it sound?'

'Mellifluous. Speaking only Latin for safety's sake, I'm tempted to say. It'll be a thinking computer, in theory. That is to say, independent thought. If it works as they believe it will then no one will ever need God again.'

Bernard forever recognised, or pretended to recognise, his social faux pas a beat too late. 'Oh, Macaffrey, obsolescence hits every field in time.'

'This is what Thatcher wants now?' I asked. 'Every time I hear it he's added a little more.'

'As a backup for Junior. Just in case. A wise move, certainly. Where is Thatcher, anyway? Why isn't he down here yet?'

'He needed to brief the guards, he said.'

Bernard stared into his screen as if attempting to divine the future from entrails. 'Stuff something in his mouth if he starts adlibbing.'

Thatcher stuck his head in through the doorway, giving us his impression of delight. 'How's everybody this morning?' he asked, barrelling in, clapping his hand on Lester's shoulder as if testing its friability. 'What's the holdup? Can't sit around here all day.'

'We *can't*?' said Bernard, harvesting folders

from his desk's fields. 'Peruse the background material, Thatcher, if you would. You've seen the agreement you're signing, haven't you?'

'I'll wing it.'

Our three guards trailed him into the office, each bedecked in identical black suits with double-breasted jackets and baggy trousers, in toto resembling the fourth-string dance line at a deb ball. Jake scratched his nose, taking care not to remove any part of it with his still-attached scalpel. Avi, seeing Lester, let his eyes lose their focus until they appeared to draw back within his head. Gus's look held so little life I thought he might have had a dentist sever his facial nerves so that he would never again worry about giving anything away.

'Never felt so up,' said Thatcher. 'Had a hell of an appetite when I got up this morning. I could've et a dog— '

'Otsuka's not Korean, Thatcher,' said Bernard. 'Make do with sashimi. Go there, talk, sign and leave. Simple?'

'It's handleable. Take care of Lester while we're away. Start pushing on that new info.'

'Everything's under control,' Bernard said. 'What isn't, will be. Come back with the agreement signed— '

'I know, I know already. Don't come in your pants about it, hell— '

Bernard's blush was so intense that he could have passed, for an instant, as Susie's brother; their shades of purple were almost identical. 'Some people are more useful alive, Thatcher. Remember that.'

'We'll see how the jury calls it,' he answered. 'Come on. It's hashsettling time.'

I never worried over Lester's safety when he left my house at night; in daylight, at Dryco, there seemed so much more to fear. He'd be with me that night, certainly; I knew that, all the same. As our quintet departed Gus radioed the lobby before boarding the elevator.

'Dryden party descending. Please prepare.'

Thatcher practically bounded off the elevator walls while we dropped to earth, in the dim light within the cab appearing to toss off sparks. 'They got the wounds,' he said, chuckling. 'I got the salt.'

Peering into the lenses affixed to the corners of the elevator's ceiling he made faces, picked at his teeth, slammed his fists against his enclosure. If I hadn't known he never touched the product I could have imagined he's done a snootful before allowing his feet to touch the floor that morning.

Jake dashed into the lobby as we landed, investigating all directions, the performance of his job giving him such mindless ecstasy as Thatcher radiated. Our route to the exit transversed the breadth of the building's lobby and then the width of the outdoor plaza. Innumerable times Gus warned Thatcher that his chosen path was forever insecurable; hearing such truth only assured Thatcher that he should pass no other way. Gus snapped his fingers; lobby guards drew up around us, shouldering guns and clutching long batons in their knobby hands. Once we exited the guards formed two long unbroken lines, forcing hundreds of late-morning passersby into pedlock while we ambled to the car.

'Jake,' Thatcher shouted ahead. 'That guy. Watch him.'

A man wearing a suit cut to appear so expensive as Thatcher's attempted to crash the line, refusing to break his stride for reasons of heaven or earth. As our barricade pushed him back he abandoned all reason, slinging his attache case to the sidewalk, aiming curses at everyone near. When Jake approached he stepped forward again, leaning in close between members of the line.

'Queer bastard!' he yelled, his tight collar vanishing beneath his billowing jowls.

Spinning en pointe Jake swung out his hand as if miming, for smaller children, the sway of an elephant's trunk. The man tumbled onto the sidewalk. Thatcher, edging by, threw himself into the car and sank immediately into the back seat's leather; breathed deep the Siberian air within. 'Good to get out among the folks,' he murmured.

Gus sat next to the driver; Jake and Avi perched in the jumpseats facing us.

'Where are we meeting Otsuka?' I asked. Such details went unrelayed while they might be overheard and put to evil purpose.

'Midtown,' said Thatcher, folding his arms before him as if preparing to sleep through a debate; he spoke into the intercom. 'How long till we get there, Gus?'

Inches of lucite and steel separated our compartment from the rest of the car; Thatcher enjoyed pointing out that were we to be bombed, some of us could survive.

'Twenty minutes,' said Gus, his voice crackling around us as it broke through the fuzz. 'Depending on traffic.'

Jake gripped the edge of his seat with his unapplianced hand so as to avoid being jostled to the floor as the car lurched across potholes,

127

swinging north onto Broadway. Once the avenue
ran one-way downtown from Columbus Circle;
Thatcher, probably for no reason other than to
show that he could have it done, decreed that its
traffic should race salmon-like upstream.

'What a wonderful world,' he said, sighing,
so seeming overcome by its beauty as to lose
all remnants of care and worry. A riot was
underway at the Federal building, several blocks
north of City Hall. Police restrained their leashed
alsatians, facing a crowd of black citizens: front-
line protestors wore knee-length coats; those
demonstrators further back carried signs, and
clubs of impromptu design. GREENASSES OUT
OF HARLEM, many of their placards read. Some
of the rest, ones hoisted by immigrants or the sup-
porters of immigrants, demanded FREE BROOK-
LYN NOW. As we glided uptown, unbothered so
long as we kept to our isolated centre lane, the
protestors moved: those in the front pulled cats
from beneath their coats and threw them onto
the dogs; the others surged ahead, swinging.

'Can't depend on cops to do shit these days,'
said Thatcher, watching as if he was interested.
'No excuse for it. Complain, complain, nothing those people've done for fifty years but
complain— '

'It's their only right, Mr Dryden.' Avi never
feared putting his beliefs into words, knowing no
one who spoke freely could be harmed so long
as the words were flung forth without matching
action.

'They got the right to work with what they're
given,' Thatcher said, concluding, 'Hell. Didn't
I?'

We bore north; Army vehicles headed south to

balm such suffering as they found. The turret of
the lead tank swung right and fired at a News4
van parked perilously close to the disturbance,
bringing forth a yellow blossom that shot hot
metal spores into the surrounding crowd. As our
car continued to rock with the concussion I turned
to look behind us; soldiers welled up from the skin
of the tanks, raising their rifles, firing into the
people blocks before the disturbance proper.

'Your news station, Mr Dryden,' Avi pointed
out.

'My Army,' he said. 'Like a son taking the car
out and wrecking it. You still got to love 'em.
Joanna, you get a chance to look over the agreement?' I nodded. 'You read the particulars? See
anything funny?'

'Not at all.'

With Thatcher's blessing the Army was at work
farther north, constructing a concrete wall from
river to river down the centre of Fourteenth
Street. They intended that each Manhattan neighbourhood would thereby be better secured from
agitators drifting in from other neighbourhoods
to assault the more productive; to live thus would
be no different from living in heaven as they saw
it, where the quieting sense of existing eternally
beneath unblinking eyes was never lost.

'You think this will take long?'

'No,' said Thatcher.

Throughout the twenties and thirties clusters
of people bundled into rags lay sleeping against
the locked doors of vacant buildings; knowing a
moment's peace, aware that few cared enough
about them to harass them.

'Why do you hate the Japanese so, Mr Dryden?'
Avi asked.

'What'd you say?'

Words sometimes stick if they're hurled with a sense of timing, and for several moments Thatcher said nothing else, trying perhaps to rationalise an explication of a belief never before challenged.

'I'm sorry, I heard you. Let me try to explain,' he said. 'Two men want the same woman. She pretends to be indifferent to both of them. Till one comes out ahead she's not going to let on how she feels about the one winning. Might not matter to her who wins.' He sat up in his seat, intent now on his lecture. 'It does to them. Maybe they're old friends. Maybe they hate each other. Could be that if they hadn't fallen into the situation they'd have never given a good goddamn what happened to the other one. Give it time. Soon enough they'll do anything to get the advantage. *Anything*. People'll do anything if they want something bad enough, period. I don't have anything against the Japanese. But they're there. They want my woman.'

'What if the woman's indifference is genuine?' I asked.

'The fight takes on its own life,' he said. 'After a while she might not as well even be there, truly. Love or business, politics or war, same difference in any situation. But sooner or later you'll be doing stuff you might find painful to remember, later on. Stuff you wouldn't want to tell your kids about. Do things you don't believe you're doing, while you're doing 'em. But to get them edge you wind up doing 'em anyway. It's in the nature of the beast.'

I could conjure in my mind an image of what West Fifty-Sixth surely had been like when I was a child. Brick apartments, fifteen or twenty stories high, would have stood at the avenues; along the byway proper old brownstones, converted livery stables, perhaps one or two small lofts would have covered the lots. Cheap restaurants and clubs would have frayed awnings extending to the curbsides. The shops of the street would know you as a customer as they'd known your mother; as they believed, and you believed, they'd know your daughter.

'Most times, that's how it works,' said Thatcher.

Otsuka's building, one of those architectural marvels that appear so sublime, alone upon the draftsperson's cold screen, took up almost the entire south side of the block. The tower, outlined with aqua neon, rose to unguessable heights; the upper floors were cantilevered over the lower and so the street knew daylight for so brief a time with every noon that were the city to be abandoned, grass would have never sprouted between the cracks in the pavement. The atrium within was so tall as the building enclosing it; the empty elevators were transparent bullets shooting up long glass guns.

'He's the only one has an office in here,' Thatcher said, eyeing the lobby guards within. 'Check it out. They're black.'

Gus identified our group; the guards directed us to enter the centre tube, their voices carrying heavy accents, and as they spoke among themselves they used a melodious Caribbean patois. Stepping into the elevator I saw that its floor was so clear as its sides. Gus stared at the ceiling, at the cables along the sides; I'd never realised that he was scared of heights.

'I don't remember Japs being real big on affirmative action,' Thatcher said.

Leaving the elevator we emerged in Otsuka's reception foyer. At once I detected the spoor of our own floor's decorators: barricades of charcoal sofas, dusty rubber plants overgrowing their ceramic pots, rough walls possessing the feel of a three-day beard. The seats of the sofas were cunningly tilted; those who waited could not linger long without sliding off. An HD monitor listed incoming figures from the Asian exchanges. The receptionist, a willow-thin Japanese woman, stood and bowed, something about her smile suggesting more of surgery than of training. When she spoke her voice came from a place other than her mouth.

'Mr Otsuka expects you, Mr Dryden.'

Taking a ballpoint from his pocket he flipped it toward her; the pen flew through her image, bouncing off the wall behind. In the ceiling we discovered the lens that produced her hologram.

'They're getting good at this shit,' Thatcher said. 'We could put that to use somehow.'

We stepped inside. Otsuka sat at his desk, his form silhouetted by the window behind him. His view was that of another window, across a space no wider than a tenement airshaft. Metal shutters veiled the opposite building's eyes. Japanese prints of traditional design were hung on the wall above a fireplace whose hearth seemed never to have seen a log. Upon his broad teak desk were a bonsai tree and a large amber lump; trapped within was a tiny frog, preserved forever in apparent mid-leap. Otsuka was so well-groomed as a dowager's corpse. His companions assisted him in rising, holding his arms when he tipped forward as if fearful that in bowing, he would break.

'A pleasure, Mr Dryden,' he said, singing with ancient and unexpectedly resonant pipes. 'Your presence is a great gift.'

'Good, cause that's all I brought,' said Thatcher, sweeping out his hand. 'My associates.'

'Mine,' said Otsuka.

His two bookends made their bows: they were mature men, with silver hair and rimless glasses; their tailored suits failed to hide their mass, and in the day's dim light they appeared to be carved from rock. All guards present sized the other sides' up.

'I am sorry Mr Leibson cannot join us today. We've worked so closely of late you will understand me when I say I sometimes think he must be one of my employees.'

'I know the feeling,' said Thatcher, rocking back on his heels as if preparing to swing. 'He runs a one-man show in our operation. Keeps him busy.'

'Sit, please,' said Otsuka, fingering a chromium nipple built into his desktop. 'Our meeting must be honoured.'

A door that hadn't been there moments before slid open, and a young woman emerged, proving her existence by the silver tray she bore. From the tray she took a crystal decanter and thimble-sized cups.

'A sixty-year old single malt,' Otsuka said. 'Hard to come by.'

'I'm not much of a drinker,' said Thatcher, tossing his drink down as he might Kool-Aid. 'From the emperor's collection?'

Otsuka shook his head so vigorously that I

feared his withered face might crumble away from his skull. 'He abstains. A gift from the late premier,' he explained. 'Where is your wife?'

Thatcher shrugged, holding his thimble up for a refill, behaving as he'd promised and not grabbing the bottle by its neck.

'Mr Leibson tells me she is an active proponent of our renewed alliance. In the past I believe she has dealt with several political appointees, I should say, from my country. This belief in equal rights for those within equal classes is so peculiarly American, don't you believe? Even now in Japan the wife too often remains simply the pipeline between husband and children.'

'That's what we got plumbers for, over here,' said Thatcher. 'She's good at what she does.'

'Perhaps my lessers are correct, I sometimes fear, and women should be kept from participating in business. They are too good at outsmarting us. The lovely woman who attends you today.' His young boy's eyes studied me as he exuded his opinions. 'She is more than your secretary, but is not your *tayu*.'

'We don't do those things here,' Thatcher insisted. 'Diseases, you know. Got to keep business risk-free, within reason.'

'She would be your *miko*?'

'Would she? What is it?'

'Difficult to translate,' said Otsuka, tapping his cheek with a thin finger, a bone sheathed in skin. 'A shamaness of graspable productivity, in the sense I use it. One who blesses the shrine of capital.'

'No, we got that covered, too,' said Thatcher. 'She's too down to earth for that feminist mystic stuff. Joanna oversees new projects.'

'And I am a new project, true,' he said. 'Still, Mr Dryden, remember that defending the spiritual quality of your business is as important as having faithful *nihirisuto* to protect your personal well-being. But forgive me, please. When I am with Mr Leibson we speak my language as if we were friends. *Nihirisuto*. Laughing samurai, you might say. Dancers at the lip of the volcano.' He examined our guards as if wondering how much they might bring. 'In my youth I kept with me always the long sword from Kyoto that Hiro now carries for me.'

The larger man, on his right, bowed lower; the scabbard's tip protruded from his jacket, obscene in its bluntness.

'But now these are the words of one who prepares to leave this world. There is no need to expend the declining energy I have when my associates may do it for me. In this setting, certainly, it seems so unnecessary.'

'Seems so,' said Thatcher. 'Trust makes the world go round.'

'And our countries have had so little trust in one another for so long.'

'We'd've preferred to settle our differences sooner, certainly. But there's no sense running into anything till you've looked to see what you're running on.'

'I wouldn't have expected you to put it any other way.'

'Past few years, your country's had it hard,' Thatcher said, failing to express in his countenance the semblance of sympathy he sought to give. 'Your people, too. It's a shame.'

'It has not been so difficult as some might have hoped,' said Otsuka. 'Persistence in the face of hardship is often rewarded.'

'Often,' Thatcher repeated.

'Still, through my foresight our industrial hollowing-out was nearly complete when this so-called Readjustment began. While we expected certain emergency measures on the part of your government, we did not foresee that the opinions of individuals would cause us to be treated as enemies. It seemed so much more unwise for you than to us, in a sense. The freeze on our assets hurt so many of your own countrymen, you know. America has been in such a perilous state since that time.'

'The sensible man who's starving can always convince himself somebody else's hungrier,' said Thatcher. 'America's never been stronger than it is today. A little adversity builds a lot of character. Think I'm broken up about it? Aren't I smiling?'

'Mr Dryden, the adversity of others has built your character. Your strength-through-joy approach is something I put little stock in.'

'Are you calling me a Nazi or what—?' Thatcher asked; I prepared to do as Bernard demanded, and squirt in conversational lubricant, but had no chance.

'A witticism, Mr Dryden,' said Otsuka. 'True, in some ways Americans would be ideal Nazis, but in the long run it could never work. Every man would insist upon being his own Fuehrer.'

Thatcher gripped the arms of his chair as if he readied to leap up and strangle his proposed ally.

'I mean no disrespect in this matter. Not everyone appreciates my humour, sir. That your Mr Leibson does counts for much in my eyes. He and

I see things as they are. My countrymen neither appreciate my belief in the individual nor my telling them what they prefer not to hear about what they choose not to see. In America the concept of individualism is at least honoured in theory. All I intended to say was that our stasis was brought about by your decline, and neither of us need to have suffered so much. Nothing more.'

'What I'm trying to say is we've finally got our house in order and once again we're ready to start helping the rest of the neighbourhood— '

'The arsonist forever returns to the scene of the fire.' Otsuka held his hands before him, as if in prayer. 'A new approach must be made by you first, Mr Dryden.'

'What approach? What are you talking about?'

'Leaving aside nearsighted economic retributions,' Otsuka said, 'I have heard stories of how you refer to my country, and my people.'

'What'd Bernard tell you?'

'Mr Leibson has been a model of circumspection in these matters, Mr Dryden. His view of all members of humanity is consistent. But a bad word shouted from a cliffside echoes off the rocks, and I have heard these echoes in several places.'

'I'm not sure what you're getting at— '

'Have you not at times called us yellow perils? Whale eaters? Monkey boys?'

'People get upset and say things— '

'Japs?' Otsuka said. 'Gooks?'

'My brother was in Vietnam,' Thatcher said, as if that explained.

'I have never been in Vietnam, Mr Dryden. Only Americans go to Vietnam. Perhaps it would be similar, and more accurate, were I to call you a Nazi in such circumstance— '

'You all don't have any room to talk,' Thatcher said. 'Way you treat Koreans. The Chinese. Things you've said about American people— '

'I treat all equally, Mr Dryden. I have said no such things. The Japanese are a homogenous people, sir, but to remain that way we shot no Ainu from trains. We imported no Koreans to sell in our cities' markets. We never beat American students to death in our universities simply for being intelligent.'

'You're still bad as we are.'

'Ours are both racist nations, Mr Dryden. But we'll have none of it between us if you want my business. This is not in the agreement but must be agreed to. You will never call me or my people anything other than Japanese again, to my face or behind my back. Is that agreed?'

'You have to understand it wasn't deliberate,' Thatcher said. 'My dad was in the war.'

'In the European theatre,' Otsuka said. 'I was in the war, Mr Dryden. When I was taken prisoner it was by Americans considerate enough not to send my skull back to a girlfriend as a token of love.'

'He could have been in the Pacific— '

'Then we might have killed each other, and where would we be today? Ours are different countries now than what they were. We must both remember that, and not view each other through our father's eyes.'

When Thatcher at last replied I barely heard him. 'That's true.'

'To share fruitfully our hegemony,' said Otsuka, 'we must trust each other as partners, if not as equals.'

138

'Agreed,' Thatcher sighed.

Otsuka smiles. 'I can drink to that. Let's do it, shall we?'

Otsuka pulled at the sleeve of his righthand associate. 'Please hand the papers to Mr Dryden. Mr Leibson has gone over the working copy with you, of course.'

'Of course.'

As Thatcher speedily read through the clauses I relaxed, and allowed my glance to drift across the prints on the wall, assuming them at first to be Hiroshige's; noted in the corner of one landscape a pair of golden arches.

'Your hard bargaining may cause us difficulties in the future, Mr Dryden,' Otsuka said.

'We'll be dead by then,' Thatcher mumbled.

'The only way to offset the thirty percent share of our profits that you require will necessitate an end to the present deflation, true, but perhaps to too great a degree. Some of my advisers believe me foolish to make such a settlement.'

'People'll have to pay what we charge, won't they?' Thatcher said. 'Long as they got something to trade we can always work something out.'

'Our retrofitted world cannot long exist on this barter system your country introduced— '

'It was my wife's idea, actually,' said Thatcher, reading the pact as he might the lease for an apartment. 'You all don't like it cause your money's finally gone like everyone else's once you get rid of what we turn loose and you don't have nothing to trade but brains and VCRs. Nobody else complains.'

'What choice do they have?'

Thatcher grinned.

'We are not so badly off as all that, Mr Dryden, and you know that.'

'I got one question. This bit about programmes employing viable personnel components of – what the hell? Southhemi states?' Thatcher reread what he'd quoted. 'People of Latin America, I suppose. I'm curious as to what your intentions are for that part of the world.'

'What is the context for your inquiry?' asked Otsuka.

'What're you going to do down there?' asked Thatcher. 'Clear enough?'

'The agreement allows only for the discussion of proposed projects. Your approval is necessary for any actions taken after the date of signing. Otherwise, certainly, we would lose our favoured status— '

'Actions already underway are unaffected?'

'Of course. Mr Dryden, you look upon Latin America as you might look upon your mother.'

'I was reborn there,' said Thatcher. 'What sort of things you got underway down south?'

'Nothing unexpected. We possess a certain amount of liquidable property there as we do in many places. Money we once had that we were unable to invest in the United States had to go somewhere.'

'I see.'

'Mr Dryden, your doubts are still evident. For a moment examine your other partnerships and see the benefits of realigning with Japan. Who else is out there with whom you deal? Europe? Because of their own so-called alliance they believe they will shortly be able to dispose of us both. So they've believed for six years, and some-day they may convince one other to believe.

140

China? You don't nurse vipers without knowing they'll strike when they choose. Russia.' He
paused; sighed, and rubbed his eyes. 'Mr Dryden,
your countries have an incomprehensible relationship. Each of your nations seems a dream
of the other. This war without war the two of
you have ongoing seems likely to bankrupt you
in time, no matter the business you believe it
creates— '

'We tried not fighting,' said Thatcher. 'Just
didn't seem natural. It's not as if there're dangers
involved. The Pax is signed and in long-distance
conflicts we both use local advisors— '

'So that your Army may be saved, to use in
battling against your own countrymen. That is
the most puzzling thing of all.'

'This incountry stuff is pennyante insurrection,
that's all,' said Thatcher. 'Long Island wouldn't
go along when the FEMA plan took effect. Too
many posses were quartered out there. They
weren't used to working inside any law.'

Most had worked for Thatcher; he never for-
gave.

'You don't see martial law still in effect anywhere
but here, do you? That's all, and that's unavoidable. We're just mopping up now. I'll be on the
winning side of the civil war this time, that's for
sure.'

'Your soldiers have been mopping for two
years,' said Otsuka. 'Your Army cannot settle
a disturbance among your own people not a
kilometre from where we sit.'

'There's just more of 'em out there than originally estimated,' Thatcher said.

'I would say America should invest its capital
and its young men in areas where they might have

more purposeful effect.'

'Well, it's our problem in any event,' said Thatcher. 'New York's got to be secure. We don't need Japanese help on that.'

'But you do in other areas, Mr Dryden,' said Otsuka. 'You need a dependable friend.'

Thatcher nodded to Avi, who handed him a fountain pen with a golden nib. Upon signing the agreement he passed it over to Otsuka, who inked in his own ideograms.

'That our age may again know reason,' Otsuka said. 'As Adam Smith wrote, economic self-interest guided by the unseen hand of God enriches the marketplace.'

'You got to watch out for that hand.'

'Our new world,' said Otsuka, reading over the signatures. 'So much clay awaits its sculptors.'

For several long moments Thatcher was un-naturally pensive, as if he already regretted having signed. 'Sometimes it takes a while to see everything in the big picture,' he said, wistfully, as if admitting to a character flaw. He folded his copy of the agreement into a neat square and stuffed it into his jacket pocket.

'Remember, Mr Dryden,' said Otsuka, smiling, showing no teeth. 'What you don't see is Japanese.'

'We have to move,' Thatcher said, standing, walking over to where I already stood. 'You'll forgive us?'

'Of course,' said Otsuka.

Thatcher nodded.

'*Go!*'

Thatcher took me down with him as he threw himself to the floor. He lay on top of me; the rug's pile scoured my face as he shielded my head with his hands. Along with cacophonous uproar I heard what sounded as the thunk of darts striking wood. I sensed Thatcher entered a state beyond consciousness; as he heard each dart take its mark he thrust himself against me. Flattening my hands against the carpet I was able to lift myself up, rolling him off me before he could attain his ultimate joy. Standing, I saw that it was done. Jake squatted atop Otsuka's desk, between the bonsai and the amber, and Avi stood where he'd been all along.

'To the elevator,' Thatcher whispered, wrapping his arm around me in pretence of concern as he got up, taking firm grips with his hand. Even his voice trembled, he was so overcome with emotions. 'Nice and calm.'

All should have been confusion and blur, but each moment seared itself into my mind, so that even now I can call up each image of the afternoon so easily as I might find a photo in an album. Otsuka's associates bore the look of dolls tossed haphazardly against the spattered window, their arms thrown back, their heads dangling. Otsuka himself appeared to have fallen asleep while in prayer, having had no more time to wait for an answer. Gus found his own rest upon the darkened carpet. From his angel's perch Jake stared down at his mentor, his face so livid as that of his friend's. Taking up Otsuka's sword from the desk, where the associate had dropped it unsheathed, he tied its strap around his waist; then he glared at Avi, appearing no less surprised than I to see him holding a gun.

'Nice and calm,' Thatcher repeated.

We drifted away then, floating across the office, into the reception area and past the ever-smiling

143

receptionist into the elevator. I'd had dreams that
seemed more real. My stomach burned as if I'd
swallowed boiling water; I couldn't stop my hands
from shaking, and pressed them between my arms
so that the others wouldn't see. Feeling wetness
on my face as if I'd run for hours through the
rain, I watched seventy stories vanish beneath my
feet as we plunged to earth. As we emerged at the
bottom I recall wondering what else Thatcher had
in mind; if another sudden episode was planned,
simply to add a fillip to the fun he'd already
had.

'Thanks a lot,' Thatcher said to the guards gathered round the information desk. 'Nice place.'

None of the guards stopped us as we walked
out the doors; no one stopped us when we walked
on, to the car. No one would stop us, once we
drove away. A haze began to cloud over my
mind, making each moment darker and ever-
colder, but rather than being engulfed within
white it was black that overtook me, deep and
limitless; as if, having been pitched out of heaven
into space's floorless pit, I discovered that not
even stars would keep me company.

Awakening again I found myself in bed, at
home, later that night. The last thing I remember
was hearing Thatcher's voice, breaking as if with
puberty, and saying only *yeah*.

8

'I hate to be in the same world with him,' I said.

Lester and I gazed out the living room window, through a lacing of dead branches toward the far-off river and the Palisades farther still. I'd never made money enough in my life to have paid for the drapes in Thatcher's house.

'Not long after we started working for him I asked Bernard if he thought Thatcher was evil,' I said. 'He said it was like asking what jazz is.'

'The mysteries come soon enough, Joanna,' said Lester, an unexpected cheerfulness hanging about him.

Thatcher's own gless so infused his holiday spirit that the day before he'd invited us to this year's Thanksgiving celebration. We were driven up; in those days the Dryden estate consisted of a couple of hundred acres running eastward from the Hudson River; a high granite wall girdled every inch. The main house dated from the turn of the last century, and had twenty rooms; for so long as I'd known him he'd planned to raze it and replace it with something cosier. While espying Thatcher's bounty I eavesdropped on the comments of guests, knowing few better paths to enlightenment in this world.

'Bernard told me not to worry about Tokyo,' a man whispered. 'Everything's under control.'

'You see the face on that new bodyguard?' a woman asked. 'The little faggot?'

'Psycho,' said her companion. 'Best kind to have, he thinks.'

A waiter glided past us, proferring a salver heavy with stunted olives and Velveeta-filled chicken livers; we declined.

'Have you heard the official explanation yet?' Lester asked.

'They're probably still working it up,' I said. 'Bernard must have taken better than I thought he would. I don't know what happened Tuesday, and yesterday they were shut up in their offices all day. What tests were the doctors giving you?'

'I don't know if I passed,' he said. 'They gave me a Bible to read. To get the story straight, maybe.'

'Probably want you to see what to avoid.'

'Why'd Bernard look so gloomy? It's not because of what happened, I can tell— '

'Usually he and Martha spend Thanksgiving at home, watching the parade and having dinner afterward.'

Macy's – not part of Dryco – had announced

that morning that they would no longer sponsor the parade, after that day's events; too many victims intended to sue.

'Bernard once told me he'd come up here on Thanksgiving only if they served up Thatcher with an apple in his mouth.'

'Thatcher needed him up here?'

'For punishment, perhaps. Doubtless we'll find out soon enough what's going on. He has something he wants us to do, I can tell— '

'Wants me to do,' said Lester. 'Why didn't Bernard's wife come along?'

'Martha refuses to have anything to do with Thatcher any more.'

'What'd he do to her?'

I shook my head. 'Some people reach their limit sooner than others.'

'Then these must know no boundaries,' he said, regarding the crowd engulfing us.

The house's rooms were not large enough to dwarf multitudes; the twenty-five present made the space feel so cramped as a subway car. They laughed and joked among themselves as if they were having a good time.

'Who are they?'

'His closest surviving business associates,' I said. 'Us, Avi, Jake— '

'They have to work even though the estate guards are here?'

'Who else to guard the guards?' I asked.

Neither of them were in immediate sight. Since Tuesday Avi had avoided me so studiously as he'd avoided Lester, seeming more fearful than ashamed. A third party had negotiated for the retrieval of Gus's body and so Jake went to Campbell's that morning before coming up,

147

bringing along his own jar in which he could carry the cremains. There'd been no autopsy; everyone knew how Gus died.

'Aren't there any family members?'

'Junior,' I said.

He sat in a chair in the corner of the room, and could not have looked less comfortable had he appeared suddenly among a mixed populace in a strange city, naked and speaking only a language no one understood.

'Their son. He's fifteen, I believe.'

'Seeing him I'd have thought he was a foster child,' said Lester, 'thrown from house to house.'

'His mother loves him, the poor thing. He's more postliterate than Jake, I can barely understand him. Thatcher doesn't want him to run the company eventually, but figures he needs to be ready to try. Susie insists upon it. That's why he wants that computer in place— '

'He's the only other family member here?'

'The only one alive,' I said. 'I don't know what happened to most of them. Bernard told me about Thatcher's brother once. He was older. He and Thatcher started the business, and then Susie came in on it. They took over the running of it after he was killed.'

'What happened?'

'Medellín was involved, as I heard it. Bernard told me Thatcher opened his refrigerator one morning and his brother tumbled out. That inspired Thatcher to do whatever it was that he did to gain control of their operation— '

'What about Mrs Dryden's family?'

'She had a brother. He worked for Medellín. They found out, after— '

'And Thatcher had him killed?'

'Susie.'

A house guard loomed behind me, tapping my shoulder; I wondered if my fellow guests believed I let slip too many family anecdotes. 'Mr Dryden wants to see you now,' the lug said, then walked away.

Taking Lester's hand in mind I walked him along, toward Thatcher's hall.

'They have family skeletons, rather than trees,' I remarked.

Jake idled in the approach to Thatcher's study, browsing over Thatcher's coin collection; gold doubloons and eagles mounted in framed panels hung above the wainscotting, and the sconces' creamy lemon light made the coins shine as miniature suns. I noticed the black mourning band Jake had tied around his sleeve.

'You all right?' I asked, stroking his shoulder; Jake never felt more than an animate assemblage of lumps. He nodded, blinking black eyes bright with red flecks. 'You got Gus this morning?'

'Solo.' he said. 'Pickupped. Did the drop bridgeways. Ashes to ashes to ashes, full fathom five.' He jerked his head toward the doorway. 'They're keen to connive.'

Avi allowed us entry, keeping out of our sight as he opened the door, locking it behind us as we came in. There'd been six windows in Thatcher's study; he'd bricked them over and tucked the bricks beneath curtains. Redwood shelves sagging beneath the weight of thousands of old LPs lined the curtainless walls. Avi reclined on a black leather divan and concentrated his stare on a spot on the beamed ceiling. Bernard paced back and forth before Thatcher's desk, his movements recalling to my mind those of the polar bear once imprisoned in the Central Park Zoo. Thatcher propped his bare feet upon his empty desk. Behind him were three filing cabinets kept forever locked, the ones that he claimed housed his most useful precautions. He spoke to me.

'Hon, you know how I hate to see people get all carried away by their emotions.'

'You've carried me as far as I'm going— ' I started to say.

'Have a seat, son.' Thatcher tugged at Lester's sleeve, and pointed to a nearby ottoman, 'You too, Joanna.'

'Are you going to listen to me? Did you expect me to verify your account to Bernard? I'm not backing you up, Thatcher— '

'Bernard, haven't I been straight as a ruler with you?'

I didn't look to see Bernard's reaction.

'Moral support's kind of superfluous at the moment, hon.'

'There's no excuse for what you did,' I said. 'None at all.'

'Tell me, Lester,' he said. 'Does dining at the table of a murderer make the guest as bad as the host?'

'Sometimes,' Lester said.

Thatcher shrugged, and held out his hands as if expecting to have them slapped. 'Smell dinner cooking?' he asked. 'Hope you all went easy on breakfast. Got a special treat coming up.'

Bernard sighed, sitting down in a wingbacked chair, giving all signs of having paced himself into a stupor. I stood before them, ever more anxious to bear witness.

'Even if you're blind to all others, Thatcher,'

I said, 'don't you think you might watch out for yourself? Don't you think you could have been killed the other day? You think of that?'

'My boys don't miss when they aim,' Thatcher said.

Avi ignored the compliment offered, and examined his nails as if searching for lingering stains.

'It's insane, Thatcher. It's immoral. I've had as much of this as I can take— '

'We were so busy yesterday I never got a chance to explain,' he said. 'It's a natural feeling you're having, thinking I've not been on the up-and-up about this— '

'Your explanations never explain,' I said. 'They rationalise, they make excuses, they lie but they never explain. What reason could you possibly have for murdering them except paranoia, Thatcher? You can't answer me, can you— ?'

'I can— '

'Bail out of your moral plane, Joanna,' Bernard said, interrupting. 'Where have you been working all this time, sweetness, a convent? None of this is new to you, it's simply your first direct experience. Every virgin suffers pain, when the moment comes.'

'It's been explained to your satisfaction?'

'The agreement is signed, after all. You shouldn't judge a book by its writer.'

'Reality's a tricky business, hon,' said Thatcher. 'No sooner do you get used to the way it appears to be it flips right over on you. You have to be ready to go with it. Once we explain this to you you'll understand why ours was the only suitable response. You're sensible as Bernard is when it comes to cold, hard fact— '

'Your facts are slipperier than reality,' I said.

'I'm not nearly that sensible— '

'You've tried hard enough to give the impression you are,' said Thatcher, 'at least in the past. You're being as hard on me as you are on yourself, hon, and that's not fair to either of us. What kind of heathern do you think I am?' His face was angelic; his eyes, so moist as a calf's. 'It's a question of getting a chokehold on reality before it gets one on you. Seeing patterns far enough ahead to make events go the way you want them to go. You got to try, at least, cause if you don't then you deserve to get anything life throws at you.' He doodled on a pad as he spoke, marking out small circles and then slashing them through with x's. 'That's the trouble most people have, being on the edge. You stay out there long enough and you're bound to get cut at some point.' He shook his head. 'Most people can't bear the sight of their own blood. Nothing more. But once you get used to your own you don't have so many qualms left about anyone else's.'

'There's no excuse for any of it, Thatcher. No reason— '

'Everyone has reasons, Joanna,' said Bernard. 'Grasp all the aspects of that verity and you either get out of the madhouse forever or never leave it again. It's up to you.'

'Listen now,' said Thatcher. 'A little background. What's the rule of thumb in interrogating those who won't give, Avi?'

'The thumbrule is that if the subject hesitates, the family will be lost,' Avi said, reciting with less élan than had Lester's students. 'If the family is absent, use their memory. If the family is present, work with them physically. If the subject has a wife, use the husband. A son, the mother.

A father, the daughter.'

'Monday night a father with daughters broke,' said Thatcher. 'One of the doctors. Spilled his guts, you could say. Seems our man Jensen is taking the air at Montefiore, up in the Bronx.'

'What does he have to say for himself?'

'Ask the turkeys in the kitchen what they have to say for themselves,' Thatcher said, laughing. 'He's more than zombified, as it turns out. An irreversible coma. I doubt he's much for idle chitchat at the moment.'

'The doctor would have claimed anything under the circumstances, I'm sure— '

'Truth cries when it comes,' said Thatcher. 'Now who do you think had him shipped up there? Old second gunman himself— '

'Gus—?'

'Got in a little too far over his head this time,' he said. 'After a while it must have affected his mind, having to keep new realities straight all the time. Working in Cuba but doing for America. Working in Mexico but doing for Cuba. Russia and Libya and Italy and who knows where else. To this day I don't think he knew who he was working for in Dallas, and would he have been surprised— '

'If he was even there,' said Bernard, in a voice less direct than was usual.

'He was there all right,' Thatcher said, reaching behind him and patting one of his files. 'I guess even you still have trouble sometimes with cold, hard facts.' He winked at me. 'In any event, it's to be expected he'd still be prone to freelance if the right commitment came through. Just wonder now what else he'd gotten into we haven't found out about yet— '

'The doctor told you Gus was involved and that's why you had Avi shoot him?'

'You think I kill people just cause I like the sound they make when they hit the ground?' he said, sighing. 'Bernard, pick up on this. I'm going to get my throat so raw jawin' if I'm not careful I won't be able to eat any turkey.'

Though I hadn't noticed before I became suddenly aware that no one in the room but Lester would look into my eyes as I saw; my wishful thinking made me think that perhaps they could no longer bear to see what they saw reflected.

'We were told,' Bernard said, 'that the poison, while of Caribbean provenance as claimed, was introduced into Jensen's system not long after Jensen arrived at Newark, more than likely by means of a needle jabbed into his neck. The poison was too dilute to have the preferred effect. Gus made a boo-boo, in other words— '

'And no doubt you've inferred that he was hired by Otsuka to do this—?'

Thatcher's face lit up as if he were my father, and I'd told him I'd gotten all A's on my report card. 'See how naturally this starts coming to you once you get the hang of it?'

'I insisted that Gus be kept viable for prolonged interrogation, not simply to uncover such facts as we could but to try as well a new method the boys have been working on,' Bernard said. 'That'll have to wait. As I knew I would be, I was overruled— '

'We'd have never got anything out of him,' Thatcher said. 'Nobody ever did— '

Bernard shrugged. 'Could have gone through Jake— '

'True— '

154

'Was Jake involved?' He couldn't have been, I realised; he was still alive.

'Ain't no mud on Jake's shoes,' said Thatcher. 'Gus did have an eye for talent, I'll give him that— '

'Even if Jake was domesticated enough to participate in such shenanigans as these Gus had no reason to involve him. It was a one-to-one action, and the fewer to know the better. So far as Jake knows at present, his teacher was killed in the line of duty. It's good for role models to illustrate the drawbacks so well as the benefits of a career.'

'You knew about this Tuesday morning?' I asked Bernard.

'It's my job to know,' he said. 'Don't give me that look, I warned you to be ready to duck.'

Their stares suggested to me that they'd long before decided I could never truly understand.

'In any event, Gus's fatal error was trying to drag the doctors into it after he screwed up. He was the one, apparently, who conceived the brilliant idea to have them forge the certificate. They carried out his wish, signing that particular doctor's name, only later realising that she was in no condition to see to anyone's death but her own.'

'See what happens when you rush?' Thatcher said. 'Never fails.'

'If the intention was to kill Jensen,' I said, 'why didn't Gus have them finish the job? Why didn't he see to it—?'

'They wouldn't let him,' said Bernard. 'Isn't that wonderful? That *our* doctors chose to abide faithfully by the Life Acts astonishes me. They've certainly never shown themselves averse to

155

thwarting such petty legalities in the past, when it suits them— '

'Bernard,' Thatcher interrupted, glancing at me. 'That's touchy. Go on with it.'

'It became a matter of principle with them, perhaps. In any event, by that point the corpus was in their care, and had been seen by too many. They had to do something. Afterward, then, this impromptu plan motored up and Jensen sped northward on the uptown express, leaving behind only an officially recorded and duly sworn death.'

'Do you think Jensen actually said anything to Gus in the car?' I asked, ignoring what Thatcher had said; trying to ignore. 'On their way over?'

'Oh. "Can you keep a secret?"' Bernard quoted, and laughed. 'It's so rare to come across people who can sound so like a bad screenplay in such strained circumstance. He did say it, none-theless. Jake slid open the divider when Jensen collapsed. Both Jake and the driver heard him say it.'

'So what's the secret?'

Neither answered.

'Haven't uncovered that minor detail yet, have you?'

'We're working on it,' said Thatcher. 'Obviously he was ready to spill the beans to somebody. I'd like to think he intended to do the right thing and tell me. He sure wasn't working with Gus, why would he have even brought it up, whatever it was, if he had been— '

'All inferences and select facts do, however, point to Otsuka's involvement,' said Bernard. 'We did trace the two individuals mentioned on the note discovered— '

'After we ascertained it was Mystic, Connecticut that was referred to.' Thatcher reached over to shake Lester's knee until Lester grimaced. Had I owned a pet I'd have never allowed Thatcher to hold it.

'Didn't Gus search Jensen's apartment?' I asked.

'Police found the note at his sister's,' said Thatcher. 'Even a blind hog roots up an acorn now and then. Avi's investigating Jensen's apartment again tomorrow to see what might have been overlooked. He lived up on the Concourse, didn't he?' Avi nodded. 'I think it was his grandmother's place. I guess it was cheap— '

'You own the building, Thatcher,' said Bernard. 'It was a perk.'

'What about those two individuals you mentioned?' I asked. 'Where are they?'

Bernard coughed, and eyed his nails as he took his hand from his mouth. 'Shot while trying to escape, sadly— '

'Both of them?' I asked. 'In both countries?'

'That struck me as kind of odd myself— ' Thatcher said.

'We're dealing with backwater elements in each port,' said Bernard. 'It's to be expected. Corrupt officials are like cockroaches, you can't get rid of them. So many things they take on themselves, leaving their superiors in the lurch— '

'But we've made the connection firm. Just haven't discovered the exact scale of the operation— '

'How convenient that the facts correspond so well to the theory,' I said.

'Isn't it, though?' Thatcher, as ever, pronounced *isn't* as *idn't*; certain speech patterns

157

of his youth he deliberately retained, that those who didn't know him might be lulled into thinking that his intelligence was less than theirs. 'I'd had my hunches. You heard him the other day, Joanna. Calling me a Nazi. Making fun of America. His talk was all sugar when he wanted to sound sweet but you could smell the vinegar underneath.'

'It's evident now why he agreed so readily to that thirty percent cut,' said Bernard.

'It is?'

'Rule of the agreement is that operations already in progress by one country won't be interfered with by the other,' said Thatcher. 'Thanks to Jensen, they have an operation in progress. So if we go and try busting it up in the usual way they can cut the whole deal cold, and at this moment that'd give 'em the edge. They've already transferred their bank accounts over to Europe and back home, isn't that right?'

'And we can't take chances on losing access to those scientists, now that they're in our grasp,' said Bernard, nodding in response to Thatcher's question. 'Susie's flying out to Los Angeles tomorrow to meet them, in fact, to be assured that they come immediately under our supervision as soon as their feet touch earth.'

'It's obvious that Otsuka could have lived with the compromises he made in order to get what he wanted— '

'Most people can,' said Thatcher.

'Why couldn't you let him?'

'Cause it's just as obvious who'd have been the next target after Jensen,' Thatcher said. 'Strike before the iron gets hot, I always say. He popped Jensen before he could spill, but he'd have known

I'd have found out eventually, one way or another. There's a Judas in every operation. Shouldn't think he'd have risked it.'

'Luckily for our agreement,' said Bernard, 'Otsuka may have been respected in his country, but there was no love lost among his folk. The problem with living successfully for so long is that after a time your enemies increase geometrically rather than arithmetically. We exchanged the traditional harsh words yesterday with his successors, and the agreement remains solidly in effect.'

'Why wouldn't it?' I asked. 'No one was hurt but Otsuka. You can't take your cut from underground activities, can you?'

'That's what we're working on now,' said Thatcher.

'What are you going to do about it? You'll do something about it— '

'Hon, you're thinking like us now,' he said, his smile so irrepressible as it was irredeemable. 'This is where you two come in, truthfully. First, go up with Avi tomorrow to Montefiore and pay your respects to Jensen— '

'To bring flowers?' Lester asked.

Thatcher stared at him as he'd once stared at me, ignoring the sass, seeing only an evanescent fulfilment of every earthly wish.

'Gus may have been talking through his hat, saying Jensen looked like he was thinking,' said Thatcher. 'If he is thinking, I'd like to know what he's thinking about.'

'If he is, I couldn't say, Mr Dryden,' said Lester. 'You expect too much.'

'Maybe he wants to get something off his chest besides his respirator tubes,' said Thatcher. 'Won't hurt to try. Joanna, you'll oversee this

159

new project solo. Strikes me you're getting damn good, handling yourself in these situations.'

'I can't, Thatcher,' I said. 'I won't.'

'Oh, don't look at me like that,' he said. 'Lester, now keep in mind he's not technically dead. I'm not saying I'd be angry if you told me there was nothing you could do but I think you're just underestimating yourself.'

'We'll have to see,' said Lester. 'What else do you want from me?'

'It's a funny old world,' Thatcher said, leaning back, stroking the arms of his chair as if they were his wife's, or even mine. 'All you can do to get out of it in one piece. Events so often occur beyond the control of mortal man. No one can predict where lightning'll strike, can they?'

'Thatcher,' said Bernard, 'speak English.'

'Say something happened to Japan.'

'What something?'

'A natural occurrence?' asked Lester.

'What insurance companies usually call an act of God, I suppose you could say.'

'You can't be serious, Thatcher,' said Bernard. 'You haven't talked to me about this— '

'It's been on the back burner. I've been theorising.'

'You can't be serious about this— '

'Look at it scientifically,' said Thatcher. 'As I understand it, Japan's a volcanic mountain range rising out of the sea, right in the middle of the earthquake belt. That so?'

'You want me to sink Japan?' Lester asked.

'You didn't hear me say that, did you?' he asked. Butter wouldn't have melted in his heart. 'Hell of a concept, though. Kind of get back at 'em for Pearl Harbor.'

'You're losing it, Thatcher,' said Bernard, brushing stray hair towards the crown of his head, as if to keep his skull warm. 'I'm not hearing you. I'm not.'

'Shit happens,' said Thatcher. 'Who'd lay the baby on our doorstep?'

'Macaffrey couldn't bend a fork using both hands,' said Bernard. 'He couldn't make dice move if he threw them. Now you want him to perform exploratory surgery on the eastern hemisphere? It'd be funny if I didn't see what your intentions are behind this. Haven't you learned anything? We have to get along with them, Thatcher.'

'Long as we've got Lester here, won't hurt to see what could be done— '

'I'm not going to listen to this.'

'You ever read that boilerplate in the agreement you drew up? Either country can take over the other's business affairs in the event of nationwide catastrophe. There's our loophole— '

'Thatcher— '

'We'd be helping 'em out, that's all. Taking control of their operations for a spell, like it says we can do. Till they get back on their feet.' Joy so enriched his voice that a singsong quality entered it as he continued to speak, as if he were crooning a child to sleep. 'If there's anyplace left to stand.'

'Psychosis I can deal with, Thatcher, I can't handle insanity— '

'You think you can have countries destroyed at your request?' I said.

He regarded me as if I'd told him the sun rose in the morning, thinking it news. 'Subtlety's everything,' he said. 'What I think's unimportant,

161

hon— '

'Enough of this,' Bernard said, rising and walking to the door.

Avi stood, as if to block his exit.

'Take a stress pill, Thatcher. Collect stamps. Do something to get your mind off things. We have enough to deal with as it is. Avi, please unlock the door for me.'

Avi looked to Thatcher, who gave his assent. 'We'll be getting up ourselves in a minute. Almost suppertime. Can't wait.'

Lester showed no greater loss of aplomb over this turn of events than he had during any other. Thatcher studied him for several wordless moments.

'Yes, Mr Dryden?'

'Thatcher,' he said. 'Thatcher, please. What do you think, Lester? You don't have so negative an attitude about this as Bernard has, do you?'

'Godness sent the rainbow,' said Lester. 'God brings the fire.'

'I don't know as how I follow what you're getting at.'

'Sometimes a challenge is taken up with interest,' Lester said. 'It's best not to offer such— '

'Who's challenging?' Thatcher asked. 'An idle thought, nothing more.'

'They'll see it as a challenge,' Lester said. 'As I understand the arrangement, that is. I couldn't guarantee what form Their response might take.'

'Christmas coming up,' said Thatcher. 'Can't tell till you try, Lester. I love surprises.'

'So does God.'

9

Thatcher bade that we follow him into the living room; we hung back as he strode forward, hoping to lessen among the others the impression that we were with him. His appearance among the guests stopped their conversation cold; lifting a hand as he sauntered in, he signalled to all that his presence should neither distract their attention nor hinder their fun. As the guests picked up their words from where they'd dropped them an almost palpable difference was noted in the volume and tone; a hitherto undetectable air of false nonchalance sharpened the now-subdued chatter, as when in a crowded subway car a lazar pushes suddenly down the aisle, thrusting a cup beneath wilfully blind travellers.

'Boy,' he said, noticing his son on the edge of the sofa, drawn deep within himself. 'Get up and

163

circulate.'

Junior shook his head; such colour as he possessed left his face. Thatcher walked over, gripped him by the shoulders and snatched him up as he might a misplaced cushion. Marching him across the room Thatcher inserted his son into a close circle of acquaintances with the manner of one driving an axe into a pie. No sooner had Thatcher moved on than Junior fled the group, flying back to his nest, brushing his arms with his hands as if to preen himself, fearing perhaps that his brief exposure might have left spores of contagion behind.

'He has so much money,' Lester said, seeming to admit an unexpected awe. 'So much must go to taxes— '

'Thatcher and Susie are exempt,' I said. 'Dryco, the company, is exempt. I'm not, Bernard's not, no one else working for them is— '

'How?'

'Part of the deal,' I said. 'Last year the IRS actually sent someone over to audit him. Someone made a boo-boo, as Bernard might say. Gus showed him out.'

'Bernard might say about what?' Bernard asked, rising up behind us as if from a cloud, clutching a drink. On the side of his glass was a cartoon of a turkey wearing a Pilgrim's hat. I couldn't remember the last time I'd seen Bernard drink, but knew I didn't want to recall. 'Try as you might, you couldn't make it up. God must have made man in His own image, it's Thatcher's only excuse.'

Judging from his breath it was evident that he sipped from a refill. I wished he'd go away without my having to ask.

'Have I offended sensibilities again? Silly me—'
he said. 'Sweetness?'

'You didn't care if I knew beforehand?'

'Of course I did,' he said. 'You might have
given away the game, had you known. Your
poker face doesn't get you through the ante.'

'I could have been killed.'

'You could have been. You weren't. God has
mercy on us all, I suppose— '

His preoccupations were writ plain on his face;
I let what he said slip from me. 'You believe
these plots of his?' I asked. 'With Otsuka? With
Gus?'

'There's evidence, Joanna. If he hadn't demonstrated to me the ground of being for his beliefs
I'd have never played along. Sweetness, it's not
professional to be taking this so personally— '

'Oh, fuck you, Bernard— '

He lifted his glass; took a long swallow. 'In
dreams,' he said, his voice trailing away.

'Thatcher means what he says?' Lester asked.

Bernard examined him as he might a spider
crawling across his desk.

'Depends on what time it is,' he said. 'The
phases of the moon. The barometric pressure.
Says about what?'

'Sinking Japan.'

'I was never consulted on it.'

'Do you think he's serious?' I asked, and
watched as his expression sagged from grim into
chopfallen, as if he were disappointed in me for
having needed to ask.

'Apparently, for now some concern as to the
little yellow people is still evident. This too, will
pass. Excepting Susie D, his infatuations linger no
longer than spring rain.' He raised his hand, and

pinched Lester's cheek. 'And some pass sooner than that. It'll pass. Everything passes— '

'He should consider what he asks for before asking,' said Lester.

'I've said as much.' Bernard drained the remainder of his drink, letting the cubes slam against his lips as if needing to punish while he comforted. The ensuing pause held a deeper silence than one employed entirely for dramatic purpose. 'Why would you care? You can't supply it, whatever he wants.'

'Bernard, go away,' I said. 'If you're mad at Thatcher, don't take it out on us. I'm not sure why I'm even speaking to you, considering— '

'So don't. Turning from us he stumbled off, ambling toward the bar, giving signs of being embarrassed for what he'd later have to say.

'Bernard,' I said, calling after him.

He lifted his hand as if to shoo me away.

'*Bernard*! Dammit— '

Lester moved closer to me, and whispered in my ear.

'Are you scared?'

'No,' I lied.

'Me neither.'

'It's unavoidable?'

He nodded. I slipped my arm through the crook of his, so that whichever of us was most tired might be supported by the other when we fell. With so little warning as when he entered the room Thatcher reappeared, throwing open the dining-hall doors and shouting:

'Happy holiday!'

The long table was so laden with tureens and casseroles, baskets and boats and bowls that the lace tablecloth was but barely visible. Between the candlesticks were five domed silver platters. The guests stampeded for their seats as if they'd been released from the starting gate under threat of fire.

'Don't shove,' Thatcher said, failing to calm them.

Susie rested, sipping from a tumbler, presiding over her side of the table, her duties of overseeing the galley slaves attended to for another year. Thatcher sat on her left, at the head of the table; Junior sat to his left. The room's high windows along the west wall allowed in late afternoon sunlight enough to wash every guest in gold.

'Everybody gets a drumstick this year,' he said. A quintet of servants raised the domes, exposing the entrée. Some of the younger children present started to cry; of the adults, all were too overcome to speak, save Thatcher. 'Don't thank me. Thank the boys at Perdue. We're taking the lead in genetic engineering and Europe can say what they want about it.'

Each nut-brown carcass bore six drumsticks. A vision entered my mind, a scene revealing a parallel world: Squanto presenting Miles Standish with giant roasted spiders, welcoming the immigrants to American shores. The sails are ordered raised on the *Mayflower*, and the fresh green breast is left to its leasees.

'How do they walk?' Bernard asked, raising his drink as if to salute. If he'd imagined that liquor might still his tongue, he had no one to blame but himself.

'I don't think they ever leave their pens. How should I know, I look like a farmer?' Thatcher tapped his spoon against his plate as if seeing what would make it shatter. 'Those of us who are still alive have a lot to be thankful for. A moment of silence, please, for those who've eaten their last piece of pie.' Hardly had we bowed our heads before his benediction continued. 'Only a couple of years ago I don't have to tell you we were facing a gloomy forecast. Just look around you today. Business in every area, up three hundred percent.' To ascend from nothing was guised, as ever, as achievement. 'The troubles across the river are nearly thrashed out. The new alliance you all've heard about with our Japanese brothers is signed, settled, and in effect.'

Polite applause of the sort that accompanies an announcement that the recording secretary is retiring followed. Two dozen chairs creaked, and creaked again; no one could eat until Thatcher finished his spiel.

'In finding the future, let's not forget where we left the past,' he said. 'Let us remember the Pilgrims, who, in looking for a better life, landed at Jonestown— '

'Jamestown,' said Susie.

'*Plymouth*!' Bernard said, his word exploding as he corrected his masters.

'Wherever the hell they landed,' Thatcher continued, 'it was on a stern and rocky shore, and they were comforted then as we are ourselves, by our wealth of spirit and by our families— '

'Speak for yourself, John Alden.' We didn't have to look to see who said it.

'What did they do when they landed?' Avi asked, shilling at an instant's notice; another requirement of the job.

'They ate, because they were hungry,' Thatcher said, his mood for oratory seeming to dwindle. 'Thanks, Lord.' The ceiling, firstly, was blessed

168

by his gaze; then he turned his eyes to Lester, anxious to cover all possibilities. 'Let's eat.'

Perhaps I had no appetite any more; the turkey might have been smoked cotton, for all it held in taste or texture. I declined a drumstick, that another might be doubly sated.

'Thanks for seeing to dinner, darlin', Thatcher said.

Susie smiled and nibbled her cottage cheese, taking one curd per bite. The strict diet she followed, that year, allowed her only white food; on her plate were several shades of pale, those of unflavoured yogurt, cauliflower, cave-grown asparagus and mashed potatoes. Most seated gourmandised as if they hadn't been fed for weeks. Neither Bernard nor Lester seemed any hungrier than I. Jake held his scalpel extended when he lifted his cup of tea.

'Dad,' Junior said, looking toward his father, and not at him. 'Bread me.'

Thatcher stared into the middle distance, as if he'd spotted an unlikely mirage. 'Bred you to speak English,' he said. 'Want to try again?'

Junior's lips moved without accompanying sound; the impression lent was that he'd had his voice erased, and hadn't yet realised it. 'Bread, Dad,' he repeated at last, attaining audibility. 'Starching's essentialled.'

'For shirts,' said Thatcher. 'I gather you want biscuits?'

Junior must have twitched even in sleep; for an instant he drew mimosa-like from the table; then, catching himself in the act of showing weakness, he quickly leanedd forward, bumping his chest against his plate, knocking his plate against his glass. The glass spilled, soaking the tablecloth.

A servant appeared, blotter rampant in hand.

'You got to be literate in the business world,' said Thatcher; I could tell by his expression that he was trying not to laugh. 'You ever going to understand that?'

'World's postliterary, Dad— '

'Listen to Bernard when he talks,' he said. 'There's talking for you. One of these days you're probably going to be his boss, and how's it going to look if your subordinates sound better than you do?'

Bernard dropped his knife and fork onto his plate, his efforts at eating ended. He said nothing that I would have hoped he might say.

'Understood, Dad. Doubledone. No ifs or maybes.'

'You fucking little idiot,' Thatcher said, rising partway from his seat, as if to take aim. 'Here's your goddamn biscuits. Don't both to ask next time if you're not going to ask in English.'

He slung a wicker basket top-heavy with rolls toward his son; Junior threw up his arms to ward off the blow. The rolls shot through the room, bouncing off the table, the walls, off the other guests. No one but the Drydens behaved as if anything were amiss.

'How the hell'd I wind up with a goddamn son so goddamn stupid he can't even talk good English?'

'Shut up, Thatcher.' When anger rushed into Susie's spirit her voice lowered until she sounded to have been born to broadcast. 'Won't you ever let him be?'

'You can only baby him so much. He's going to have to find out what a tough world this is darlin', he can't be as stupid as he looks— '

Junior could bear his parent's opinions no longer; without a word he leapt from his chair.

'Where you think you're going? Come back here, goddamn your ass— '

He tripped before he'd gone five feet, falling into one of the immovable house guards stationed around the table. Junior punched the man in the sides and stomach, flailing his fists to no evident effect; then, he dashed from the room.

'You have to speak to him in public like that?' Susie asked; anger increased her hunger, and her rate of intake, and within moments she was spooning food into her mouth as one starving. 'In front of these people?'

'You're smothering the little bastard, darlin',' said Thatcher. 'Mark my words, he'll turn out funnier than he already is 'cause of you, you can bet on it— '

'Well, he won't be like you— '

'What'd be the matter with that?'

'Just shut up, Thatcher, please shut up— '

'If he just talked normal like a normal person— '

'It's fucking Thanksgiving, Thatcher, so shut the fuck up— '

'I know my holidays,' he said. 'Don't you be telling me to shut up— '

'I'll tell you— '

We waited to hear what she threatened to tell. An aphasic look passed over her face, as if she was unable to say what her brain insisted she should relate. Lifting her chin as if for a facial exercise she rubbed her neck; pushing herself from the table Susie slapped her knees with her hands in an offbeat rhythm. When she coughed it came without sound.

'Darlin'—?' Thatcher asked, staring dumbly at his wife; she pointed to her throat. 'Sue—?'

'She's choking,' Avi said.

No sooner had he said it than he reached her, lifting her from her chair as she slumped. Encircling her waist, clasping his hands across her stomach, he shoved up and in, attempting to dislodge what she'd aspirated.

'Help her, dammit— ' Thatcher shouted.

Susie flopped in Avi's arms as if she was stuffed with rags; closed her eyes as if to hold back tears. She showed no signs of recovery; Thatcher jumped from his seat, and, without warning, began hitting Avi in the face as if it was his fault that she so suffered, his frustration total, his rage absolute, screaming without words, slapping as Avi squeezed. Cuts opened above Avi's eyes; blood reddened the corners of his mouth, and I turned away. Avi seemed oblivious to Thatcher's blows as he undertook his work; appeared almost at peace, as if he felt he received the payment he deserved for all that he had done.

'Get away,' Thatcher shouted, shoving Avi aside, embracing his wife in his own arms, applying so vigorous a grip as to lift her feet off the floor. Her purple lightened with grey undertones. As they grappled there without sound I thought how like the scene seemed to be some private drama glimpsed briefly through a window in the night; by the crowd's noise I gathered that they were not so detached as I.

'She's dying—'

'Oh, God, Susan— '

'Help her.'

Her arms dangled, her fingers snatched at air, her toes turned inward, brushing against the floor;

a feeling so reprehensible as it was human entered me, and at that moment I knew I would be glad to watch her die, that I could have no trouble hearing, no problem forgetting, this scream in the night. Then, awakened as if by a different siren's sound, I felt Lester take my arm.

'Together,' he said, without speaking. 'It has to be. Come on.'

As in a painfully clear and fully recollected dream we glided across the room. Thatcher held his wife closely, as if to keep her soul from escaping; he'd so exhausted himself that we had no trouble, pushing him gently aside. We lay Susie down upon the floor; Lester knelt before her, between her legs. I took my position behind her, propping up her body, putting my arms around her waist, clasping my hands beneath her heavy breasts.

'Close your eyes,' Lester said, placing his hands upon her temples.

Her perfume was sharp in my nostrils, a fragrant blend of spice and oranges, a clove-stuffed potpourri worn as if to ward away the plague. My hands grew ever-warmer as I pressed them into her flesh; warmth rose through my arms, over my face, sent a column of fire rising up my spine.

'Push,' Lester said.

Without warning my memories burned through my walls.

Push.

The smell of cloved oranges suffused the room's antiseptic air, overcoming alcohol's refreshing sting when I breathed in, holding open my mouth as if I were drowning, and wished to sink all the sooner. The room's lights were so bright I thought they must be trying to set my eyes aflame, that I might never speak later of what I saw. When I moved my head, first to one side, then to the other, I glimpsed my face, framed by askew haloes, reflected in surrounding mirrors. Susie readjusted me, taking hold of my head in her hands, turning my face toward hers. My eyelids seemed weighed down with lead; as she kept her unwavering watch over me I believed, looking up, that she had been suspended from the ceiling, and wondered why.

Push, Thatcher said.

Like a train, Gus said. Breathe in. Out. Gets air in the head.

Push, the doctor said.

Susie held me firmly, as if suspecting I might try to turn my head too quickly, and so snap my neck: she offered no consolation, whispered no assurance; took, I fancied, rather than brought, comfort. I couldn't see what was happening; the notion came to me that they'd decided to dissect me, for want of better to do. Glancing toward my feet I found that I couldn't see them; my legs served as framework for a snow-white tent; heads bobbed beyond its peaks, as if an encampment were climbing in. Susie pressed her hands against my skull as if to pop out my eyes. I began not to notice so much, after that; the pain elsewhere grew too great. My thighs shivered with the touch of chilled metal; I imagined them taking up shards of shattered mirror in order to scrape me away.

Push.

A baby, I thought, realising I was pushing without thinking; though I couldn't feel my body I felt too well the pain. I'd never known how large the smallest baby might feel. My pelvis seemed to be coming apart; I clenched my teeth together, wishing I had something to chew. Looking up I stared directly into Susie's inverted eyes, so black and still that they could have been shaped from obsidian. I hurt all the more, once it was done.

A boy, I heard Thatcher say.

Competition, said Susie.

'Push.'

Opening my eyes, feeling her shivers as she rasped out an unending cough, I allowed her to pull away. Blots of wet potato smeared Lester's shirtfront. He fell to one side; blood streamed from his nose as if he'd haemorrhaged, and he lay on the floor hyperventilating, shaking as if too much voltage had shot through him. Thatcher helped Susie to her feet; I crawled over to Lester, gathered him up and cradled him in my arms, and pressed my hand beneath his nose to halt the flow of blood. What remaining sense of time I retained disappeared as I sat there holding him; I would have been content to remain as we were, frozen in our pose unto eternity.

'Mother,' he said, seeing me, not seeing me.

I smoothed his hair; a moment longer and the bleeding stopped. Thatcher and Susie made noises that could have been those of laughter or of tears; I couldn't tell and had no desire to look. That I could be, in these circumstances, a bringer of life struck me as being incomprehensibly unfair, knowing as I did that having stolen one person from the grave, I'd allowed another to be led closer to his own.

'You okay?' I whispered.

He nodded, not opening his eyes, resembling a newborn kitten as he lay there. The room's

silence jarred me into more mundane consciousness; raising my head to see where everyone had
gone, I saw them all still there. They stared at
Lester; even Susie looked up from her husband's
bosom long enough to glance our way, as quickly
turning back toward him, her features holding
so much anger as of shame, and not a sign of
gratitude. I could only imagine that, having seen
the face of her angel of death, she recognised it
as one she'd known all along.

'God bless,' said Thatcher. 'God bless us. I was
right, Susie, I was right. Wasn't I? I was right.
God bless— '

'God damn,' Lester whispered, so that only I
could hear. Bernard edged closer to us, holding
his drink, keeping his distance, his face no less
pale than Lester's. He looked down upon us as
if from a mountaintop, for the first time since
I'd known him seeing through me as he stared
at another.

'Hallelulah,' he said.

If I hadn't known better I'd have sworn he
understood.

That night, later on, Lester and I talked our
hours away.

'Everyone does have their reasons,' he said.
'As do They. In neither case is everyone satisfied,
or even helped.'

'Why have I stayed so long as I have?' I asked.

'You had to,' he said. 'Where would you have
gone?'

We lay in darkness in my lightless house; we
didn't have to see each other in order to talk.

'What would you have done?'

'I know now what I could have done— '

'You didn't know then,' he said. 'Don't allow blame to lay its head in the wrong bed, Joanna.'

'There were things I could have done,' I said. 'That is the greatest sin. To see evil and do nothing.'

'The sins of the parents are best taught to the children,' Lester said. 'So little is expected from Them by us, and vice versa. Once and only once will change come overnight. Until the day comes you fight as you can, when you can. Until then, you get by.'

'You almost sound like Bernard— '

'Even a blind hog roots up an acorn, now and then.'

'I've spent years trying to be like him,' I said. 'Even like the Drydens. I shouldn't deserve any better than they deserve. Avi knows that, he's accepted it. You saw him this afternoon— '

'He does as he does for different reasons,' Lester said. 'Why are you so hard on yourself?'

'I've always thought someone should be,' I said. 'I wanted her to die. For what they did.'

'A human response to human acts. It's understandable.'

'Not to me,' I said. 'Not now, not any more. Not to me or to you or— '

'Understandable to Them,' he said. 'Joanna, the godlike in humanity is bad as well as good. The evil that lives in people more than meets its match in Theirs.'

'That's no excuse,' I said. 'I've brought so much of this down on myself. Some of my friends always said I must be an emotional masochist.'

'Most people are,' he said. 'I suppose I am. Don't you think a certain masochism is essential in a messiah? A certain sadism on Their part is

177

sure unavoidable.'

'But now I see how much I could have done differently— '

'When he was alive the other afternoon Gus told me something,' Lester said. 'He believed that if he hadn't gone to the knoll that day history since then would have been very different. Therefore he thought he was the one to bear ultimate responsibility for why the world is the way it is, today.'

'He told you that?'

'In so many words.'

'What did you say?'

'I asked him if he wasn't unsure whose shot was truly the one that killed. That it could have been Oswald, after all. He told me, it didn't matter, he was there, he could have done something else. The more he talked the more it became clear to me that he was as troubled for having to bear the guilt without receiving recognition as over anything else. I told him that as far as I understood it, neither he, nor Oswald, nor even Kennedy could have been there and everything would still have happened as it did in the long run. That didn't improve his mood, but I suppose I could have predicted that.'

'If so much is predestined by Them then why do They give us what we perceive as free will?'

'It is free will as to how we get there. It's all in the perspective. It's always more worthwhile to consider how much worse it all could have been.'

'How?'

He had no answer; I suspect he knew, but saw no need to say. 'What did the Drydens do to your baby, Joanna?'

'I don't want to think about it— '

'You thought about it earlier today,' he said. 'The baby was unplanned?'

So much of my life seemed to have happened so long ago, in another country, to another person, as I supposed it had. As I grew older the sense of disconnectioon pervaded my spirit, the feeling that moments existed only as they occurred; when certain stray memories eked their way into my soul they were therefore, up to a point, easy enough to slough off as nothing more than vague recollections of shows once seen, of books once read. Only when my guard slipped accidentally, as it had that afternoon, or deliberately, as it did now, could I again relive a life consciously lost.

'I'd broken up with Avi but hadn't told him yet,' I said. 'About the same time Thatcher had to go on a business trip to Buenos Aires. Bernard wasn't able to make it. I was sent in his place, I'd only seen Thatcher once or twice before then, and never for so long a time. During the flight down he noticed me, I guess. He fished with all his lures. He seemed so different then, so charming, so— '

'So he hooked you,' said Lester.

'At forty thousand feet,' I said. 'I'd come to suspect that I was sterile, but I wasn't. At first I thought I could get an abortion. The only way I could have made the connections was through Thatcher, and he wouldn't hear of it, as I've said— '

'He knew it was his baby?'

'There was the possibility it was Avi's,' I said. 'A fifty-fifty chance.'

'He knew that.'

I nodded.

'And Susie?'

'Nothing happened when she found out, which surprised me. I'm not sure how quickly she noticed the relationship. She was always running around doing something and at that point Thatcher was still subtle about it. So, the longer I was pregnant the more I wanted to have the baby, whosoever it was. By the time I went into labour I wanted my baby so much. I'd taken such good care of myself, I quit smoking, I didn't drink— '

'What happened?'

'They'd told me. Thatcher told me. He said he'd see to it that I had the best doctor in the company. I wanted a natural childbirth and he said no problem. Gus was my Lamaze partner. We'd practice in the office at lunchtime. They took me to Beekman when it was time. Susie and Thatcher and Gus. Avi knew I was pregnant, of course, but I swore I'd had genetic testing done and discovered it wasn't his, and of course I hadn't, I didn't want to know. I didn't want to lie to him and I did.'

'Then?'

'They put my gown on me. Stuck something in my arm while they were— ' While they were shaving me; while Thatcher shaved me. He'd asked if he could, and no one minded but me. 'I was so doped up. I remember lying on the table. I remember having my baby, and then I passed out. That's what I remembered.'

'I know.'

'When I woke up again it was in recovery. I was the only patient. Thatcher was there. I asked him where my baby was.'

I paused; he said nothing. I didn't want to

continue, but I did.

'I never even got to hold him,' I said. 'He told me later it was Susie's idea. At the time he just said things happen. She'd insisted, he said later. He went along, whosever idea it was. They didn't want to let me see him but finally did. He was all wrapped up. He had dark hair. Like Avi.'

'Why did she— '

'To prove a point, maybe. To put me in my place. Maybe she did it just for the hell of it. Who can say?'

I started to cry, and then I couldn't stop; he held me, and I sobbed without ceasing for most of the rest of the night. No sooner had my memories bolted than I locked the door behind them at last; their odour would forever cling, their prints still scar the places they'd been.

'How could I do what I've done?' I finally asked. 'I stayed with them. With him. How could I do that—?'

'If you can't say,' Lester said, 'no one can.'

We lay there without speaking for long minutes after that, watching the room appear in all its form as dawn approached, lifting the veil from a new day's darkness.

'Joanna?'

'What?' I said, barely hearing myself.

'Even when people try to do right it so often turns out wrong. It's in the nature of things,' he said. 'For the longest time I wondered why They didn't just end it all and start all over again fresh. It seemed such a lost cause. I didn't think we deserved another chance. It came to me, after a while, how different Their outlook must be, and as I thought about it I got the perspective you need sometimes. Theirs is greatness, but by

its magnitude it must be so provincial. Who was
Leonardo, next to a tree, or Tolstoy next to a
tidal pool? What's Mozart, compared to a star.
Rome, compared with the moon? The words of
philosophers set against the mechanics of the
planets' spin?

'In the end I realised that even so we must be
worthiest of all, to hold our own when judged
against such perfection. Why else would They
bother? Now They know the time has almost
come for Them to interfere with us toward more
direct purpose, though They know that holds its
own peril. They're ready to throw the dice of the
universe.'

'Then what must the Messiah do?'

'Think with Their mind, and see with our eyes.
Then, finally, everyone involved can understand.'

'There wouldn't have been any other way to do
this?' I asked.

'Why is the sky blue and not green?' he asked.
'I don't know, Joanna. I guess not. Sometimes
you know, you don't know, you understand, you
can't understand— '

'There's too much now that I know without
understanding yet,' I said. 'This way, then, and
no other?'

'I have to be truthful,' he said. 'I'd have preferred another way, myself.'

'I love you, Lester,' I said, not expecting a
response; no longer wishing for one, certainly
not hoping for one. 'Why must it be so unavoidable?'

'Cain and Abel,' he said. 'Jesus and Judas,
Kennedy and Oswald, Nazis and Jews. God and
Godness. Without the dark, would the light seem
half as bright?'

10

'Did he elaborate this morning?' I asked Lester as we rode through the Bronx, passing the abandoned stadium, driving through the Army-guarded courthouse district. The street was blocked on our left, where a building's facade, feeling the tug of years, slumped onto the pavement to take its rest. We sat in the back of the car; Avi sat up front, considering all we cruised by, seeming deaf to our worlds. 'I hardly saw him. What did he have to say?'

'Not a lot,' Lester said. 'He thanked me again. I don't think it was for helping Mrs Dryden. It was like he was thanking me in advance for what he thinks I'll do. I tried to remind him that I had no say in the matter, but all he did was smile and nod his head.'

'Once he conceives his reality everyone's stuck

with it,' I said.

'Did you see Mrs Dryden before she left?'

'She avoided me. Didn't appear very pleased about much of anything, but then she so rarely does. She didn't even look at her newspaper.'

'Has she already taken off?'

'Her flight wasn't leaving until late this afternoon.'

'You think this has been his plan all along, in the event he thought he had something more than what he expected?' Lester asked.

'Who knows?' I said. 'It'd be so unlike him to have a specific goal in mind. So often he just waits to see what heaven'll drop in his lap— '

'Or on his head. He's so confident he'll get what he wants.'

'He always is,' I said. 'Do you really think They'll have a response to his request?'

'Under the circumstances a response is demanded. As to what it might be— '

'What if we weren't— ' I began to say; stopped, halfway through my sentence, and picked up anew. 'Would They involve Themselves if They didn't have to?'

'Possibly. I've never understood Their criteria. Why They send church buses off roads into rivers. Why steeples blow down in windstorms. Why so many saints died young. Perhaps They might have, perhaps not.'

The streets around us appeared not to have been swept for years; where windows weren't boarded over, or shuttered closed, they had been broken out, leaving over the sidewalks an icy frosting of bright broken crystal, a diamond-paved road. As Brooklyn and Queens were now part of the no-man's land across the river, and as

184

Staten Island had seceded years before, the Bronx remained the only borough other than Manhattan still existing under the nominal aegis of the government of the City of New York; yet, the Bronx was to Manhattan as a colony might stand in relation to its ruling empire: a strategic outpost whose inhabitants could be easily overlooked, whose defences required constant supervision.

'There'd be any number of things They could do, I suppose— '

'Limitless,' he said. 'Godness would leave the details to God. That's where His interest lies, after all.'

My father's family were from the Bronx; it was so hard to imagine anyone living here, much less distant relatives. My grandparents lived near the Hub, at 149th and Third until they moved to Co-Op City. The rot they'd escaped trailed them, but didn't catch up until they were long gone. What had been the south Bronx was now nothing other than sweeping acres of brick left to erode back into the earth from which it had been taken, a post-industrial compost heap. In the north Bronx, and along the border, the neighbourhoods were indistinguishable from those of southern West-chester, far from Thatcher's estate: that is to say, they were decrepit, overcrowded, dangerous and awaited a perpetually-delayed rediscovery. There were Army personnel stationed throughout the Bronx, for no reasons other than to secure the southeast corner against assault from Long Island, and to protect the homes in Riverdale so many officers had commandeered for themselves. The population, it was believed, had proved so efficient at killing itself off that assistance from the Army was seen as unnecessary; the average

Bronxite's life, in those days, was twenty-three. Jensen entered half-life at twenty-seven.

'Where is everybody?' Lester asked, seeing along the Concourse nothing more than endless blocks of emptied buildings.

I shook my head. On ground floors along this stretch signs were posted upon rusted window-grates and locked doors, familiar signs seen throughout the borough, each of standard design, each bearing the yellow grin and pro forma notification: PROPERTY OF DRYCO. NO TRESPASSING.

'I wouldn't think he'd find this a sound investment.'

The further north we drove, the more people we saw; one or two per block began to appear. 'He has plans,' I said. 'He started buying it up several months ago. You know the wall downtown, around the Battery?'

Lester nodded.

'He foresees the water rising high enough one day to warrant moving the operations up here, Bernard tells me. He'll tear it all down eventually, I suppose, and I hesitate to think what he'll build in its place— '

'Did he make everyone leave?'

'Not everyone,' I said.

More natives came into view; remaining residents huddled at street-corners, slumped against doorways, clung to lampposts as if expecting the wind to rise and carry them all away. They seemed only partially real, as if the uncertain conditions under which they lived caused them, over time, to fade away even before they might be erased. In the lot of an abandoned gas station a cluster of thin women watched two older men circle around each other, lifting their arms over their heads, performing some manner of ghost dance upon the asphalt plain.

'Thatcher believes you can bring Jensen out of his coma, I'm sure,' I said. 'What do you think?'

'I'd think that were he to come out of it Thatcher would only kill him when he was done with him. I doubt he'd want to be reawakened, considering.'

We turned onto Gun Hill Road; in those days, a most appropriate name. The hospital buildings rose before us, appearing as an embassy within a war-torn country. Surrounding streets were secured by countless guards; atop stacks of sandbags were head-high coils of razor-edged wire. Our driver edged us past concrete pyramids and steles that erupted at unpredictable intervals through the road's pavement. At each of several checkpoints we were allowed passage, and moved to the next station. Through our car's insulating walls I grew conscious of a distant whirring, the sound of a swarm of locusts.

'We're going in the front?' I asked; we seemed to be driving by it.

'The emergency room entrance is safest,' Avi said, speaking to us through the intercom. 'We had no information at the office as to how we reach the experimental floor.'

'I thought we ran it.'

'That doesn't mean anyone at the office knows anyone about it. We'll stop and ask at the desk once we get inside.'

Looking out the window as we rounded one last corner, I saw the source of the oncoming noise. A covey of Emergency Medical and police

helicopters were settling down, one after the
other, across the way in a vacant lot smoothed
down by repeated landings. The breeze whipped
up by the rotors lifted the dry soil toward heaven,
spinning it into dust-devils.

'Stick close,' Avi said as we got out of the
car and walked swiftly into the hospital, granted
admittance through the emergency room's elec-
tronically-locked bars.

The Bronx's missing population suddenly rose
up around us: hundreds were jammed into the
waiting room, crammed in shoulder-to-shoulder
along benches attached to the walls, lying in
heaps, on stretchers or on blankets aligned in
haphazard rows upon the floor. Children's high
crescendoes rose in atonal counterpoint against
adults' hushed drones. Hospital staff stepped
warily through the crowds as if over a mine-
field, handing out forms, taking temperatures
with digital thermometers, giving small cups of
water to the overheated, slipping drugs to those
who'd come ready to bribe. Nine television sets,
none working, hung from the ceiling, attached
to a grotesque chandelier; their pulsing screens
served to sedate and smooth that portion of those
awaiting who chose to look up.

Avi tugged at an extern's sleeve; the man
coughed, sounding tubercular.

'How do we get to the experimental floor?'

'No English,' he said, in that language.

We'd only stepped over the first patients when
those from the helicopters began to arrive. With
the others we stepped aside, allowing the parade
of newcomers to enter.

'Out of the way,' an orderly screamed, pushing
a gurney stacked three deep across the floor.

'Nurse! Get 'em ready back there.'

'Yo, yo, watch your back, watch your back— '

'Nurse!'

An unending stream of gurneys carried in the newest casualties: young blacks, Latinos and police, men and women alike, those who were old enough to be called men and women. Those police who were still on active service came in to assist in clearing the way for their own, kicking aside people lying on the floor along the walls in the event that the space they occupied might be needed. Those on patrol swung their clubs with impunity, surely estimating that it was safe to do so, so long as medical personnel were so near.

'Avi, get us out of here,' I said. 'This is dangerous— '

'Legal danger, though,' he said. 'Stay with me.'

A supervising nurse came forth to greet one of the police captains, and together they walked from patient to patient, making their judgements. Orderlies hustled away each gurney that bore a policeperson, once the captain ascertained the condition; civilians weren't sped off with such fervour. The nurse paused at each to await the captain's word before marking, or not marking, upon each patient's forehead the mark of solace, the purple X of triage. A young man whose legs were gone below the knees wailed so loudly as to drown out all others' screams. The captain patted his head.

'We want this one,' he said to the nurse, and the youth was moved along.

They walked to the next gurney: a woman lay there, her ankles cuffed to the metal bars supporting the mattress; her hands were tied above her head.

189

'What about her?' the nurse asked.

It was impossible to guess what the woman might have done, and the captain didn't say; before I could look elsewhere he raised his gun and shot her in the head. Those in the room who were able, or whose television-induced trance was not too deep, threw themselves to the floor. I held Lester tightly as we followed Avi to the admittance desk.

'You saw that,' I said. 'You saw it.'

Lester had no reply; there was nothing that could be added. The captain and the nurse continued on their rounds.

'Excuse me,' Avi said, shouting through the protective mesh that ran from desktop to ceiling. No one looked up. 'How do we get to the experimental floor?'

'Take a number,' a nurse shouted back, gesturing to a machine bolted onto the desktop, the same sort of device delis have to keep their customers under control.

'Where's the elevator to the experimental floor?'

'There's no experimental floor.'

'How do we get to it?'

'Lester,' I said, looking around, unable to forget the woman's face as she lay there, when the captain shot her; she hadn't appeared even remotely surprised. 'Can't something be done? This is unbearable— '

'In these situations it isn't right to help one without helping all,' he said. 'It'd hardly be possible— '

'Why?'

'It'd be like sending a hundred times the normal current through a kitchen appliance. There's no getting around it. I'm sorry, Joanna, the spirit is willing but the flesh is weak.'

'If there were an experimental floor,' Avi said, spotting a different nurse as she emerged from behind a row of dented filing cabinets, 'how would you get to it?'

'Down that hall, fifth elevator on the right,' she said, pointing.

Avi smiled, and wrapped his arms around us; we walked toward the hall. The captain and the nurse walked ahead of us; the woman's face could have been pressed against mine, so sharp was the memory. My brain felt as if it were on fire; the captain's knees buckled, as if he were dizzy, and at once overcome by what he had done. I knew there was no guilt in his soul; the nurse slipped an arm around him.

'Joanna,' Lester said, shaking me. 'No.'

The captain stood without moving for a moment; shook his head, and continued on. We edged past them, and counted off the elevators until we found the right one. As its doors slid apart, revealing within walls so white they seemed not to be there, I found myself wondering if we'd discovered a way by which we could go much further than we'd expected, or even hoped.

'What's wrong, Joanna?' Avi asked.

'This is such an awful place,' I said. 'It brings out the worst in everyone, I suppose— '

'People wouldn't get sick unless they brought it on themselves— '

'Avi, shut up.'

We ascended; I looked to Lester, who stood close by me, patently aware of what I'd felt, and continued to feel. 'There was no reason for what

191

he did— '

'The captain?' Avi asked. 'In his mind there must have been. People lose their grip sometimes, that's all.'

'Even divine retribution is less than divine,' said Lester, touching my hand. 'Don't ever forget that.'

'We have to take precautions,' Avi said, removing his wallet from his pocket, holding it open before him that his Dryco ID might be visible at a glance. 'Stay behind me, in the corners. Make sure you can be seen. Hold your arms in front of you, palms out.'

When the elevator stopped, the door opened; Avi yelled 'Dryco!' and thrust his wallet forward as if it might defend.

A large man in a blue uniform balanced what appeared to be a cannon against his paunch, levelling the weapon at Avi's midriff. A younger man wearing a suit stepped up and plucked the walled from Avi's hand, smiling as if he'd happened upon autumn's last perfect apple, still hanging from its tree.

'Easy,' he said to the armed man, and, still smiling, handed Avi's wallet back to him. 'Safe better than sorry. Accompanied?'

'Obviously,' said Avi, guiding us out into the entrance hall.

I looked more closely at the guard's gun, knowing nothing of artillery than what I'd seen at play. It resembled half a dozen shotguns bundled together and tied with two handgrips. 'In a hospital you're using this sort of thing?'

'Firepower plus,' said the overseer. 'Ready-made for reprisal events.'

'We're here to see Jensen,' Avi said. 'He's a

persistent vegetable. Arrangements were made. Which is his room and where is it?'

'328,' the man said, taking badges that bore our logo upon a forest-green field from his pocket, handing them to us. 'Thirty minutes top permissible. Wouldn't want to overstimulate.'

'The last thing we want,' said Avi, pinning his insignia to his lapel.

The man pressed a button, and a buzzer rang; a steel door rose up, disappearing into a slot in the ceiling. The walls of the long hall beyond were painted sky blue; soft-edged patches of white idly spaced across the azure represented clouds, so near as I could tell.

'What did you mean, persistent vegetable?' I asked.

'Referring to his state,' Avi said. 'They're exact in their terminology around here. It's good to go along.'

'What sort of gun was that?' Lester asked.

'A topbreak,' said Avi. 'Six 20-gauge magnum barrels fixed and mounted, revolving and firing in sequence. A tube in the centre squirts hydrochloric acid.'

'Since when do you know from guns?' I asked.

'You learn.'

A flock of doctors sailed down the hall, giving no evidence that they considered us worthy of study. Their long white coats billowed behind them, resembling clumsy wings. As we moved through the hall's bends and turns we began coming upon doors left partially open, or completely ajar; each room held no more than two patients, fast in their beds, nursed by machinery. Some were hooked up to dialysis units; others slept beneath translucent tents.

'What sort of experiments go on on an experimental floor?' Lester asked.

'All kinds, I'd think,' said Avi. 'Ask the experimenters. This looks like the place. 328, wasn't it?'

This door was shut; he rapped once against its wood, and then again.

'Is it locked?'

'Would it matter?' Turning the knob we opened the door; we walked in. The windowless room was soaked in unshadowed fluorescence; one unknowing might have thought medical science knew no higher aim than to preserve the tans of those convalescing. Jensen lay naked on his back, atop a heated mattress. Three machines attended to his needs; wires ran from their mantles and attached to clamps on his forehead, arms and legs. From his scattered parts tubes drained into bottles, bags and jars. In the screens of his caretakers I discerned nothing more than glowing lines and phosphorescent flashes. He had an erection; I wondered briefly whether his condition caused it, and then I noted the bend of his catheter, curving up and then down again, appearing after a time no more remarkable than a bishop's crook.

'Did you know him?' Avi asked.

'No,' I said. 'He's so young. They hire them so young nowdays.'

'They're more impressionable, fresh from college.'

The muscle with which Jensen's body was padded assured me that he'd never done a day's worth of physical labour in his life; his flesh could have been hardened foam, shaped to suit. I'd known several co-workers in my time who'd suffered coronaries while struggling to apply bulk suitable enough to convince their supervisors that they could handle the strain of an executive career.

'I guess it's up to you at this point,' Avi said. 'All right, Lester?'

Until that moment Lester had waited at the room's threshold, as if to approach too quickly without suitable preparation might disturb whatever mood needed first to be set. Walking over to the bedside he pressed his fingertips against Jensen's forehead, careful not to dislodge the wires. Jensen's eyes were open, but it was apparent he couldn't see; the pupils were so small as to be absent. As Lester made contact we listened to the machines' vespers: the beeps, the pings, brief gasps of static and a soft choral hum.

'Any luck?' I asked.

Lester suddenly drew his hand up, as if in probing for something dropped he'd jammed his fingers into a wall socket.

'What was it?' Avi asked. 'What? What'd you see?'

'Who're you?' A stranger's voice, coming so unexpectedly that, before we turned to see who it might be, I considered that perhaps Jensen was awake after all, employing ventriloquism to make us go away. 'You going to answer?' the woman asked; she was tall, and wore a candy-striped uniform. She wore her hair in cornrows and had forearms more muscular than Jensen's. 'You family or what?'

'We're with Dryco,' Avi said. 'So was he. We came to visit.'

'Everybody on this floor's with Dryco, hear them tell it. You all may own the place but that doesn't mean you can run around here like you were home.'

'We intended no trouble— '

'No, none of you all ever do. You know how easy it is to be spreading diseases to somebody in his shape? You may just have the sniffles but it'll be pneumonia when he gets it. Then who you think'll have to deal with the mess?'

'I'm sorry,' I said. 'We'll leave— '

'Not so fast. I'm saying be careful. Long as you're here, one of you give me a hand flipping him.'

'Why does he need flipping?' Avi asked.

'Even on these special mattresses they get bed-sores if you're not careful. Let 'em lie too long in one place, they draw all in on themselves. Wind up looking like a pretzel if you're not careful and then you got to break their arms and legs to straighten 'em out again. So, you got to turn 'em. Once, twice a day. About all you can do.' She regarded her patient. 'Somebody's glad to see me this morning,' she said, yanking the catheter free, and then beginning to unclip the other wires, and some of the tubes.

'Are you the floor nurse?' I asked, reading the name on her badge so that I could call her by her name, and not find myself treating her only as a creation of the hospital. 'Nurse Cordero?'

'No, I'm paramed. Wouldn't have minded going to nursing school but who's going to pay the bill?' She detached the last connections and removed the intravenous tube from his left arm's vein. 'All right. I'll get his legs, you put your hands under him. When I say go, turn him over on his right side. Okay?'

'All right,' said Avi.

'Do you attend him every day? I asked.

'Doctors attend, I just clean up after 'em. This's the only chance I get to relax, making the rounds up here.'

'Has he ever shown signs of consciousness?'

'No. Stiff as a board. He'll blink his eyes sometimes if the lights dim but that's involuntary, you know these PVs. Ready now? Get your hands under there. Don't want to bruise anything useful. Okay, go.'

They folded him in one smooth motion, as if they were making an oversize omelette. Lester had said nothing since removing his hands from Jensen's head. He'd picked something up, that much was evident; he'd returned to his place by the door as if he'd managed to convince himself that, given the proper moment, he might yet be able to break away. Nurse Cordero began reinserting the tubes, and reclamping the wires.

'A week or so ago I had a day off. Not long after they brought him in. Girl who's on duty when I'm not told me he started mumbling about something— '

'Did she say what?'

'Nothing she could understand,' she said, wielding the catheter so deftly that she could have been threading a needle. 'She told the doctor in charge that she thought he might be coming out of it. Told me he got on the phone to somebody real worried like before she even got out of his office. But when I came in, next morning, he looked just the same to me.'

'Which doctor was that?'

'Whichever one was in charge, I don't remember. Around here one's as good or bad as the next.'

After hooking up one final cord she paused, and wiped the perspiration from her forehead with the side of her hand. 'Well, I'd think he's had about as much visiting'll be good for him. Never can tell how the outside's affecting the inside.'

'No,' I said. 'What do you mean?'

'Got to keep him fresh. You know.'

'I don't follow,' said Avi. 'Fresh for what?'

'Recycling. Next week. That's what I've been told— '

'What are you talking about?' I asked. 'I don't understand. Recycling what next week?'

'What he's got,' she said. 'You said you're with the company, you ought to know. Word passed along this morning gave the okay.'

'Okay to what? What recycling?'

She stood back; nodded that we follow her as she left the room, and we did. 'Maybe you all don't understand how it works up here,' she said. 'Some of the folks up here, the doctors find 'em most useful to keep them like they are. Others, though, there's not that much they can find out from 'em no matter how long they're around, and there's new ones coming in all the time. Only got so much space up here, no matter how much they talk about future expansions— '

'What are you getting at?' Avi asked.

'When they're young and healthy like he is, and have no relatives, and we've had a chance to flush the poisons or the drugs out of their systems, nine times out of ten a lot of 'em'll still come in handy. Once the go-ahead's given they cut off the machines and then they— '

'Distribute the parts to worthy recipients,' I said.

198

'Within the company, as I understand it,' she said. 'Cost-effective, I imagine.'

'Then he's to be put up for auction?' Avi asked.

'First come, first served, long as they can afford it. Memo came over from your office this morning, I was told. That's why I was so rough on you at first. He's in perfect shape at the moment, excepting— '

'You just wanted to keep him that way,' I offered.

'You understand,' she said, and looked him over as he lay there. 'They always take the best-looking ones.'

After she let us out, closing the door behind us, we stood in the hall for several moments, saying nothing. Avi's bearing made me aware that he was certain something was going on that he knew he could never be part of.

'Come along to his apartment with me,' he said as we started to leave. 'Let's see what we find over there.'

'How long has Dryco owned the building?' I asked as we stepped from the car onto the Grand Concourse at 167th Street. We crossed the broad sidewalk to the building's entrance, crushing beneath our feet glass vials so empty as the boulevard.

'Over a year,' Avi said. 'It belonged to one of the realty companies he obtained.' With little effort he forced open the building's broken door. 'Jensen moved in when his grandmother died. I think he was the only one still living here. Dryco kept the utilities hooked up.'

The lobby was only large enough to be called

unassuming. Ochre paint peeled away from the lower reaches of the walls; above that watermark was graffiti surely scrawled on while I was still at college. In making our way to his apartment we passed the elevators; none were working. Someone had pried the doors from their frames and left them lying on the cold stained tile.

'This one's his,' Avi said, drawing from his jacket a bracelet ringed with keys, and beginning to unlock the door's seven locks. Jensen's flat was in the rear of the building, on the ground floor; I gathered that it faced the smaller street running just to the east of the Concourse.

'They never let on they'd be putting him up for sale,' I said, attempting to judge Avi's reaction, to see if he'd already known.

'I'd imagine they estimated he should be put to some use,' he said. 'It's understandable.'

'And convenient,' I said. 'Did Bernard have anything particularly in mind that you should be looking for?' I leaned against the wall, having certified beforehand no roaches scurried nearby that could take advantage of my proximity. There were no roaches, which was something other than unusual.

'Evidence,' said Avi, shoving his way in.

As we entered I knew a sudden notion that I'd been there before; remembered visiting, as a child, an elderly aunt who lived on the Concourse some twenty blocks to the north. Her apartment had been no different from Jensen's, speaking strictly of layout: within was a small foyer, a kitchen and bath, two bedrooms and a living room sunk two steps below the level of the other rooms.

'Do you think he was here much?' Avi asked,

looking around.

'Why do you ask?'

At once I realised why, when my eyes adjusted to the dim. Brown curtains hid casement windows, dyeing all in sepia. If the Metropolitan Museum's curators ever chose to admit into its collection of period rooms one representing the Eisenhower era, they could have never found one more perfect than Jensen's; his grandmother's, I should say. An armless sofa stretched along the right side of the living room, its boomerang-shaped legs lifting its sections no more than a foot from the floor; the drawers of a Danish Modern cabinet bore no matching blond-wood handles, none that were visible. A floor-to-ceiling pole lamp appeared braced in such a way as to support the ceiling; what appeared as an artist's oversized palette bore stubby legs, that it might be used as a table. A wall clock resembled a splattered melon thrown against the plasterwork. Black aluminium bookcases contained scores of old paperbacks; along their top shelves were photographs in faux-brass frames.

'No disputing taste,' said Avi.

A film of dust coated everything, as if it had been applied in careful layers to serve as protection. Walking across the room to one of the bookcases, coughing as I drew in breathes thick with unsettled dust, I took from the shelves several volumes. *Pride and Prejudice*'s cover showed a busty Regency wench wielding a whip, and I hesitated to imagine the workings of the art director's mind. When I opened *The Flying Saucers Are Real*, the cover's cellophane epidermis scaled loose beneath my fingers, and the pages crumbled into flakes of brown snow.

'Who's pictured?' Avi asked, coming over, puffs of dust rising with his every footstep. Within moments we were all coughing.

'It must be his family. Her family. He's in this one— '

'The kid?'

'Look at the ears. That's him.'

There were no other shots of Jensen; in this single image he sat on the lap of an older woman; she sat on the living room's sofa. He looked too young for elementary school. She wore a simple flowered frock; one arm was thrown over him, to keep him from sliding away. At first I thought she hadn't washed before having her picture taken.

'Must be his grandmother,' Avi said.

'What's that on her arm?' As I stared into the photo, attempting ro raise its image into life, I found myself unable to distinguish smudge from shadow.

'Numbers,' Avi said. Looking again, I saw them.

'They didn't do that everywhere, did they?' I asked. 'Maybe she even knew your father— '

'No.'

The other, older photographs were taken a world away, and preserved seconds of years long lost. Though I was no photographer I knew at once that their earthen tones had been weathered in, and not painted on. In the largest shot, a man with moustache, bowler and boutonierre stood with a woman wearing a cloche, and a long coat; judging from her waist I imagined she'd had several children. They'd been captured in the midst of a square cobbled over with stones no larger than a young girl's breast; piercing the sky behind their heads were ornate spires, eight-gabled roofs, filigreed stone and the statue of an angel hewn into a facade.

'I think that's Prague,' I said. 'Though it's prewar. Could be anywhere over there in that case, I suppose— '

'They'd have been hidden somewhere,' Avi said.

'The pictures?' I asked, looking over the rest; there were twenty-odd photos, and different people in each. Only the shot of Jensen and his grandmother appeared to have been taken in America.

'Buried, maybe. Stuffed behind bricks in a chimney. That's how my father saved a couple of things.'

'And come back for them later.'

'If they could.' Avi sighed, and turned away. 'I'll be quick,' he said. 'I feel like a thief.'

He walked up the two steps and disappeared behind the bedroom doors. Lester sat on the edge of the sofa; I sat down beside him. The yellow-brown light strained through the curtains made the room seem sealed within amber.

'What's in his head?' I asked.

'It's easier to say what isn't there,' said Lester.

'Say it, then.'

'Nothing involving Japan, or that fellow Otsuka. Nothing about Gus, except an impression of surprise. Nothing about his family or anyone who might once have been close to him. He did want to tell Thatcher something. I couldn't tell what, exactly. Something he saw. There was a hatred there that didn't leave room for much else. That sort of thing tends to linger.'

'Hatred towards whom?'

'A general rage,' he said. 'To Bernard, to some

degree.'

'What was it that he saw?' I asked; Lester sat within a faint cloud, seeming to stir dust by the act of remembering. 'You acted like you'd been burned when you were in there.'

'Some memories hurt more than others.'

'Did you see what he saw?'

The rumble of a truck, or of some heavy vehicle, pulling up and coming to a stop sounded through the window, seeming some distance away. Doors slammed as its riders climbed out.

'I saw what remained,' Lester said. 'I gathered it was a recent memory. It lay too close to the surface, though I gathered he'd been trying to dig a hole for it, and hadn't dug deep enough. There wasn't much. He stood on a dock. I think it was a dock, or a pier. There was water, and boats. He looked down on a boat. Someone lifted a hatch cover— '

'What else?' I asked. 'Lester, tell me— '

'In dredging another's memories you haul up a lot of mud,' he said. 'There was a disconnection then, and then another picture. There were people. They seemed to be dead. Then I think he must have changed the channel, as it were.'

Whoever had parked outside wasn't coming in, I didn't believe, or they would have already broken in the door the rest of the way; I heard truck-doors open once more, and then murmurs of conversation too distant to make out. Children were laughing.

'This has something to do with all of this?'

'Without question.'

'Was there anything else?'

'The soul remains trapped for only so long in such conditions,' Lester said. 'Afterward, it's like digging up a bone and then trying to imagine its animal.'

Bile rose from my belly up my throat when I heard a crash in the other room; as I leapt up I realised it was only Avi, emptying drawers that he might rifle Jensen's more disposable fragments. Lester sat as before, moving no muscles but those which allowed him breath. At that moment he looked so beyond any attentions I might offer as had Jensen. A child shouted, out on the street; I walked over to the window, curious to see. Spiders dropped onto my fingers as I drew back the musty curtains, and pulled apart the dust-blackened blinds. A white van bearing on its side a red cross made a U-turn in the middle of the back street. No one who might have made noise was visible. As the van drove away, heading southeast, I eyed the cross more closely; where red nave met red transcept a small yellow circle fit neatly into the interstice.

'Lester?' I asked; he didn't answer. 'What's wrong?'

'It's the time,' he said. 'Nothing more. Is Avi all right? He looked so uncomfortable when you mentioned his father.'

'They're just like this,' I said, holding up two fingers in a sign of victory, or of peace. 'They're from different worlds, that's all.'

'His father was in a concentration camp?'

'His father,' I said, 'and his father's first wife, and their children and families. He married Avi's mother after the war. He told me they met in a displaced persons' zone.'

'Most people do, I suppose,' he said.

Avi stepped out of the bedroom just then, his hands smeared with dust and dirt. He held several sheets of paper, folded in such a way as to hide the writing. When he looked at us he appeared oddly calm, for the first time since we'd encountered Lester: as if, having been at first frightened by a shape in his room at night, and unable to cry for his mother, he'd strengthened his will enough that he might look more closely and, having allowed his eyes to readjust to the dark, saw at second glance that the shape was nothing that could bear harm; found at last, upon rising, that his terror came solely from misperception, a trick played on the eye by his soul.

'What were you talking about?' he asked.

'Your father,' Lester said.

Avi appeared, for an instant, as if upon rising he'd discovered that sometimes something does lurk in rooms at night. When he recovered he proceeded as if he'd been told no more than the time.

'What happened to him, you mean?' Avi asked. 'He lived. That's what happened to him.'

'Where was he?'

'They put him in Auschwitz first,' Avi said. 'Then he was sent to Maidanek.'

'And then?'

Avi said nothing for a moment; stared at the papers in his hand. 'There's no purpose in the telling.'

'There was a purpose in its occurring,' said Lester.

'The Allies were closing in,' Avi said, his face holding no expression, his voice carrying no inflection as he told Lester; once he'd told me, using similar phrasing, and like tone, and I could only think that he recounted it as he'd heard his father tell it to him. 'The Germans moved a thousand prisoners from Maidanek, deeper into Germany. The prisoners were all men and my father was one of them. They reached a small town on a cloudless day. The soldiers had orders to get rid of the prisoners. They locked them in a big brick barn and set fire to it. The prisoners screamed. My father said they screamed so loud that finally even God heard their prayers. It rained. The fire went out. Most of them were already dead. My father, a few others, they lived.'

He had nothing more to add, not immediately; we sat in the room, watching the light fade around us as the afternoon drew to a close. After a short time more Avi spoke again, directing his words toward Lester, as if I wasn't even there. 'I know there must be a purpose to everything,' he said. 'But where's the purpose in that?'

'Would you be standing here telling the story to me if there'd been no purpose?' Lester asked.

'Where's the purpose?' Avi repeated. 'What was God's intent? Can you say?'

'Only God could say,' Lester said. 'Godness draws what good She can from evil. So her tears saved enough for a minyan.'

Avi closed his eyes; forgetting for the moment what he was, he seemed to remember, for an instant, what he had been. Lester crossed the room, that he could stand beside him.

'Do what you must,' he said. 'It's your job, Avi. You know that.'

Avi opened his eyes, and nodded his head; started to close his hand, as if to crumple the papers he held. When he saw Lester demurring he stopped, and folded them over one more time, and slipped them into his jacket.

'Lester,' I said, 'What is it?' I don't know why I asked; I knew.

'Mr Dryden will have to see these, Joanna,' Avi said, patting his pocket. 'He has to. I'm sorry. Lester's right.'

I followed them out of the apartment, down the hall and into the street. Avi held Lester close to him as he guided him into the car, into the back seat; for the only time during the years I worked for Dryco I sat up front where the guards always sat, protecting us without cease until the time came to take us away. I wanted to hold Lester; I feared I could never recall the feel of his touch, years later, though I knew it was foolish of me to have such fears. The sunset was so beautiful that it hurt to see. God favours details, truly; Godness appears only in absences, and I saw not sign of rain.

11

Three hours later Jake and Bernard hustled me into the car; Thatcher was already inside. When we went back to Dryco I'd been locked in my office, as if I'd try to get away. Thatcher had come in to sit with me a while; after so long he departed, leaving neither explanation nor conclusion behind.

'What are you doing to him? Where is he?'

'You've got to let us handle this, hon,' Thatcher said. 'You taking this more seriously than you ought to.'

'I don't want to hear it,' I said. 'What were those papers Avi had? Will you please tell me something other than lies for a change?'

'What else can we offer, sweetness?' said Bernard. 'I prefer to give you truth when you seem capable of dealing with it. You know that.'

'The papers show that Lester was approached by Otsuka's boys earlier this year,' Thatcher said, staring through the windshield at the narrow street before us. 'He's admitted that, now. Told us it went no further than that, and we have no reason to think otherwise. Said he didn't even realise until the other day that they might have even been connected to Otsuka. Says the ones who did the contacting weren't Japanese. It's not a pretty tale.'

'It appears Otsuka heard the same stories as we did, and proposed similar options through his agents. He simply didn't woo with such intensity as did we, and he certainly hadn't such good bait. Call it a hunch but I doubt that theology played much of a role in their actions. I'd think it could prove difficult driving messianic delusions into Shintoism.'

'I still think it's funny none of the Europeans got into the act— ' said Thatcher.

'Perhaps they tried,' said Bernard. 'When all these lovers come calling, what's a boy to do?'

'If he had nothing to do with them after that what difference does it make now?' I asked. 'Why are you doing this?'

'He could have gone along,' said Thatcher, by way of explanation. 'He just didn't.'

'Macaffrey is rather too intent on keeping secrets,' said Bernard. 'That's not necessarily a useful trait if he's to attain the sort of position some around here would have him attain. It's a matter he should have found appropriate at some time to mention to us, and he didn't. He said nothing to you, I'm sure.'

'Certainly not,' I said. 'This is insane. Nobody

keeps more secrets than you two.'

'A number of which he's discovered since signing on, you'll agree. And he does seem uncannily adept at making inferences regarding situations best left alone. There's no way around it, Joanna, the teacher needs a lesson of his own.'

'Even a messiah can't think he can get away with anything he want to do,' said Thatcher. 'We hear anything from Susie yet? Shouldn't she be there by now?'

'She's only just landing, Thatcher. Give it until nine or nine-thirty. Let her get there, pick them up and get back in the air.'

'I just asked— '

'What are you doing to him?' I repeated. 'Where is he? Tell me!'

'Please calm down, hon,' Thatcher said. 'We're going to see him now. We had him taken over to the Tombs. They've got some new techniques in development over there Bernard thought could be productively applied. I gave the go-ahead.'

'You're going to torture him,' I said.

'What kind of people do you think we are?' Thatcher asked. 'We won't do anything to him that'll hurt him physically.'

'Think of it as motivational training,' said Bernard.

'Then what does it involve?'

'It's what some refer to as neopavlovianism,' said Bernard. 'We leave him with a few lasting impressions. Nothing new. Simply reinforcing what's already there, in the event he ever starts to stray— '

'What is it, Bernard?'

'Elegant, you could say. We recreate for the

subject a key event in the subject's life.'

'What sort of event?'

'Ideally, a childhood trauma. They can come in so handy, later on, if put to worthy purpose. If the subject chooses to bury the memories of the event, however, that causes any number of problems later on. Tends toward dysfunction. The doctors believe this treatment will be helpful not only for us but for the subject as well— '

'Lester,' I said, interrupting. 'Not subject. Lester.'

'You say tomato,' said Bernard. 'In any event, by enabling him to re-experience his chosen trauma, by lifting it fresh to the surface of his mind, he's given a second chance to deal with its previous effects, using the knowledge and – oh, how do they put it? – life experiences. Using those to understand what happened in a more adult way. Everyone's better off afterward, surely.'

The Tombs was in the Criminal Courts Building, on Centre Street, not far from Dryco headquarters. Years ago criminals awaiting trial were held in cells on the upper floors; when the new jail was built to the north of the older structure, those upper floors were renovated for new uses, through a joint effort of the city government and Dryco.

'Behavioural science is such a growth industry,' Bernard continued. 'I'm told this particular technique is one proving especially useful, conjoined with traditional psychiatric approaches, though I don't have to repeat to you my qualms concerning psychiatry. The only Freud I appreciate is *schadenfreude*. Still, now that something more scientific has been added to its mix— '

'Better 'n television, I'd think,' murmured

Thatcher.

'What have you done to him so far?'

'A brief isolation,' Bernard said. 'He was given a light sedative, to assist in calming him before the next step. He's being readied for a little walk down memory lane, that's all.'

Our car pulled into the garage that had been built below the new jail. The elevators that rose through the old building, leading to the Tombs, could be reached from there through a series of secured tunnels that ran under the street, beneath the structures.

'You ever been here before, hon?' Thatcher asked.

'For jury duty,' I said. 'Six years ago.'

'It's a fascinating place, whatever you've heard. You know how shaggy dog stories shed.'

'The new computer's mainframe will be installed here, in fact, directly above the interrogation floor,' said Bernard. 'It's a good central location.'

The elevator reserved for Dryco's use took us up; when we emerged we entered a hall that appeared so washed of personality that it could have been any office building. Discarded monitors, keyboards and desks were piled high along the walls, farther down; the lights flickered and hissed, and smelled of burning tar. Police and men in cheap suits went about their business until they saw Thatcher approaching; then they'd flatten themselves against uncluttered walls until we passed, Bernard and I coming directly behind him, Jake bringing up the rear. We reached what appeared to be the end of the hall. Bernard, stepping forward, pressed a light switch; the wall blocking our progress slid out of sight, revealing

a shorter hall beyond, and two unmarked doors.
'That one leads into the staging area,' said
Bernard, nodding to the door on the left, opening
the one on the right. 'The observation room.
Shall we observe?'

'Stay back here, Jake,' Thatcher said, and Jake
took his place by the door, once we entered,
inside with us but at a proper distance.

As we walked in we saw ourselves walking
toward us. A mirror: one so high and wide as the
room, serving as barrier between staging area and
observatory. An oak table was placed perpen-
dicular to the mirror, and the table's chairs were
turned away from the door. Two men wearing
those long white coats were already in the room;
I gathered that they could be called doctors. They
shifted in their chairs, that they might greet us.

'Frank,' Bernard said, shaking hands with the
older of the pair, a man in his late fifties with a
red, wattled neck. His cheeks were scarred with
pockmarks; his white hair retained enough blond
to its strands to give his crown greenish undertones. 'How's he holding up? All progressing?'

'His injection was administered twenty minutes ago,' Frank said. 'As mentioned, optimum
timeframe begins about now and lasts for an hour
and a half.'

'Shouldn't think it'd take that long,' said Thatcher, pulling out a chair for me that I might have
a seat. 'This is Joanna, folks.'

'Oh, he mentioned you,' said Frank. 'You've
made an impression on an impressionable mind.'

'She has that tendency.'

'What are you shooting him up with?' I asked.

'Let's let our old junkies here explain,' said
Bernard. 'Medical terminology rings so false

within my ear. Howard?'

'The patient receives 450cc's of pentathline blended with a small amount of metalysergic,' Howard, the younger doctor replied.

Something about him reminded me of the boys I knew in high school biology class, the ones who liked to help the teachers pass out the new-pithed frogs.

'Pentathline enables the patient to recall repressed information in infinite detail while metalysergic's hallucinogenic properties allows him to believe that events described are events occurring.'

'Chemical hypnosis, in a sense,' said Frank. 'If you were to tell him a match was being applied to his arm, a blister would rise on the skin.'

'When actual events taken from the patient's life are recounted to him, the combined chemicals produce in the mind a substantial and ongoing reality completely unrelated to true physical surroundings.'

'*That* sounds better than television if you ask me,' added Bernard.

'And there's no unwanted side effects noticed afterward?' Thatcher asked.

'None noticed thus far.'

'What are you going to make him remember?' I asked.

'Allow him to remember,' Bernard said, correcting me.

He opened a folder lying atop a small pile stacked upon the table and, pulling from it two reproductions of newspaper articles, handed them to me. The clippings were from the Lexington, Kentucky *Herald*; their dates were twenty years distant.

DOCTORS THINK MIRACLE CHILD WILL
SURVIVE,

and,

LESTER TO TESTIFY IN MOTHER'S TRIAL, D. A.
SAYS

'Sending his own mother to the slammer,' said
Thatcher. 'What a world.'

'They had to send her someplace— ' Bernard
said.

'Please explain these,' I said, letting the copies
drop down upon the table.

'He didn't even tell you,' Bernard said. 'See
what we mean about his fondness for secrecy?
I'd almost call it a fetish. There's been so much
he hasn't been forthright about— '

'One day Lester's mother went a little funny
in the head,' said Thatcher. 'You know usually
in cases like this they kill themselves right after,
but not her. Seems like she was just too damn
sure she was right. Teaches you never to argue
religion with anybody, that's for sure— '

'Her sense of purpose persuaded her to plead
neither guilt nor insanity. She discharged three
lawyers before setting her sights low enough.
Young Macaffrey was the only witness for the
prosecution, and once he recovered the trial began. His testimony was given in closed session,
with only the lawyers and judge present – they
were considerate enough to take his age into
account – but one can't help but suspect that
none of it much lightened his probable mood.
She was convicted, and sentenced. She filed no
appeal and so went up the river, or wherever it

is they go in Kentucky. Six months later a fire of suspicious origin gutted her cell. She was in it, at the time.'

'Suspicious?' I said. 'How?'

'Only cause of the fire they could come up with was spontaneous human combustion,' said Thatcher.

'Not a favourite of coroners,' said Bernard. 'It was put down as— ' He paused; thumbed through the stack until he found the document he sought. 'Death by misadventure,' he read. 'So Macaffrey was put, briefly, in the care of the commonwealth, poor boy. He was given a remarkable number of tests pertaining both to his intelligence and to his personality. He had no surviving family and after a time they began shooting him through a series of foster homes. He was in those from ages ten to fifteen, all the while being periodically tested. Emotional fractures were noted, along with a keen but somewhat unbalanced intellect. He fooled them enough even then that at one point he was given the Rhine test for ESP. Results were inconclusive, which hardly surprises— '

'And it seems he was put in homes where the fathers had lots of time on their hands,' said Thatcher. 'He got beat pretty regularly in one of 'em, sounds like. He seemed pretty content in another one but the family moved to Houston to look for work and the agencies responsible for his well-being wouldn't let 'em take him along. They put him in a place where when the father wasn't beating him he was molesting his daughters. That was when Lester was fifteen. Don't know how old the daughters were, or if he knew about it, or did anything if he did know.'

'We know he ran away,' said Bernard. 'For four years after that we have no record as to what he did, or where he was. Ten years ago he emerged from his desert and came to New York, living here in perfect obscurity until the yen to fulfil this perceived role of saviour of Loisaida came over him. The rest, we know. Frank, what have this week's tests told us? Why don't you recap?'

'A pervasive disassociation is seen,' said Frank. 'Perhaps predisposing the subject to schizophrenic disorder over the next few years. Manic-depressive syndrome in its purest manifestation is not found though he would seem to experience bouts of severe depression interspersed with episodes where his messianic complex would seem to be more pronounced. His words demonstrate unmistakable signs suggesting ethylithic mythomania— '

'Run that by me again,' said Thatcher.

'A tendency to identify oneself too closely with historic events,' said Frank. 'Believing that one's actions effect one's society, now and in the future, and even in the past. Bear in mind that in most studies of even the so-called great, psychotic propensities are always noted. We can say— '

'We can say he's not the sort of fellow we'd like to have our daughters bring home,' said Bernard.

'You still don't give him enough credit,' said Thatcher.

'He's overspent what he had.'

'We'll see,' said Thatcher. 'Can we get on with this? I don't want to miss Susie when she calls.'

'Very well.'

The room darkened at once; in the next second,

a white light reflected through the mirror we faced, the gleam of the sun striking a glacier. The mirror's glass was two-way; the other room, the staging area, was lit so evenly, and painted so white, that Lester could have been sitting a foot or a mile away, so absent was perspective. He'd drawn his knees tight against his chest, and clasped his hands around his knees. His laboured breathing came as roar, over the intercom. Avi entered that room; he stood in the far left corner, wearing a knee-length coat. Two mannequins were close by; half mannequins, truly, resembling sewing dummies with unsculpted heads. Their plaster torsos were mounted upon wheeled tripods.

'Having all source material at hand,' said Bernard, sitting next to me, picking up a wireless mike, 'court transcripts, police reports, photographs of the house and of his family, testimony given and newspaper accounts, we can begin. Keep in mind that a certain role-playing is essential on the part of the interrogator, and unavoidable on the part of the subject.'

'Bernard,' I said. 'This isn't right. How can it help him?'

'It'll give him something to keep in mind.'

'You're punishing him. You're not helping him.'

'Punishment is a Biblical precept, I believe,' he said. 'Onward and downward. Lester? Miracle boy? You still with us?'

Distance notwithstanding, I could see how his eyes were so dilated that all blue was supplanted by black. He looked across his white world, his head wobbling loosely upon his neck, as if, having once been removed, it hadn't been properly reattached.

'How old are you, Lester?'

'Twenty-nine,' he said. With one hand he mussed his hair, as if attempting to comb it. 'Think so. Don't know.'

'We must be as a child to enter the kingdom of heaven,' said Bernard. 'You're nine years old.'

'Nine,' Lester repeated. 'Nine years old.'

'Very good. Do you recognise where you are? Look around you.'

'Where am I?' he asked.

'In the living room of your parents' house. Now you see it, don't you? See the big fireplace over there? A big stone wall? Three brass plates hanging over the wooden mantelpiece? See the slate hearth and the butter churn? That's right. What else do you see?'

'The andiron,' Lester said, reading a swatch of white wall. 'A little bench. The dog's basket.'

'Every family should have a dog,' said Bernard. 'What's you dog's name, Lester?'

'Snoopy.'

'Original,' said Bernard. 'Considering your father's profession I'd have thought it might be Saint John the Divine— '

'Mr Leibson,' Frank said, lowering his voice, shaking his head. 'Don't want to confuse him unless it's necessary.'

Bernard cupped his hand over the microphone's tip. 'My fault,' he whispered in return. 'Lester? Has Snoopy been acting funny this morning? Almost as if he knew something was wrong?'

'Uh-huh.'

'Someone else in the house hasn't been themselves lately either, have they? Who's the trouble-maker?'

'I'm twenty-nine,' Lester said.

'You're nine years old, Lester. You know what today's date is?'

'No.'

'September the nineteenth, 1978. Who's the troublemaker, Lester?'

Lester drew himself into a ball, and pressed his face against his knees. 'Momma.'

'Is your mother acting funny? What's she up to?'

'She won't come out of her room,' he said. 'She won't let Dad in.'

'Poor Dad,' said Bernard. 'Is your sister at home?'

Lester nodded once, and stopped.

'Her name's Betsy? How old is Betsy? Twelve?' Hearing no answer, Bernard shifted into a new line of questioning. 'What's Dad up to right now?'

'He's in the den. Writing the sermon. For to-morrow.'

'That's right,' Bernard said. 'Today's a Satur-day. He's listening to music as he writes.'

'Yes.'

'Reverends should always be reverential of clas-sical music,' Bernard said. 'What's he listening to? I'm sure he's not much for serialism. Nor any of that heavy romanticism, clogging the arteries of the soul.'

'Mr Leibson— '

'Choral music is so much more inspiring.' Music rose in volume over unseen loudspeakers, filling both rooms. 'Gregorian chants, was it? Bach? Taverner? Our sources aren't so clear. Let's say Thomas Tallis. Isn't that lovely mu-sic? What do you think of when you hear it?'

'Angels,' said Lester. 'Millions of angels flying around.'

'Must be worse than gnats,' said Bernard. 'You don't have any trouble seeing the room now, do you?'

Lester shook his head; he didn't.

'So dog's in his basket. Sis is in her room, Mom's in bed, Dad's communing with spirits and all's right with the world. What are you doing? Were you reading?'

Avi knelt, and slid a book across the floor; it skidded to a stop near Lester's feet. Seeing it, he reached across and picked it up. His hair was wet with perspiration.

'Quite a reader for your age, I suspect. What are you reading now?'

'Stories,' he said, examining the jacket. 'Edgar Allan Poe.'

'Good bedtime reading, I'd think. Isn't that awfully hard reading for a boy your age?'

'I like it,' Lester said. 'They say it's too hard for me at school. It's not. Dad thinks it's good that I read.'

'I suppose your mother has her own opinions.'

'She used to think it was good,' said Lester. 'She says Dad pushes me. Pushes everybody.'

'Push comes to shove after so long, doesn't it?'

'They've been fighting a lot lately.'

'About what?'

'Everything.'

'About religion? About God?'

Lester nodded.

'Didn't they once believe in the same God?'

'Yes.'

'Your father's an Episcopal priest?'

Lester nodded, again.

'Once they believed in a God of love? Now your mother believes in a God of wrath? Each to their own, I guess you could say. Kind of complicates matters unnecessarily to have such duplication, I'd say. What did your father once call your mother, Lester? You know big words, you can say it. What did he call her?'

'Charismatic.'

'Sounds kind of like a disease,' said Bernard. 'Like rabies, perhaps. God bites the believer and leaves them foaming at the mouth. Dad doesn't think much of this, does he?'

'I hate to hear them fight.'

'Do you pray at night for God to make them stop?'

Lester nodded his head, and then rested it against his knees again, as if its weight was too great for him to carry unaided.

'Some prayers God answers, Lester, but I suppose you found that out. What's the weather like today?'

'It's been pouring out.'

'I gather you mean rain. What they call a frogstrangler in those parts? What time is is now? You see the grandfather clock? By the door to your sister's room. What time is it?'

'Two-thirty.'

'Here comes your sister now,' Bernard said. 'See her?'

'No,' said Lester, hiding his face. 'Stop it.'

Bernard sighed and took a photograph from one of his files; held it before him as he continued. 'You see her.'

Avi gently pushed one of the mannequins toward Lester; it rolled across the floor on well-oiled wheels, and stopped just short of where

223

Lester sat.

'Stop,' Lester repeated, still averting his eyes.

'Don't you love your sister?' Bernard asked. 'You haven't seen her in so long. You haven't forgotten what she looks like. Skinny little thing. Taller than you. Straight brown hair and braces. Green eyes. You see her.'

Lester cried. 'Stop!'

'You're a big boy now, Lester. It's all right— '

'Stop it, Bernard,' I said. 'Look at what you're doing. Stop— '

Thatcher grasped my arm; pulled me nearer.

Lester raised his head an looked at the mannequin, smiling through tears.

'Bets,' he said. His smile faded. 'Betsy. Talk to me.'

'Cat must have her tongue,' said Bernard. 'She wants to know if you're hungry, Lester. She'll fix you whatever you want to eat. Are you hungry?' Lester shook his head. 'She doesn't mind. What's she wearing, by the way?'

'A white sweater,' Lester said. 'Blue jeans. Sneakers with pink laces.'

Bernard smiled. 'Such an eye for detail you're developing. What does she usually fix you to eat on weekends?'

'Grilled cheese sandwiches.'

The odour of toasting bread at once permeated the rooms.

'Almost smells good enough to eat, doesn't it? Now you're both in the kitchen, talking about your parents. Isn't the kitchen a homey place? Shame that your mother insisted upon painting the walls that awful red. Almost like blood, isn't it? You're sitting at that big round table in the centre of the room. What communion does your

224

family take there?'

'We have family meetings,' Lester said. 'Every Wednesday night at seven. After Dad watches the news.'

'I suppose you discuss family problems at family meetings. Haven't had one for a few weeks though, have you?'

'Momma doesn't like to be around us any more.'

'You don't say. Why's that?'

'She says our sin rubs off on her like dirt.'

'Saturday's bathday,' said Bernard. 'You and your sister hear something now. You hear your father open the door to his den and come out. The music's much louder than it was.'

There came a corresponding increase in volume in our rooms as well; voice upon voice swelled the chorus's sound.

'What do you think he's going to do?'

'Try to get Momma to come out?'

'What makes you think that?' Bernard asked.

'That's what he's always trying to do. She never comes out till she wants to. He's upset. He's yelling at her through the door.'

'She said something to him, probably. Do you know what she said? Or why she won't come out even now?'

Lester got up, and wandered over to the mannequin representing his sister; stroked its unfeatured face. He circled round it, looking her up and down with nothing more than child's intent, seeing so much that he'd lost years before, seeming deaf to our cries.

'Lester,' Bernard said, more sharply, holding the microphone so intently that he might have been masturbating. 'Tell me why your mother

225

won't come out.'

'She thinks we're trying to hurt her.'

'Would you hurt your mother?'

Lester made no direct response; he touched the mannequin once more, and then started edging away. 'She says we're bad for her soul.'

'Does God tell her that?'

'She says Jesus does.'

'You Macaffreys are so popular with the boys upstairs,' said Bernard. 'What does Jesus tell your mother?'

Lester shook his head; wouldn't, or couldn't say.

'Your parents are still yelling at one another through the door? You and Betsy creep over to the kitchen door, don't you? You can hear what they're saying but you can't see them.'

'Betsy can.'

'What is your mother saying to your father?'

'She says Dad blesses too many animals and doesn't think about us.'

'Animals?' Bernard asked. 'Foxhounds, you mean?'

'No.'

'You mean when he blesses the animals in the nativity set at Christmas?'

Lester held his hands against his ears as if to deafen himself to all he heard.

'What animals, Lester? Do you know?'

'People who live in the city,' he said. 'She says if they were supposed to live at all they wouldn't live like heatherns.'

Lester pronounced the word as Thatcher did, with the extra r.

'Jesus tells her that? Shame on Jesus. Does your father agree?'

'He says she needs help,' Lester said. 'Like the people do, but in a different way.'

'God helps those who help themselves, I'm told.'

'She tells Dad God helps when he wants to.'

'She's wise in her generation,' said Bernard. 'What happens now?'

'She starts screaming. But she's not afraid. She's saying curse words. Saying things about us.'

The smell in the room changed from that of toasting bread to that of burning bread. 'What is she screaming about? What is she saying about you?

Lester sank to his knees upon the white field as if collapsing in the face of a blizzard, believing it was time to freeze. He wrapped an arm around the mannequin's tripod. I acted without considering; grabbed the microphone from Bernard and shouted into it.

'Lester, don't listen. Don't. Don't listen to it.'

Thatcher clamped his hand across my mouth; no sooner did he have me silenced than Bernard wrested the microphone from my hand. It struck me that he seemed willing to break my fingers to retrieve it if he had to. As Thatcher relaxed, somewhat, Bernard picked up, extemporising.

'Did you hear your sister just then?'

Lester lay on the floor, weeping, nodding his head.

'She has your best interests at heart. What does your mother say the rest of you want to do with her spirit?'

'Take it to hell,' Lester said. 'She says we're already burning and we're trying to take her down with us.'

'Take her back, I'd say,' said Bernard. 'Smell something burning, though, don't you? Is it you? No? You two forgot all about those sandwiches.'

'Bets runs over and takes them off the stove.'

'If you'd been paying attention to what needed attention none of this would have happened, would it have?' Bernard asked. 'But you had to be more concerned with someone else's business— '

I flung out my leg, trying to strike Bernard, but was too far from him to do more than brush his trousers with my shoe.

'Yes— '

'See what happens when you don't give consideration to other people's wishes?' Bernard waited until Lester had stopped wailing, that he might hear his words over the sound of sobs. 'You're still having to learn that, aren't you? Well, well. What does your father say now?'

'Nothing.'

'Your mother's door opens. You hear it open. What does your father say?'

'Put it down,' Jake said. 'He says put it down.'

'Put what down?' Bernard leaned forward, his eyes moist with much that wasn't sad; he began breathing through his mouth, as if his lungs were too excited to hold enough air. 'What's the next thing you hear, Lester?'

'Nothing— '

'Your sister saw, Lester. What did she see?'

'I don't know— '

'You do know,' Bernard said.

'Nothing, nothing, nothing— '

'Tell me!'

'*No!*'

The second of the two mannequins was on the

far side of the room still, near Avi; without words of his own he pulled a shotgun which had been circumcised at each end from beneath his coat and fired both barrels, taking his cue. The concussion tore at our ears; before I heard the sound I watched the torso disintegrate into uncountable splinters, blackening the walls as they embedded themselves into that pallor. Lester curled himself against his sister-mannequin's wheels and screamed, long and loud. Thatcher let his hand slip from my mouth in his moment of being overcome by the drama; I sank my teeth into the webbing between his thumb and forefinger.

'Goddamn you,' I said; before I could move more than a foot away from Thatcher, when he released me, I found Jake at my side, slipping one of his hands into my clasp, placing the tip of his scalpel at the juncture of my jaw and neck.

'Please, Joanna,' he said. 'Don't.'

'*Jake*,' Thatcher said. 'No. Just keep her back.'

'Are we quite finished?' Bernard asked, turning away from his microphone.

Thatcher wrapped his handkerchief around his injured hand; I hadn't drawn blood.

'Keep her quiet, Jake,' he said.

I thought I heard a knock at the room's door; no one else gave signs of having noticed. Bernard tapped the mike with a finger to make certain the equipment hadn't been damaged by the concussion. The music changed; Tallis's forty-part motet spilled its waterfall of voices over us. I watched Avi reload.

'Here comes the chopper to chop off your head,' Bernard said, deepening his voice from its natural low baritone into one suitable for a cartoon wolf. 'What's the matter, Lester?'

'Please stop— ' he said.

'You both hear footsteps again,' said Bernard. 'They're not your father's footsteps. Whose are they? What does your sister do?'

'Makes me hide. In the pantry.' Unexpectedly, seeming as a fish cast from water onto land, he began rolling across the floor, coming to rest against the wall opposite from Avi; between them, not three feet from where he lay, was his sister-mannequin. 'She stands in the door. In front of me.'

'You see her white sweater. You hear the footsteps coming closer, and then you hear them stop. What does your sister say?'

He got no answer; Lester stared up at the mannequin, his eyes so bright with fear as any animal's.

'Thatcher,' Bernard said; caught himself. 'Lester! What does she say?'

'Stop it,' I repeated, attempting to demand, rather than plead; plead I would have done had I thought the response would have been any different.

The rap came again at the door. Jake pressed his scalpel against my neck enough that I might know its coldness. 'You see what you're doing to him. You know it. Stop— '

'Answer me,' Bernard said, his smile reflecting shine from the room's constant light.

Thatcher lifted a finger of his unharmed hand to his lips. 'Hon,' he said, 'Must be a hell of a mind trip for him.' He winked at me. 'You might learn something yourself if you pay attention.'

'Lester!' Bernard shouted, and Lester's reaction was to flatten himself into his wall as if wishing it might swallow him up. Avi took aim.

'What does she ask your mother? What does she ask your mother?'

'*Why?*'

In science, an astronomer might say that the mannequin's head went nova. A hail of papier-maché rained down upon Lester, surrounded him within a growing cloud of plaster-dust. As he screamed again he began banging his head against the wall as if he tried to smash himself and so put an end to his scene. I slung out my arm, pushing Jake to the floor, and ran to the glass; pounded my fists against its thickness, would surely have broken through had not the doctors and Thatcher, and Jake dragged me away, pulling me across the floor, struggling to take me from the room. As he gripped my arms Thatcher whispered into my ear as if to pass words of love.

'No, hon,' he said. 'It might be dangerous, interrupting them.'

As I heard the music again I remembered the angels I'd been shown.

Spem in alium nunquam habui praeter in te, Deus Israel

I have never put my hope in any other than you, God of Israel

'Your sister's sweater now matches the walls,' I heard Bernard say, sounding no more mirthless than he ever did. 'How're you doing in there, Lester? Is this any way for a messiah to act?' Again, Bernard set aside his mike, and spun round in his chair to face us. 'Would you please keep it down back there?'

I tried breaking free again, getting no further than before; Jake restrained himself, as if in these circumstances he found it impossible

231

to bring an easy end to the confusion. When Thatcher and the doctors got me into the hall we collided with the policeman who'd been knocking at the door.

'Mr Dryden, sir,' he said, handing Thatcher a thin sheet of white paper with stripped-away edges. 'Emergency, sir. For your attention.'

'Your mother sees you, Lester,' I heard Bernard say.

'Teletype?' Thatcher muttered to himself, glancing over the paper. 'Who'd send anything by— '

Allowing the sheet to flutter slowly to the floor he turned on his heels; opened the door that led to the staging area, and went in. Plucking the paper from the air before it landed, I read; realised at once why he'd left. In my mind I understood his intent.

'Do you see her?' Bernard said.

FLASH   GET OFF   NXR
NXR 57E–LA #*($894 FLAH   FLASH
FLASH FLASH FLA

EARTHQUAKE 9.1 RICTER STRUCK S C ALIF
EPICENT LAx22993((((((

GET OFF   GET OFF AND STAY   OFF

MORE MORE MORE STRUCK 5 30 PST PLS
RPT PLS RPT MORE

THOUSANS DEAAAAAAAAAAAAAA

As I entered the room I saw Thatcher violently twisting the shotgun from Avi's hands. Lester crouched now, near the mannequins' wheels, tracing his fingertips through the powder and crumbs on the floor. There was a dent in the wall; his hair appeared coated with reddening snow. For once he looked so old as he was.

'What are you doing, That— ' I heard Bernard say.

I was reminded of classical scenes of apotheosis; Lester lifted high in the air, flying upward, his arms and legs free of gravity if not inertia; neither seraphim encircled him, nor did cherubim sail round his head; the white sky against which he ascended misted over in a fine red shower. As if in the approach of a tornado pain pressed into my ears; when the sound resounded it came as thunder, deep within the midst of the gale. A thousand bells rang through my head as its noise decayed. Lester made his descent, tumbling from heaven; a babe pitching earthward, end over end. As he landed I ran to him, hearing nothing but chimes abuzzing my brain; I knelt, soaking my clothes in his blood, knowing I could not close the wound in his side. There was nothing to be done that hadn't ensured that it would be done.

'You *idiot*,' Bernard screamed. 'Thatcher, you fool. What are you doing— '

'You killed her,' he bellowed, so consumed by anger he didn't appear to notice Avi yanking the gun away, and slinging it across the floor, allowing it to slide far from reach. 'Saves her one day, kills her the next. Fucking lying sonofabitch— '

'*Thatcher!*'

'She's dead, she's dead, I know she's dead— '

'What's he talking about?' Bernard asked. 'Thatcher, you idio— '

Jake entered the room, stopping for a second

when he saw blood; moving forward again after his pause. Avi tried to steer Thatcher away, holding his arms as he led him out. 'You and your God,' he shouted. 'She's dead, I know it. What'll I do?'

'Killing him's not part of the treatment,' Frank said, his voice calm, what I could hear of it; sense, rather than truly hear.

Feeling the music continue to play, I found Lester's pulse.

'What'll I do— '

'God, Thatcher— '

'Japan,' Thatcher shouted out to anyone listening; even I could hear. 'Japan, Japan, I said Japan— '

Lester's eyes opened as I clasped him; his lips moved, issuing no words that I could understand. Fearful that my moments' deafness would keep me from knowing what was left to say I lowered my dead ear until it rested against his lips; heard nothing, still. Bringing up my arm I readied myself to place my hand over his reopened scar; lifting his own hand, he pushed mine away. Blood came with his words when he finally spoke.

'Please,' he said. 'Momma.'

'Joanna,' Jake said; he stood behind us, nearby. 'Endtime. Never need to suffer overlong.'

Endtime it was. Not letting go of Lester's hand, scooting out of Jake's way, I nodded, knowing that it was the spirit, and not the act, that mattered; I gave my blessing to the euthanasia Gus had taught Jake so well. Avi, coming back now, crossed to where we were and stared at us. My hand was wet with Lester; I thought there could be nothing more left in him but his spirit.

'*Shema Yisroel*,' Avi began, in his father's

tongue; as he prayed, I added my parents' voice to his psalm.

'Hear us O Lord,' I said, 'the Lord thy God is one God.'

One in act, in form, if not in spirit; God, Godness, if the act is despicable, how can the spirit save? Jake extended his little finger; its blade shone in the pitiless light. Reaching around Lester's head, he found the spot he sought; as Lester left I felt such heat rise through me; shortly I thought I should at last combust, and know my flames growing hotter and brighter, until in my incandescence I would burn down the world around me and all who live in it.

'Joanna,' Avi said. 'Let's go.'

Their hands hold the sun, but never burn; Their eyes stare into the fire, but never melt. Their plans proceed as They desire, and not as we would wish them to proceed; neither can Their actions be judged as we judge our own, nor can They undo what must be done. For the time there was no more reason for Them to answer than there was for us to ask. Take such comfort as can be taken, knowing that those who are gone can never know how much you miss them; Their most difficult lesson is that only by living briefly with others will you at last learn how to live with yourself. They were Two who once were One and would be One again, once the day came. That day, I knew I had to go; I had mouths to feed.

12

One day a woman told her daughter a story. 'Once I was walking down the avenue and I saw myself coming toward me.'

'How is that possible?' her daughter asked.

'Spirits break through from the world of confusion sometimes,' she said. 'Before she could say anything to me I walked up to her and told her, "You don't belong here, you. Begone!" She disappeared like fog in the night.'

The notion of such comminglings disturbed her daughter. 'How do you know you didn't send her out of the world of confusion?'

'Angel,' she said, 'once you know there is a world of confusion you're no longer in it.'

Susie's body deplaned the next morning and, walking on its feet, strolled calmly back to her

236

car; the scientists arrived that afternoon, under separate cover. Her plane had prepared to land at the moment the earthquake struck, shaking the field, rocking the control tower; the pilot turned the plane around, that they might reach more solid ground, and so they landed in Salt Lake City. Thatcher was pleased.

No one claimed Lester's body and so he was buried on North Brother Island, in the potter's field, on Monday morning. There was no service, not that he would have desired eulogies, nor even wanted me to attend; there would have been no point. As he was being to lain to rest I was meeting Bernard, in a coffee shop on Cedar Street, safely anonymous, alone within the world.

'Look at it this way, sweetness,' he said. 'Even if he'd been the messiah it would have come to this eventually, don't you think?'

'Tell me what's been going on, Bernard,' I said. 'After much longer you won't be able.'

'Taking more of an interest in your work?' he asked, appearing not entirely pleased. 'I'd have never guessed you cared.'

'What I'm saying is that lying comes too naturally to you now,' I explained. 'I'd appreciate it if I knew you respected me enough to tell me the truth, one more time. Like you did, once.'

His coffee's waves broke over the rim of his cup as he lifted it to his mouth. 'Ours has become a world of artifice, after all,' he said. 'Mirrors and smoke and mirrors. The question isn't so much what sort of reality can be made, but how much of any reality may be dealt with. Perhaps we should have asked your boy if you become a saint when nothing surprises you any more.'

'You don't,' I said. 'Were those papers Avi

found forgeries?'

'He did confess to having been approached— '

'Lester always had his reasons for doing things,' I said. 'When did you have them slipped up there?'

'Thanksgiving morning,' he said. 'The Irish boy that worked for us last summer, I had him run them up.'

'What's real and what's not, Bernard?' I asked. 'You even keep Thatcher in the dark about it, don't you?'

'Wouldn't you say it's his element?' he sighed. 'You'd be dealing with this soon enough, I suppose. Once I begin programming that damned computer I won't have time to turn around. Please bear in mind, though, that particular aspects of this situation can be told to no one present, beyond this table,' he said, looking around; in those days a place such as the one in which we sat was still, usually, safe. 'Those who break silence so often wind up broken. You know me too well to know that isn't a threat of mine.'

'Bernard,' I said, 'what's truth?'

'I lose track sometimes,' he said, looking out the window. 'What appears so simple at first can become so complicated. In any event, then. Jensen was involved in a project. He intended to go public about the nature of that project. You'll need some background— '

'You and Susie are involved in this?'

He set his cup down, spilling coffee into his saucer. 'What sort of tricks did he teach you?'

'Call it a hunch. What project are you talking about?'

'You know as I do that were it not for the problem in Long Island there'd be no need for

238

the Army to be in New York any more. Each year they become more maladjusted, more hardened toward the populace they've been paid by Thatcher to protect— '

'This has to do with something?' I asked.

'With everything,' he said, rubbing his eyes with his hands. 'It's so typical, isn't it, that for the past thirty years each President makes the ones who came before look so much better, no matter what they've done? Even that fool Charlie. By managing to get himself nailed up as he did his example has since convinced Susie that were our own huddled masses allowed to breathe free they'd swim across the river, march through the streets – carrying heads on pikes for suitable dramatic effect, certainly – and, upon catching up with our employers, hang them up by their feet, Mussolini-style. Soon after we started working there Susie told me that an essential aspect of my job was to make certain that the Army would remain in New York for so long as she was alive. Precautions, nothing more.'

'Hasn't the Army grown to appreciate its duties?'

'The big boys never imagined they'd have such a time of it here. No one in the Defence Department foresaw a local insurrection turning into a prolonged guerilla war going on just upstream from Washington. A living room war in the truest sense, you could say. They step up their operations, the insurgents step up theirs. It's not generally known that aerial bombardment has been ongoing over there for the past eleven months.'

'You can hear it at night,' I said. 'They thought people would think it was firecrackers?'

'Probably. The point is, by rights one third

of the Island's estimated population should be
dead by now. That's not counting the thousands
who left after the accident. So, after a specified
number of years, with a steady attrition rate
being dealt upon a fixed population, it would
seem that a prediction could be made concerning
a not-too distant settlement, or victory. There'd
be stragglers, certainly, not unlike those Japanese
soldiers in the Pacific that so impress Thatcher.
Nonetheless, were nature to take its course, the
mopping-up could be probably completed within
ten years at most. I pointed this out to Susan.
She repeated her demand. She's crazier than he
is, you know.'

'So what did the two of you come up with?' I
asked.

'I came up with it,' he said. 'A plan by which
the Army would never run out of opposition.
Jensen was put in charge of overseeing the plan.
I oversaw Jensen. She had, and has, no desire to
know facts, they're so inessential to her beliefs.'

'So will you tell me about this plan?'

He nodded, and sipped what remained of his
coffee. 'A traffic network was already in place.
Jensen was handy with Latin American affairs.
All that was required was a readjustment. Fall,
chips, where you may. At the time a select group
was chosen who might, in the event of inadvert-
ently revealed facts, be held responsible— '

'In which event Otsuka was to take much of
the blame?'

'At the time we had but a limited understanding of his true influence within his country. Our
fault. You kill as many birds as you can with the
stones you're given.'

'He was in truth uninvolved, though— '

240

'In this? Of course,' said Bernard, chewing on one of his nails so intently that I thought I should order breakfast for him. 'Suddenly he becomes the key to settling our difficulties or should I say Thatcher's difficulties with Japan. Everything started falling apart, not long after— '

'What was readjusted, Bernard?'

'Cargo,' he said. 'The network continued transporting cargo from south to north along standard routes. But a different product was shipped.'

'What product?'

'Thatcher's xenophobia is an awful thing,' he said, resting his chin in his hand as he propped his elbow on the tabletop. 'These immigration quotas he's insisted upon for the indefinite future. Can you begin to imagine the potential going to waste, forced to remain in the wilds? For better or worse, Joanne, America is still better than most. Even now most of the world would move here if they could. Granted, that says more about the world than about America, but yet, I knew there had to be a way to give at least a few to have a chance as well— '

'You're moving people?'

'He nodded. 'In small boats. They have supercharged engines and Stealth siding to elude Navy patrols. The cost Guard never touches anything of ours and never has, so them we don't worry about.'

'Shipping them from Guyana to Connecticut.'

'That's one route,' he said. 'Each boat carries from seventy to one hundred and fifty-five, depending upon the layout of the decks. It's a three-day trip, generally— '

'Three days and a twenty-five percent loss during the trip,' I said. His fingertip began to bleed, as if he were stricken with an errant stigmata. 'I suppose Jensen went to Mystic not long ago. Maybe to one of the other ports. A shipment came in while he was there and he went to inspect the cargo. Is that what happened?' Bernard appeared more than unnerved, that I'd become so accomplished at inference as Lester. With idle, unwounded fingers he straightened his necktie. 'Then he decided to go public.'

'It was his own fault, in the end,' said Bernard. 'As I've told you, you have to delegate responsibility. You have to. Like you, he didn't always follow the advice that was most sound.'

'Who was he going to tell?' I asked. 'Who couldn't you have bought off? Who would have cared enough to wonder?' He didn't answer. 'Thatcher? You don't mean he really doesn't know?'

'Susie's always told me he'd disapprove,' Bernard said. 'She says it's as important that he never find out as it is that the Army not leave. That's easy enough to accomplish, of course, so long as everyone behaves as they should behave. When Jensen developed this newfound aversion to his project he let me know how he felt. Perhaps I didn't treat his opinion with as much respect as he believed it deserved. Before he left for Chicago he let his feelings slip in such a way that it became evident to me he was preparing to tell Thatcher, upon his return. Well, we couldn't have that. At my request Gus killed him for being a spy for Otsuka. At least, that's what I told Gus.' He tapped his fingers against the side of his head. 'That excuse served as well for Avi, when Gus's turn came.'

'Why did you drag Lester into this?' I asked.

'Why was it necessary, as you saw it?'

'He insisted upon leading Thatcher down roads there was no need for him to be travelling. And you're well aware of my doubts concerning that entire operation. Doomed from the start. It seemed a convenient way to kill two birds with one stone, and I don't mean that literally.'

'Killed or driven mad,' I said.

'Certainly not the former,' he said. 'Not necessarily the latter, but— '

'You enjoyed doing that to him, Bernard. Why? How did he hurt you?'

'I didn't like what he was doing to you,' Bernard said. 'I never meant that he should be killed. I'm not Thatcher, for God's sake.'

The weather that morning was winterlike, in the traditional sense, as it once always had been in November. It no longer felt appropriate to the season. I said nothing, neither denying nor agreeing; there was little that Bernard so despised as much as silence.

'I'm not Thatcher, Joanna,' he replied, as if it were one of Avi's less obscure mantras, a chant with which he might heal, a litany to sway the hearts of the heathen, a song sung silently in the brain, reminding him of where he'd been, and who he was with, when first he heard it.

'Let me see if I understand this,' I said. 'I suppose you got much of your cargo from South America, but I can't see Dryco so limiting itself. Where else, Bernard? The Caribbean, I'm sure. From Africa? Asia?'

'People will do anything to come to America.'

'When they already live in the Bronx?' I asked, recalling that white van's red cross. 'When they reach Mystic, or wherever else they're taken,

243

what happens?'

'They're transferred into smaller boats— '

'Those who survived the trip.'

'Yes, those,' he said. 'They're offloaded in stages, at night, along the North Fork. Then the boats go back.'

'Leaving them on the beach to enjoy their new life in America?'

'Joanna— '

'What's the survival rate for the first week, Bernard?'

'Please keep your voice down— '

'It's not only men, I'm sure. Or adults, even. I'd think it would be most cost-effective to transfer whole families. Any package deals offered?' He looked away from me. 'Weekend rates? Can't you see what you're doing?'

'Yes,' he said. 'What chance do they have where they were? What opportunity? They have a chance here, Joanna. They really do. In any situation the best always come out of it all right. What chance would they have otherwise?'

'Have you ever seen them being brought in?' I asked. 'Have you?'

'It's an untenable position I'm in, Joanna,' he said. 'You try to make the best of it. Bring profit out of loss when you can. Draw good from bad— '

His words sounded so rational, so heavenly, that had I not seen the face from which they issued, nor known the act, I might have been confused as to whose spirit spoke, to what purpose, to the living. 'You've managed to keep the Army from discovering this arrangement? I shouldn't think they'd think much of it.'

'Several commanders in useful positions have

enough of a notion to take their payment and keep quiet,' he said; taking another drink from his cup his face sagged, discovering it had gone cold. 'They believe it's useful, having a training field so close. Prepares the boys for anything, one told me— '

'Did the shipments stop during the confusion, at least?'

'Never, he said. 'Always ongoing.'

'With Susie's knowledge?'

'With her blessing,' he said, 'though without details, whenever possible. If I didn't know better I'd swear I believe it upsets her.'

It was nearly nine, I saw, reading the clock on the wall; almost time to go. There were several people I still needed to see.

'Everything can return to normal now,' he said. 'The caravans bark, the dogs move on. I'm sorry, Joanna. At least I think I can say you'll get over this.'

'That's safe to say.'

'It strikes me that you've grown into your position,' he said.

The restaurant began to empty out; the food was nearly gone, and they would receive no more until noontime. Bernard glanced at the window, at the multitudes passing.

'Oh, Joanna,' he said. 'The world would be such a lovely place without these people in it.'

Returning to the office I found all progressing as it always did; secretaries typed memos, mailroom staff brought deliveries, comptrollers oversaw the growth of ever-increasing numbers, bookkeepers peered at their terminals, assistants stood round the coffeemakers, pouring fresh cups. From seven continents came calls and faxes and messages, and the Dryden Corporation continued upon its appointed task, to remake the world in its image, to join what was once apart, to separate what was meant to be together. Avi sat on one of the sofas in Thatcher's waiting room perusing magazines, awaiting his cue. He didn't see me when I came in; he stood when he heard me speak, his manners, as ever, unfailing.

'Thatcher's in?' I asked Lily, his secretary. With a jerk of her head she nodded toward his door, and continued typing at her keyboard, her eyes set upon her screen. She wore plastic splints attached to her wrists, so that her arms could have more support, if no less pain, while she typed.

'He and Mrs D,' she said. Before I went in I paused to see what Avi had to say for himself, and to say what I needed to him.

'You're all right?' he asked.

I nodded.

'I was concerned.'

'I'm sure. How is Thatcher and the little woman?'

'Very happy,' he said. 'Celebratory in a quiet way. They're going over some new projects, I believe. You'll be told shortly, no doubt.'

'It won't matter,' I said. 'I'm giving notice today. I'm leaving, Avi.'

His expression remained so stolid as it ever was; his eyes alone revealed the surprise he felt. He cocked his head to one side, as if adjusting for deafness, and knowing where best he could ascertain what he heard. 'When? When did you— '

'I'm leaving as soon as I quit,' I said. 'I'll be here another hour, maybe.'

'What'll you do? Do you have anything else to do?'

'Yes,' I said. 'I have to leave, Avi. This sort of thing isn't what I'm meant for. I'll be fine.'

'What they did to him,' he said, forgetting his presence at the event. 'It wasn't right.'

'You were doing your job,' I said. 'I don't hold it against you.'

He shifted his weight from foot to foot as he stood there, now almost seeming anxious to break away, to begin another conversation with another person, or perhaps only to return to his work. 'It does seem he was something other than what we were led to believe.'

'He was,' I said.

'You'll have to give up your apartment,' he said. 'Where'll you stay? Joanna, you can't live on the street— '

'I'm going away for a while,' I said. 'It's hard to say when I'll be back in town. It won't be very long, but— '

'Will I see you again?'

'I don't know,' I said. 'Perhaps you shouldn't expect to.'

There were moments, during the time I knew Avi, when his transcendent enclosure – his aura, one might put it – would without warning disappear, leaving him as helpless as an oyster removed from its shell. He knew such a moment, just then, and said nothing; I knew how he felt.

'It's my life, Avi. You say I have to accept it for what it is, and it's not here. Not any more.'

'People adapt,' he said, 'It takes time— '

'They try to adapt,' I said. 'Some do better than others. Give my best to your father. I'm sorry I never met him.'

247

'It's as well,' Avi said. 'He wouldn't have liked you.'

I shrugged. 'There's something I'm sure you know that I need to tell you.' He stared into my eyes, for once, possibly, not seeing in them a reflection of himself. 'When he sees the right moment, Jake'll kill you. He knows what you did.'

'I am aware of that,' he said. 'I don't want to know when it'll be before it happens— '

'I wouldn't tell you if I could,' I said. 'Just one day you'll not even know he's there. Then— '

'There's a better way?' he asked, and shrugged.

I kissed him and walked toward Thatcher's door.

'Take care,' he said. 'Find peace.'

'I have.'

As I entered his office I saw both the Drydens behind his desk, she perched next to him; their feet touched, propped as they were upon its surface. There was nothing so heartening as seeing two people together who so personified that Platonic ideal, that those whose souls were split apart in the life before birth might, through predestination or serendipity or happenstance, find one another in this world and so rejoin their spirit. Several seconds went by before my presence intruded upon their silent rapture; had I desired, and had I learned better my corporate lessons, I could have killed them both before they even said hello.

'Look who's here,' said Thatcher. 'Hon, how you doing? You okay?'

I nodded.

'You sure? Ready to get back to work yet or you think you need a little more time off?

Just tell me, what's today? Monday? Come in tomorrow, don't worry.'

'I won't be in tomorrow, Thatcher,' I said.

'Well,' he said. 'We do need to get the train back on the track around here but if you need—'

'I'm resigning.'

'What was that, hon?' he asked. 'Didn't hear, exactly—'

'You did, Thatcher. I'm leaving your employ. Effective immediately.'

'Wait a minute. Come on in here and sit down. Talk to me about this.' He turned to his wife, who sat still beside him, looking no worse for her stumbles at the edge; without a word to him she stood, smoothed her skirt and picked up her newspaper.

'You'll be missed,' she said to me, her look focused upon the distance, seeming more than one who had merely chosen blindness; resembling, almost, one of Lester's children, born without eyes but taught never to seek the light.

Once she closed the door behind her Thatcher patted the warmed seat next to him.

'Communication's the key in business, hon. Talk to me.'

'I'll stand—'

'Then stand closer. Have you thought about this? Don't you think this might be a little rash?'

'I've been thinking about it for some time, Thatcher, and I've made up my mind. There's nothing left to talk about. I only wanted to give notice—'

'Mighty short notice,' he said. 'You haven't got anything set up elsewhere that I've heard about.' His statement came as declaration rather than question. 'What's made you do this? What set it off?'

'You have to ask?'

He acted utterly baffled; his feigned behaviour came more naturally to him than the actual – had supplanted it entirely, I'd come to believe.

'Joanna,' he said. 'I told you I was sorry, and I meant it.'

'You mean it as you say it, Thatcher. Then it's gone.'

'Something snaps in my head when I think something's the matter with Pussums,' he said, using the name I knew he used for his wife when he dealt most intimately with her; twice, with me, he'd cried out that name at the crescendo of his joy, surely forgetting in that moment that I was even in the room. 'Who else did I have to go after, then? Who'd I have to blame, hon? You can't blame God.'

'You mean you can't kill God.'

He shrugged, but had no answer; perhaps he had someone working on it even as we spoke.

'I don't know what else to tell you,' he said. 'Even if he didn't seem to be making himself especially useful it was still counterproductive— '

'That it was.'

'My temper'll get me in deep one day,' he said. 'I just thought she was gone. What would I do?'

'One day she will be gone,' I said. 'What then?'

'You don't think I'm upset about this?' It was reassuring to see such consistency in one man's soul. 'You know how I am. I try to let my emotions out but they just spill out all over the place sometimes. Something like this shouldn't be the thing making you— '

'I said I'd been thinking about it anyway. I

can't do the job any more, Thatcher, and it's
time for me to go. Nothing either of us can say
will change that.'

'You should keep your options open,' he said.
'It's a bad world out there if you don't have a
helping hand, hon. Getting worse all the time—'

'You'd see to it if it wasn't, of course—'

He held out his hands, as if to take mine
from me;' opened them, palms up, in a display
of supplicance. 'Omelettes need eggs, hon. Omelettes need eggs. How're you going to get by?
You need anything?'

'No,' I said, dropping my apartment keys and
my corporate signifiers onto his desk, keeping for
the moment only the card that allowed me access
into my office. 'I have to clean out my desk and
then I'll be going.'

'You've left me speechless,' he said, leaning
back in his chair. 'It's all too sudden.'

'Things happen, Thatcher—'

'Joanna,' he said, 'something I've always wanted to say—'

'What?' I asked, not yet leaving; certainly it
shouldn't have been hope that caused me to linger, one second more.

'I never really did think you ever put your
heart into this, hon,' he said. 'You got to give
whatever you do your all. You can't go halfway
and get anywhere.'

I almost laughed; didn't; couldn't. 'I'll stop
off in Security so they can remove me from the
records. I'm aware it's required.'

'I'd have trusted you to do that, hon,' he said.
'It'll be hard living without you.'

'You'll manage.'

He smiled, and nodded to himself. It always

pleased him when he found people so accepting
of his worth. I closed his door, and walked to my
office.

Desks breed trash as closets breed hangers; from
the drawers of mine I drew and disposed of a
hundred restaurants' matchbooks, long-forgotten
memos from Finance concerning medical bills,
programmes from events that were unimportant
at the time, and less so now; old disks, empty
boxes once housing pens, three dozen copies of
my resumé in its various states. A memo Bernard
sent to me on our first day at Dryco marked a
page in the Executive Health Plan Guide; he
wrote it, having not yet ascertained if the offices
were bugged.

At least we're working.

The page marked concerned obstetrical care. Into
the bin all of it went; what I had at home could
now be dispersed so easily, as Jensen's had been,
as his grandmother's had been, as Gus's would
be. Memories in hard copy so transmogrify with
time: notes fade until the words written are not
so unreadable as incomprehensible; letters of love
undergo a reverse metamorphosis, dropping their
brilliant wings within safely sealed cocoons and
emerging, if broken into, as something to crawl
over the skin at night; only photographs, as those
in more natural cultures believed, catch a shard
of the soul of the one photographed, the one
nonetheless visible only to those who were there
at the time.
    'Joanna.'
2   Jake startled me, knocking on the doorframe

of my office's entrance; he clung to its side, as if fearful to enter without an invitation.

'Come in, Jake. It's all right.'

'Why the open road?' he asked, stepping in cautiously, as if uncertain who else might be in there with me.

'It lies before me,' I said, placing my purse beneath my desk. In it were snapshots, combs, two dozen credit cards, my licences, my makeup, one hundred new dollars, my earthly possessions, all unnecessary. 'Come to say goodbye?'

'To escort out,' he said. He'd had a new cast applied, I noticed, a simpler splint free of obvious hazard. 'Forgive what was necessary.'

'Don't look so sad, Jake,' I said. 'Your face will freeze like that. You did what you should have.'

As he stood there, making no reply, I thought he might be wondering, not understanding why, why he should disagree. I shredded my superfluous documents.

'I'll miss you overmuch.'

'I'm sure you miss Gus more than you'll miss me.'

'No,' he said. 'Permanent expectations. Why waste the look when you won't see the bullet?'

'That's so.'

'You vizzed ahead?' he asked. 'That they'd take Macaffrey?'

'It was too late to stop it, even before it happened. You understand that?'

He nodded. 'What now?'

'Getting out of town. A clear life ensuing,' I said. 'What strength I have's my own.'

Jake smiled, knowing whom I'd quoted. 'Flying?' he asked.

'You know a better way?'

His grin was that of a boy much younger than he could ever be again. The windows in the Dryco building were hermetically sealed so that on days when the air conditioning faltered the place might quickly become more unbearable than it already was. As Jake sat on the couch to await me, I walked across my office, to my own window, one not nearly so large as any of Thatcher's. The drapes had to come down to be laundered anyway.

'Joanna,' he said. 'What's desired? I'll do— '

I climbed up, stepping into the niche between wall's edge and windowpane. Reaching high above my head I disconnected the hooks and the veil dropped away. From my new vantagepoint I saw city, land, ocean and sky; saw the curve of the world and the unceilinged sky.

'Joanna,' Jake said. 'Head floorways. You'll fall— '

Lester came to earth, lived and died. Who doesn't? I didn't.

'*Joanna*— '

So through winter morning I flew on alone. A snowfall of glass showered down, chiming as it drifted toward the street far below. Sparrows and gulls and doves circled round me, their wings so like those of angels. The mist of the clouds wet my face as if I cried; cried for my friends, for my parents, for the millions of this city of God; for those who were lost, for those who would never be found; for Lester.

If I shed tears, they were ones of joy. There could be no separation from him; that which once was one would soon be one again. On the desolate isle a river's width away I'd wait until

the day came, and so return, that our world
might be recovered: our sick, wonderful world,
our blessed world that wept for its mother. On
our first night together Lester told me what I
once knew I'd hear; I'd always wanted to hear,
and see, and remember all I'd known. You're the
Messiah, he told me, and I remembered, and I
knew. You're the Messiah, he told me; I'd always
been the Messiah.